Though vacations can be murder on our pocketbooks, who doesn't love them? That sublime feeling of time away from the soul-sucking vagaries of life comes around far less often than most of us desire.

In this riveting collection—each story set against the backdrop of idyllic vacation spots in Southeastern Virginia and the Outer Banks of North Carolina—darkly motivated but otherwise ordinary folks undertake erratic and unpredictable actions with nary a display of remorse, proof positive that cold-blooded murder never takes a holiday.

—Lauran Greathouse Strait
Executive Director/President of the
Board of Directors at Hampton Roads Writers
Author, Writing Instructor, Workshop Facilitator

Coastal Crimes 2
Death Takes A Vacation

EDITED BY
TERESA INGE & YVONNE SAXON

WILDSIDE PRESS

To Skip.

CONTENTS

INTRODUCTION, *by Teresa Inge* 7

A TASTE OF WINE AND MURDER, *by Teresa Inge* 9

GRANDMA CONNIE'S STRAWBERRY PIE, *by Michael Rigg* . 19

NOTHING QUICK ABOUT IT, *by Dawn Brotherton* 33

IT'S ALL IN THE FAMILY, *by Maria Hudgins* 45

SILVER BELLS AND BULLET SHELLS, *by Allie Marie* . . . 55

HAPPY DAYS AT THE HALLVIEW CEMETERY,
    by Max Jason Peterson 59

COTTAGE FOR RENT, *by Allie Marie* 75

THE INFLUENCERS, *by Judith Fowler* 83

CARAVAN AND CHALICE, *by Max Jason Peterson* 95

SILVER FOXES FIGHT BACK, *by Sheryl Jordan* 114

THE EXPERT IN THE ROOM, *by Judith Fowler* 128

RIDESHARE MURDER IN OBX, *by Sheryl Jordan* 135

A DEAD BODY IN THE HALL, *by Penny Hutson*. 145

THE HALLOWEEN HIT, *by Kimberly R. Thorn* 160

ACKNOWLEDGEMENTS 167

ABOUT THE AUTHORS 168

INTRODUCTION

Get ready to travel to mysterious vacation destinations in the second volume of *Coastal Crimes: Death Takes a Vacation*, compiled by members of the Sisters in Crime, Mystery by the Sea chapter.

Set in and around Virginia, each of the fourteen stories transports readers across a rich, unique, and deadly landscape in the Coastal Plain of Virginia, North Carolina, and east of I-95.

This collection includes vacation getaways from the shores of Virginia Beach to the Eastern Shore, and the Outerbanks of North Carolina.

So, pack your bags to visit premier destinations filled with mystery, murder, and a coastal view.

—Teresa Inge
Co-editor and
Anthology Coordinator

A TASTE OF WINE AND MURDER
TERESA INGE

"GET UP, JENNA!" Tess Harper yelled at her best friend passed out on the couch.

Jenna opened her eyes and rubbed her throbbing head. "What time is it?"

"Five o-clock. You've been sleeping all day."

Jenna Carson twisted her aching body into a vertical position and frowned. "How did you get in here anyway?"

"The door was unlocked. I'm serious, Jenna. I needed you at Coastal Events today. You missed a retirement lunch for an important client. I'm already regretting hiring you as a bartender." Tess had taken a chance on her sometimes-unreliable friend as a bartender for her event planning business.

Jenna ran her hand through her long, brown hair and shrugged.

Tess pushed a pair of cowboy boots, an empty bottle of rosé, and a Post-it note to the back of the couch and sat down. She snatched the note, read it, then slapped it against Jenna's arm.

"Is this why you didn't show up for work?"

Jenna grabbed the Post-it. "Nick broke up with me last night."

"I'm sorry that happened. But you need to pull yourself together. We have events coming up and I need you to bartend."

Jenna lumped on the couch. "My life sucks. My boyfriend dumped me on a Post-it, and all I do is bartend for a bunch of drunks, and work at events that I can't join. I'm burned out. Ugh!"

"That's what we do. We plan weddings and events in North Carolina's Outer Banks for our local and out of town clients to enjoy." The OBX was the local vernacular, referring to the Outer Banks off the east coast of North Carolina and a mecca for beach vacationers and wedding destinations.

"Besides." Tess softened her voice. "Bartending is your chosen profession and you're the best bartender I know. You've got to snap out of this, or you'll lose it all. Now listen up. You need to be at Coastal Events by three o'clock tomorrow for the wine tasting." Tess turned toward the door. "And clean this place up. It reeks of wine."

* * * *

Tess arrived at the Coastal Events venue in Nags Head, a small town in OBX. Inside, she took a moment to enjoy the view of the Atlantic Ocean through the floor to ceiling windows. The ocean was the perfect backdrop for any event, such as the annual North Carolina Vineyards Wine Tasting coming up. Tess thought about how Jonathan Grandy of Grandy Vineyards had selected her to host the event here this year and how it would help grow her business. She was taking the role seriously—Jenna better not mess up.

Allison "Allie" Martin, the event coordinator, approached Tess with an iPad in hand. "The vendors are setting up their products at the tasting tables. Oh…and Beau is here." Allie was referring to Beau Ellis, Tess's ex-musician-boyfriend. Along with Jenna, Allie was one of Tess's best friends. It was a fresh start for the three of them after they had solved the murder of Tess's brother Robert "Robbie" Parker, who Jenna had dated.

"What is the final vendor total?" Tess asked.

"Thirty. And they all paid their hundred-dollar vendor fee." An incoming text buzzed on Allie's phone. She tapped the screen with her index finger. "There's an issue with a vendor's table. Gotta go." She rushed off to solve the problem.

As the vendors finished setting up, Tess walked toward Beau as he tuned his guitar in the corner of the room. "Thanks for playing tonight."

Beau placed his guitar in the stand. "Appreciate the gig."

A moment of nostalgia swept over Tess as she thought back to dating Beau when she arrived in OBX. His rugged good looks had caught her attention, but his late-night gigs had gotten the best of their relationship. She had forgiven him and moved on to make her business a success. She remembered his talent after seeing him perform at a private party in OBX recently and hired him to play at today's wine tasting.

Beau stepped closer. "Care to join me for a glass of cab?"

As much as she wanted to catch up on old times, she had to make sure the event was on track. "I can't now…but how about a rain check?"

"You got it."

As Beau headed toward the tasting tables, Tess scanned the room for Jenna. It was three o-clock and attendees would arrive at four. "Jenna Carson, you better be here," Tess mumbled.

"Excuse me?" Jenna appeared wearing a little black dress paired with red cowboy boots.

True to form, Jenna looked more like a beautiful, rich client than a bartender. It was easy to understand why Tess's brother Robbie was attracted to her. But unfortunately, that relationship was not meant to be.

Tess worried about Jenna being stressed out. All three women were trying to rebuild their lives in OBX, but Jenna seemed to be having the hardest time. Keeping her busy was one way Tess could help her. "Please place these on the registration table in alphabetical order, then you are needed at the bar." Tess extended a box of stick-on nametags toward her.

"Who's working registration?"

"Allie. But she's handling the vendor tables right now. The guests will be here shortly."

An hour later, as guests sampled wines, Donna Martino, Jonathan Grandy's assistant, rushed toward Tess. "You put us at the wrong table and Louie refuses to switch tables with us. What are you going to do about it?" Donna demanded, fisting her hands on her hips.

As Tess made her way behind the tasting tables, she observed Louie Patrick of North Carolina Wine in a heated discussion with Jonathan. Kym Lee, Jonathan's girlfriend, stood behind them.

"Frankly, you always get the center table and most of the sales. I pay a fee to be here as well, so I'm not moving," Louie said.

Both men turned toward Tess with their hands stretched out for a solution.

She took a deep breath, her gaze searching for Allie. "Since guests are already at the tasting tables, it's too late to change now. But in the future, when a table is assigned, you must take it."

As both men stormed away, Tess rubbed her head and paused for a moment to listen to Beau perform. His music was soulful and relaxing.

Donna approached Tess. "I see you handled table gate well." Her voice dripped with sarcasm. "But now you have a new problem. The hors d'oeuvres ran out. I would think you would focus on the event and not Beau."

Tess glared at Donna. "I'll take care of it."

"Too late. I already handled it." Donna turned on her sensible heels and walked away.

A tension headache forming across her skull, Tess headed to the registration table to find it closed. She grabbed an extra tray of hors d'oeuvres from the kitchen, where she found Allie directing Nick Kent, Jenna's ex-boyfriend and owner of the North Carolina Food and Beverage Delivery Service, to the designated drop off space in the kitchen. Despite the breakup of her two friends, Tess often used Nick's service for her events.

Tess turned toward Allie as Nick pushed the hand truck out of the kitchen. "We've already run out of hors d'oeuvres, as Donna smugly told me. How's it going with you?"

"Crazy busy. I helped the vendors with their tables, Wi-Fi connection, then checked in the guests, and helped Nick drop off the supplies."

"Can you place these on the food bar?" Tess extended the tray toward Allie.

"Sure thing. Leave it to Donna to spot that. She wanted Grandy's to host this event, so she'll savor any mishaps we have."

"By the way. There was a mix-up with Jonathan and Louie's tables. Louie got the center table that was assigned to Jonathan."

"I'm sorry that happened. Everywhere I turn someone has a question or needs something." Allied pushed hair strands away from her face. "I'll stay close to the food bar and tables," she offered.

Tess realized that Allie would need help with future events. She also noticed Nick and Jenna talking at the corner of the bar just as Jonathan stepped up to the food bar. Better to apologize now, she thought as she walked toward him. "Sorry for the mix up."

"Frankly, you under delivered. We ran out of food, and you didn't handle the table situation well." Jonathan reached for a crab cake from the tray and popped it into his mouth.

"Sometimes these things happen," Tess said.

"Not on my watch." Jonathan took a sip of wine and turned his back toward Tess. He suddenly began coughing and wheezing and gasped for breath. His glass hit the floor and shattered. He grabbed the table, toppling the serving tray and scattering crab cakes everywhere. His body jerked as he hit the floor by Beau's feet.

Beau stopped playing his guitar and knelt beside the portly vintner. He placed his fingers against his neck. "He's dead!"

* * * *

Coastal Events was off limits to anyone but the police until the investigation was complete. Four days after the deadly event, Tess eased her restored 1968 Ford Bronco into the parking lot. She was eager to return to work and try to recover from the disastrous wine tasting.

As she entered the building, she picked up scraps of yellow police tape clinging to the door and walked past the abandoned tasting tables, all with the vendors' products waiting for the tasters who would never appear again. She noticed a light in the kitchen and made her way to turn it off. As she did, she knelt and grabbed a receipt on the floor near the edge of the refrigerator, balling it up for the trash. She heard two knocks on the door and stuck the paper in her pocket as she opened the door to find a man in a blue suit waiting there.

"I'm Detective Trace Jansen." He moved his jacket aside to show the badge clipped to his belt. Is Tess Harper here?"

"I'm Tess Harper, the owner of Coastal Events."

"I've been assigned to the case, and I have a few questions for you."

"The police already questioned me," Tess said.

"I have additional questions. Have a seat." He pulled a pen and small notepad from his jacket pocket as Tess sat at a table. "Let's get the facts straight, Ms. Harper. You were talking to Jonathan Grandy when he collapsed?"

"Yes."

"According to Louie Patrick and Kym Lee you argued with Jonathan twice at the event. Once, at the tasting table then again at the food bar. Can you elaborate?"

Tess wondered why Louie and Kym revealed this information when Louie's argument with Jonathan was far worse.

"Like I said on Tuesday, Jonathan was upset that my coordinator had accidentally put the wrong name tent on his tasting table."

"Why?"

"Because he didn't get the center spot."

"What's the big deal about that spot?"

"More people gather there, thus generating more income."

"Did the argument escalate?"

"It wasn't hard to argue with Jonathan. He was very controlling."

"So, it's not hard for you to argue with people. Do you have a temper?"

"That's not what I meant."

"Then what?"

"I decided to apologize to Jonathan and approached him at the food bar later."

"And...?"

"He collapsed, but I don't know why."

"According to the autopsy report I just got back, he died of anaphylaxis."

Tess's eyebrows knitted together. "I don't understand."

"Jonathan had a fatal, allergic reaction to peanuts."

"We didn't serve peanuts."

"He ingested them through the crab cakes on the food bar."

"How?"

"The peanuts were crushed and mixed into the cakes."

"How can that be?"

"According to a source, Jonathan ate from a tray of crab cakes you gave to Allie Martin to place on the bar. Is that correct?"

"No...I mean yes." Tess remembered Allie placing the tray on the bar.

"Did you put peanuts in the cakes?"

"No!" Tess's legs shook as she repositioned herself in the chair.

"Did you kill Mr. Grandy?"

Tess's lip quivered. Could he see her tremble? Was he going to arrest her? "No!"

* * * *

The next morning Tess stumbled out of bed, still shaken after what Detective Jansen told her about Jonathan's death. Up to now, she'd thought he had died of natural causes. How had the peanuts gotten into the crab cakes? He'd questioned her extensively, but she still had no idea what had happened.

She showered, clicked on the news in her home office, and jumped onto the treadmill. The screen flashed, "Wine and Murder," with Tess's photo beside it. She grabbed the remote and turned up the volume.

"Tess Harper, owner of the Coastal Events, was questioned by police for the murder of North Carolina winemaker Jonathan Grandy." The reporter described how Tess and Jonathan had argued and how Jonathan had collapsed after their deadly encounter.

"Omigod! They think I murdered him." Her thoughts raced to Jonathan's body on the floor. *Why would someone kill him? And why were they accusing her?*

* * * *

The day had arrived for Jonathan's funeral. Tess, Allie, and Jenna entered the small chapel in Nags Head. After signing the guestbook, the three women slipped into a back pew next to Louie Patrick. Tess noticed Beau and Donna chatting in the corner.

"How's it going?" Louie asked Tess when she settled beside him.

"I've been better," Tess said.

"Yeah, I caught the news. But one thing…"

"What?"

"The police paid me a visit."

"Why?"

"They wanted to know what you and Jonathan argued about."

Kym stood at the end of the pew next to Allie, her eyes red and swollen. "Didn't think I'd see you all here."

"Our condolences," Allie said.

"I just hope the police arrest *her* soon." She glared at Tess.

"She didn't kill Jonathan," Jenna said in a loud whisper. Heads turned in her direction.

"Everyone knows she wanted Jonathan out of the way so she could take over the event in the future."

"That's not true," Tess said.

Beau began strumming his guitar and Donna took a seat nearby.

"Looks like the service is starting." Louie motioned toward the front.

Kym scooted up the aisle into the front seat, sending another glare toward Tess.

Louie slid closer and patted Tess's leg. "Don't let her bother you."

Unable to concentrate, Tess scanned the chapel during the ceremony. *Do others think I killed Jonathan as Kym suggested?*

* * * *

Since news of Jonathan's murder, several clients had cancelled their events with Coastal Events. With business down, Tess ate a light lunch while checking email.

The doorbell jangled. She closed her laptop and headed to the front counter. Donna stepped into view. "I could have emailed this to you, but I wanted the pleasure of showing it to you in person." She placed an invoice on the counter. "I highlighted the items that you overcharged for the event. I would think you would pay more attention to your billing."

Tess read the invoice and took a deep breath. Allie had processed the itemized charges. "I'm sorry for the error. I'll look into it."

"I have something else."

"What?"

"I got word that Jonathan died of anaphylaxis. And since he was allergic to peanuts, do you know how they got into the crab cakes? I specifically requested no peanuts."

Tess repositioned herself at the counter. "I don't know."

"Well, you can bet the police are going to find out."

As Donna left the shop, Jenna entered and walked to the counter.

Tess looked her over. "You look awful."

Jenna rubbed her throat. "Wine!"

"Are you okay?" Tess walked behind the bar, popped a cork, and poured Jenna a glass of rosé.

Jenna guzzled the wine. "I know it's early, but I needed something to calm my nerves. Someone just attacked me in the parking lot."

"Omigod! Why didn't you come get me?"

"Because it was a little hard with someone's arm around my throat."

"What happened?"

"When I shut the car door, he came up from behind me, yanked me to the ground, and tried to take my keys before running off." Jenna pushed her glass toward Tess.

"Did you get a good look at him?" Tess refilled her glass.

"No. But I did notice a blue fish tattoo on the guy's arm."

After reporting the incident to the police, Jenna sat at the bar to calm her nerves while Tess and Allie stood at the front counter correcting the Grandy invoices. Louie entered the shop.

"What's up?" Tess asked.

"I wanted to talk to you all about Jonathan's girlfriend Kym."

"What about her?"

"I'm hearing rumors that she's spending money left and right."

"What do you mean?" Allie set the invoices on the counter.

"As one of Jonathan's beneficiaries, she'll get a big insurance payoff. She already bought an expensive car, fancy clothes, and tickets for a cruise. It's almost as if she's glad he is...gone."

Jenna slid off the bar stool and moved closer. "Are you saying Kym had something to do with Jonathan's murder?"

"I just don't know." Louie shook his head.

"I did find something curious." Tess reached into her purse and grabbed the crumpled receipt that she had found and held it up.

"This is from the corner store. I found it by the fridge. It's for wine and peanuts but it's not mine."

"What does that have to do with anything?" Louie said.

"I don't know, but I intend to find out."

* * * *

The media continued to cover Jonathan's death, and Tess disliked the attention and suspicion against her. On a hunch, the three women paid the merchant a visit to check on the receipt and purchase a few items for an upcoming event. Though the clerk verified the purchase was for wine and peanuts, he refused to provide any further information, and the girls were back to square one.

* * * *

Tess, Allie, and Jenna prepared the veranda for a food and wine tasting she had booked months earlier. The event was sponsored in part by Outerbanks Tourism to promote local merchants. She was glad the town did not cancel the event since several merchants had come right out and told her the police had been by asking them questions about her and Coastal Events.

That afternoon, Nick rolled his hand truck into the shop. "Where do you want these?"

"Where are the other boxes?" Tess counted only three boxes on the truck.

"They're not ready. I have to go back and pick up the remaining wine."

"You can put these in the kitchen."

Nick lifted the boxes onto the table and whirled the hand truck around. "Be back soon."

As guests mingled on the veranda, Tess, Allie, and Jenna sat on bar stools talking to Louie as Beau played guitar.

Kym made her way toward them. Tess had invited her, hoping to clear up Jonathan's murder.

Donna appeared holding a glass of wine. "I didn't think you could attend, Kym."

"I just got back from a cruise." Kym smirked.

"Must be nice." Donna gulped her wine and turned away.

"I see Donna is her usual sweet self." Kym crossed her arms against her chest.

"Uh oh…looks like the wine is running low," Louie said.

"Nick is supposed to deliver more wine but there are boxes in the kitchen I can grab." Tess slid off the stool and headed that way. As she grabbed the box in the kitchen, a hand reached over her.

"Thought I would help you." Louie stood behind her, blocking the exit.

She noticed a blue tattoo under Louie's thin white shirt. She remembered Jenna's attacker had the same tattoo.

She shoved the box toward Louie and moved away from him. "You attacked Jenna? Why?"

He grabbed her arm. "I knew you were getting close when you found the receipt. But you couldn't leave it alone when you asked the merchant about it. He called to let me know my transaction was being questioned since they sell my wine there. So, I attacked Jenna to get the keys to your store to destroy any evidence."

"But that doesn't make any sense." Tess searched his eyes. "You killed Jonathan? Why?"

"He was constantly trying to one up me in business. I had enough of him running me down to get his own way."

"I know he was difficult, but that's no reason to kill him."

"There's something else. Jonathan was trying to purchase half of the vineyard from my sister, so I had to stop him."

"I don't understand."

"My sister was in debt. I couldn't afford to buy her out. She hated Jonathan but caved in since he had the money." Louie stepped closer. "I put peanuts in the crabcakes and killed him and now I have to kill you." He placed his hands around her neck and squeezed tight.

Tess couldn't breathe. She felt her eyes bulge from her head. If she didn't do something, she was going to die. She reached into the box and grabbed a bottle of wine. She wrapped her hand around the bottle and slammed it against Louie's arm. Louie reared back, snarling. Tess ran toward the door. He grabbed her skirt and yanked her to the ground. Tess fell against the door, landing by the tasting tables. Louie jumped on her back. Dazed, Tess struggled to get free.

Just when she thought it was over, Louie fell off her back. Tess looked around to see Nick whirling his hand truck against Louie's body with Jenna and Allie standing behind him. Wrenching herself free from the weight of Louie's legs, Tess scrambled to her feet.

Donna, Kym, and Beau appeared in the doorway, their mouths as they took in the scene.

Tess raced toward them. "Thank God. Call 911. Louie just confessed to murder."

* * * *

Tess listened to Beau play the guitar at a small gathering three weeks after Detective Jansen arrested Louie. With business back on track, she had hired Donna to handle billing due to her attention to detail and she'd lost her job when Grandy Vineyard and North Carolina Wine were purchased by a group of investors. This allowed Allie to focus on coordinating events and to avoid future mistakes. While Kym continued to travel and spend Jonathan's money, Jenna and Nick reunited since Jenna had a more positive approach toward their relationship, bartending, and the business.

Tess clinked glasses with Allie and Jenna. "Our hunch paid off about Louie."

"Here's to future sleuthing," Allie said.

"Count me in," Jenna added.

Tess had just one unfinished item of business. She grabbed a bottle of cabernet and an extra wine glass and approached Beau during his break. "I'll take that rain check now."

GRANDMA CONNIE'S STRAWBERRY PIE

MICHAEL RIGG

THIRTEEN-YEAR-OLD Riley Newton glanced at her grandma driving the olive-green Gator-brand utility vehicle. Connie, who self-identified as a with-it grandparent, had told Riley to "forget the Grandma" business when they were alone. Plus, she played "a mean acoustic guitar"—Connie's words—and sang about bizarre stuff, like a magic dragon who lived by the sea. And her frequent F-Bombs, dropped mostly when Riley wasn't in the room, added to the charm.

Eccentric—even weird sometimes—Connie didn't look like a criminal, much less a killer. And especially not with her gray hair flowing in the summer breeze as she wrestled the steering wheel. Riley bounced and swayed in silence, while their Gator traversed the ruts and potholes pitting the gravel path on Connie's farm. Overhead, seagulls' screeching mews underscored how close Pungo, a rural section of southern Virginia Beach, was to Back Bay and the Atlantic Ocean.

Even hardened criminals looked like normal people. At least according to the Nancy Drew detective novels in Connie's library. But there was no doubt about it. Mayor Stubbins had died right after eating Connie's homemade strawberry pie a couple of weeks ago. A coincidence? Seemed unlikely. And one of the most basic lessons Riley learned from reading the Nancy Drew books was that appearances could be deceiving.

Riley glanced at her grandmother again. Enough stupid thoughts. Connie couldn't be a murderer. How could she—how could anyone—kill someone with a piece of strawberry pie? Besides, Mom and Dad wouldn't leave her with a dangerous person, would they?

"It'll be like a vacation," Mom said, when they dropped her off two months ago.

"But why did the Navy have to send you both away at the same time?" Riley had exhaled a dramatic sigh, playing with her mom and dad's emotions. "How dumb is that?"

"Well, sweetie," Dad told her, "it's unfortunate, but sometimes it happens."

"Besides, it's only a few weeks," her mom added. "It'll be over before you know it."

Dad had looked especially guilty when he brushed the hair out of her eyes. "Just as soon as one of us gets back, we'll come get you. We'll plan a real vacation."

So much for her parents' promises. A real vacation? She wouldn't bet on it. The first day of school drew closer with each new sunrise. They couldn't go on much of a trip once classes started. And if her parents didn't get back in time? She'd have to go to Princess Anne Middle. Barf-a-roni. Maybe it'd be okay if her with-it, guitar-strumming, f-bombing grandma turned out to be an assassin. She could just put Riley out of her misery.

"Here we are." Connie pumped the brakes, and the Gator skidded to a stop. She looked at Riley. "Penny for your thoughts?"

"What?"

"Oh, it's just a saying. An old-fashioned way of asking what you're thinking about."

"Not much." Riley didn't mention the whole put-me-out-of-my-misery thing. "Pungo's too boring to have anything to think about."

Connie smiled. "I understand. Spotty internet. TV on the fritz. At least you have Nancy Drew to keep you company."

Riley nodded. The fictional teenage detective didn't have internet or television, either, at least in the musty, hand-me-down volumes she'd been reading. "Right, Nancy Drew."

"You know, a lot of those are the same books I read when I was your age. And so did my mother when she was a little girl. Over the years, we've added new ones, of course."

"Really, your mom read them? How about my—"

"Your mom, too." Connie pointed at Riley. "So, young lady, you're the fourth generation of amateur sleuths in this family trained by Good Old Nancy."

Riley sighed. "Well, that's something, I guess."

"Exactly," Connie said. "And if that's not excitement enough, there's always the bees."

"Yeah, the bees." Riley rolled her eyes. "THE B-E-E-E-E-S."

"Come on, Little Miss Negativity, put on your veil and gloves. And make sure that bee-suit is zipped-up tight. A couple of stings and you'll remember how exciting they can be."

Beekeeping. Another tradition passed down from generation to generation, just like Nancy Drew. Connie was an expert. The farm and honey-making had consumed her life in the dozen years since her husband, Riley's grandfather, died. Connie had taught Riley tons this summer about agriculture and operating an apiary, but there was so much more to learn.

Connie's "Bee Yard" had six honey-producing hives. Not exactly high tech. Six sets of stacked wooden boxes, each with a copper-plated roof and positioned on a raised platform about eighteen inches off the ground. The Yard sat near the outer edge of her property, adjacent to neighboring fields of corn, soybeans, and strawberries—Pungo's signature crop. Connie surrounded the hives with beds of flowers, including Black-Eyed Susans, Riley's favorite. A variety of sources of nectar and pollen added to the sweetness and flavor of the honey.

Bees could distinguish colors, so Connie painted the boxes. The first stack—the first hive—was fire-engine red. The one next to it was white, plain old white. And rounding out what she called her "All-American Trio," was a blue one—navy blue. The next three were red—a much darker red than the first hive to avoid confusing the bees—then orange and yellow. Connie often said that she planned to finish the rainbow, starting with a seventh hive next spring, this one in bright green, maybe with some sparkles. Connie's colorful, flower-encircled Bee Yard stood in stark contrast to the two seemingly forgotten hives Riley had discovered a few days before, while exploring the woods behind Connie's house.

Connie lifted the roof off the fire-engine red hive—one of the patriotic grouping—and placed it upside-down on the ground. The buzzing inside the boxes intensified, as if the occupants were sounding an alarm and preparing for battle. She put each box in the stack on the ground until she made it down to the very bottom hive—the brood box.

She turned to Riley. "Hand me the smoker, won't you, dear?"

The smoker looked more like an ancient coffeepot, sort of like the ones the scoutmasters used when her troop went camping. But it had an oddly shaped hand-pump and extra-long spout.

"Thanks." Connie pressed the pump and small, cloudlike whiffs of white flowed from the elongated spout into the brood box—where the Queen lived and performed her most important function, laying eggs.

Riley's nostrils flared at the faint, burned-oak odor. "Does that make them calm?"

"Actually, it's a trick, remember?" Connie handed the device back to Riley. "It makes the bees think there's a fire nearby and that they might have to flee the hive. They prepare to leave by filling up with honey and don't feel like stinging. They sort of forget that I'm here."

"Oh, yeah, that's right. I remember. But it sounds mean. Scaring them and all."

Connie smiled. "Maybe a little. But it's nature's way. We're not here to harm the colony."

"What are we doing today?"

"Same as we've been doing each week since you've been here. Medical doctors would call it a wellness check."

"Right," Riley said. "Like we're making a house call."

"A wonderful description." Connie reached into a pocket in her bee-suit and pulled out a small, yellow-handled tool shaped like a miniature crowbar. "We'll make sure all the bees are doing well and the Queen is still laying eggs."

Riley smiled. "And we need to make sure they're getting enough water and sweet syrup, and maybe add a bee-patty."

"Excellent, young lady."

Riley took an internal victory lap. Maybe she was finally getting the hang of it.

Connie pulled a wooden frame out of the brood box that contained a plastic insert covered in bees and looked at it. She glanced at Riley. "Someone's been paying attention." Connie sniffed the frame, then placed it back in the box and removed another one. "There's more to beekeeping than many people think."

"Like me." Riley pursed her lips. "I always thought that the bees got enough to eat and drink from flowers and plants."

Connie continued to remove the inserts and inspect each bee-covered frame. When she finished the bottom box, she placed the second hive box on top of it and started her inspection process anew. "They do, for the most part. But that's usually only enough to keep the colony alive. We're trying to make the bees produce extra honey for us to sell. It's called building the brood. More bees mean more combs filled with honey."

She paused and looked at Riley. "And that means more honey for me to use, instead of sugar, when I make my pies."

"Your secret ingredient, right?"

"Yes, ma'am. And don't you go tattling about how I work my honeybee magic."

"Your secret's safe with me." Riley raised her right hand, her middle three fingers pointing toward heaven, her thumb holding her pinkie finger against her palm. "Scout's honor."

"That's settled." Connie chuckled. "And now back to the bees. They're like humans in some ways. They need energy from carbohydrates. That's where nectar comes in. They turn nectar into honey. And they need protein. They get that from pollen. But during parts of the year, there might not be enough nectar and pollen. Normally, there's enough during summer. But I'm worried because it's been so hot and dry. And they need more carbs and protein because they're working harder."

"So, you want to give them extra to be sure?"

"Bingo. We're supplementing what they get from nature, sort of like taking a multivitamin."

Connie used her hive tool—the yellow-handled mini-crowbar she'd taken from the pocket of her bee-suit earlier—to space the frames in the top hive box, the super, closer together. "Everything looks and smells healthy. No rotten wood. No mites, and there's enough water and sugar solution." She looked at Riley. "Would you hand me a bee-cake?"

Riley reached into a nearby waxed-cardboard carton with a cartoon-like drawing of a honeybee on it, placed above the words:

A-Bee-Cee Brand:
Queen Bee of Protein Patties

She presented Connie with a golden-brown packet that looked like a flat, rectangular pancake. "Is a bee-patty the same as a bee-cake?"

"That's right, dear." Connie removed the paper covering the patty, set it on top of the super, and replaced the lid. "Done and done. Off to the next one."

And so it was with the other hives. Pull out the internal frames, check on the bees—especially the Queen—and make sure they had enough water, sugar solution, and a bee-patty.

"Well, that's that." Connie placed the last frame back in the yellow hive, her inspection now completed. She looked at Riley. "Bee-patty, please."

Riley peered into the carton. "Sorry. All gone. We used the last one on the orange hive."

"No problem. It's lunchtime anyway. I can whip up a batch of patties from some dry-mix pollen-substitute I have back at the Bee Shed. Easy peasy lemon squeezy. We can run one out to the Yard later and store the others in the freezer. That'll do until I can order some more pre-made patties." Connie wiped sweat from her forehead with a blue bandana. "Let's go home."

The road always seemed smoother on the journey back to the house. An opportunity for Riley to collect her thoughts.

"You seem quiet," Connie said. "Beekeeping got you tuckered out?"

"Not really." Riley sighed. "Just thinking."

"Okay." Connie smiled. "I've got another penny to spend."

"Aren't you worried about what happened to the Mayor?"

Connie's forehead wrinkled. "How's that, dear?"

"He died after eating your strawberry pie."

"He had a heart attack, dear."

"But, still, Grandma. I mean Connie—"

"He was an ornery cuss." Connie gritted her teeth. "He wouldn't approve permits for this year's Strawberry Festival." She exhaled a loud sigh. "Besides, he was too fat. His time had come." She glanced into the distance. "Must have been something special about that single piece of my award-winning strawberry pie to kill that tough old buzzard."

"The police questioned you and everything. Weren't you scared?"

"What's to be scared about?" Connie smiled, sort of. It was more of a smirk than a smile. "They didn't find anything out of the ordinary, did they?"

"Well, I guess not."

"Or else your old granny would be in jail, right?"

"I suppose." Riley's face warmed. She hadn't intended to accuse her grandmother of murder, but that's what she had just done.

"And the Virginian-Pilot reported that the Medical Examiner concluded it was an accidental death by heart attack. He even tested for standard poisons, like arsenic." Connie's eyes seemed to sparkle, as if she were extra proud of herself. "So, what's to be scared about?"

Riley pursed her lips. "Secrets of the Strawberry Pie. Sounds like a Nancy Drew mystery."

"A budding author." Connie smiled. "I can hardly wait to read about how I did it. Offed the Mayor that is."

"Well, I didn't mean… I don't think… How could you?… How could anybody?… It just sounded funny. You know, the book title."

The Gator rolled to a stop near Connie's back porch. She winked at Riley. "Okay, let's have some lunch and then get after those bee-cakes."

Riley's phone vibrated. "Hi, Mom." Riley nodded as she listened. "Tonight? That's great." Riley looked at Connie. Salvation was just around the corner.

"About nine o'clock? Got it. Connie—I mean Grandma—is right here. I'll let her know." She paused and nodded as she listened. "Love you, too. Later."

"Wow," Connie said. "I've only got my assistant for a few more hours. We'd better get cracking."

Riley bit her lip to keep from yelling, "hooray." No more bees. No more Nancy Drew. And no more boring old Pungo. But something still nagged at her. What about the Mayor and Grandma Connie's strawberry pie? It didn't add up. Something seemed wrong, but what? Maybe her mom would explain things, help make sense of it all.

Within thirty minutes, the pair finished lunch and walked to Connie's Bee Shed, a combined workshop and business office. The small, barnlike structure sat in one corner of the yard, maybe a hundred feet from her back porch. The shed abutted a small forest, an eerie copse that scared Riley whenever she ventured into the shadowy thicket. It was where Connie kept the other two hives—the ones she had never mentioned. Except for the creepy forest, the backyard was another garden spot, filled with bushes and shrubs and a few flowers. There were azaleas, rhododendrons, swamp laurels, buttercups, oleander, and a lot that Riley didn't recognize. On top of being a master beekeeper, Connie had a green thumb.

And Connie was right about making bee-patties being easy. She mixed a couple of cups of 'Dr. Brad's' brand pollen substitute powder with a cup of white sugar and added water until it formed a thick glob, almost like modeling clay. Riley sat on a hard wooden chair next to the table where Connie worked.

"When the weather gets colder," Connie said, as she continued to mix the pollen substitute, "I make bee candy. It's the same basic recipe, except I use extra sugar instead of the pollen powder."

"What's bee candy for?"

"In late fall and winter, there's little nectar because the flowers aren't producing much. So, the bee candy's a substitute to provide those extra carbs."

"Neat. Maybe I can come back over Christmas break to help."

"I'd like that." Connie smiled and pointed to a nearby shelf. "Hand me the Healthy Hive, dear."

Riley grabbed a small brown bottle with the word Healthy, printed in green, above the word Hive, printed in gold, on the light-purple label. On the shelf next to it were many other containers, all with interesting names.

"Here you go."

"Thanks."

Connie measured a tablespoon of the liquid and poured it into the bee-patty bowl.

"Smells a little like bug spray." Riley's nose wrinkled. "What does that do?"

"It's a supplement for the hive to protect it from various things and give the colony a boost."

"What about the other stuff on the shelf? I mean, there were these two bottles of stuff that seem—"

"Like what, dear?" Connie focused on mixing the supplement into the claylike compound.

"One was Oleander Oil."

Connie looked up, as if she'd been surprised. Her forehead wrinkled.

"And the other one was Essence of Rhododendron."

"Oh, those?" Connie's face reddened. "Don't worry about them. They're for later."

"For the bees in the woods behind your house?" Riley surprised herself with the question. But it made sense. That's near where the rhododendron and oleander plants were.

"Um…" Connie glanced to her right and paused, as if searching for the correct words in the air. "I didn't realize you knew about those two hives."

"I found them a couple of weeks ago when you told me to go outside and explore."

"Of course. I remember."

"So, are the Oleander Oil and Essence of Rhododendron meant for the hives in the woods?"

"Sort of. It's more for the plants than the hives."

"Oh?"

"I spray it on the buds in spring," Connie said. "And it's supposed to help them flower and produce more nectar. The bees make honey from the nectar."

"Do you just use it for the plants around the hives in the woods?"

"Yeah." Connie swallowed hard, as if choking back on something important.

"Why?"

"Well, that's where the rhododendron and oleander plants are." Confirmation. Good, but a little worrisome. Something still seemed off. "Why don't you paint the hives in the forest?"

Connie exhaled, moved to a chair near Riley, and sat down. "It's a long story."

"Okay." Riley grinned. Time for a zinger. "Do I need to offer you a penny?"

"Not necessary." Connie frowned. "Do you know my full name?"

"It's Connie Robbins, right?"

"Robbins is my married name. It's your Grandfather Walt's family name."

"I see."

"My maiden name is Constance Grace Whitehurst."

"But you go by Connie."

"Right."

"Grace is a pretty name."

"And a very historical one, too."

"Wow."

"My middle name comes from Grace Sherwood, a distant relative."

"Who's she?"

"They called her the Witch of Pungo." Connie rolled her eyes. "Over three-hundred-years-ago."

"A witch?" Riley tilted her head to the side at this new, startling information. "Did they burn her at the stake?"

"Not exactly."

"What happened to her?"

"She was a widowed mother of three boys, and independently minded."

"What does that mean?" Riley paused. "Aren't women supposed to be independent?"

Connie nodded. "Farming in those days was very hard. There wasn't any machinery or scientifically altered crops. And even after her husband died, Grace was successful in agriculture, when others failed to grow anything."

"That's impressive."

"She was a midwife, too."

"She helped babies be born?"

"That's right, dear."

"That's impressive, as well."

"And she learned how to use native plants as medicines to heal humans and animals."

"Sounds like she had a green thumb and did all sorts of impressive things, like you."

Connie smiled. "That's very kind of you—"

"Well, I mean it."

"I appreciate that, dear." Connie placed her hand on Riley's. "I just hope no one accuses me of being a witch."

"So, why did people say Grace was one?"

"Maybe it was fear, or maybe it was jealousy. They claimed she cursed their crops and even caused women to have miscarriages. Things that only a witch could do." Connie formed air quotes with her hands when she said *witch*.

"But it wasn't true, was it?"

"Well, they put her on trial for witchcraft."

"How do you prove someone's a witch?"

"They took off all her clothes and tied her up. Then they weighed her down and threw her into the Lynnhaven River."

"They drowned her?" Riley wanted to drop an F-Bomb, like Connie often did, but bit her tongue. "How did they know she was a witch? Didn't she get a trial?"

"That was the trial. It was called witch-ducking. If the accused—Grace in this situation—drowned, it meant she was innocent, because she had no dark magic to save her."

"But if she survived, she must be a witch, right?"

"You're quite the detective," Connie said. "Grace untied the ropes, swam to the surface, and, voila, they declared her a witch."

"Well, that's effed… I mean…messed…up."

"Right, it's—"

"A real no-win deal."

"Exactly," Connie said. "They put her in jail for a half-dozen years. She returned to Pungo and lived near Muddy Creek for over two decades."

"Wow. At least they didn't burn her at the stake."

"I suppose that's something, dear."

"But Connie, what do the beehives in the woods have to do with Grace Sherwood?"

Connie looked at Riley, or maybe past her, as if trying to figure out how to change the subject again. "Local lore says that Grace took up beekeeping when she returned from jail. And as the hive grew, she shared bees with her family and friends."

"Did the hives in the woods come from Grace?"

"That's the story passed down through the years."

"Are the bees over three-hundred-years-old?"

"Oh, no. Of course not." Connie shook her head. "A honeybee's lifespan is only a month or two. But the cycle of life for the hive continued all these years. Some people believe the current bees are the great-great-great—you'd have to add over a thousand greats—grandchildren of the original swarm."

"So why don't you paint their hives?"

"Tradition, I suppose." Connie shrugged. "Maybe out of respect."

"Respect for Grace?"

"Yeah. And for all those generations of women in our family who kept the hives going." Connie held out her open palms and rolled her eyes. "Maybe it's kind of silly."

"But why don't you sell the honey? Wouldn't honey from a three-hundred-year-old hive linked to the Witch of Pungo be really valuable?"

"Maybe. But there's a problem."

"Like what?"

"Bees make honey from the nectar they gather from the plants around them."

"So?"

"And the honey gets its flavor from the nectar."

Riley puzzled over the connection. How could bees collecting nectar be a problem? That's what they're supposed to do. The next question came to mind, almost as an instinct. "Are some kinds of nectar bad?"

Connie nodded. "Ever heard of Mad Honey?"

"No. What's that?"

"Nectar from certain plants produces honey that's toxic to humans, but not bees."

"You mean poisonous?"

"That's right. It's called Mad Honey because it can make someone who eats it feel like they're going crazy or make them sick." Connie paused. "But Mad Honey isn't usually deadly."

Riley closed her eyes for a brief second as she contemplated whether to ask the next logical question. Nothing ventured, nothing gained. She might as well go for it. "Do rhododendron and oleander produce the poisonous nectar?" She peered at Connie, waiting for her reply.

Connie looked at the ground and then up at the sky but didn't make eye contact with Riley. After several seconds, Connie turned her gaze to Riley and pursed her lips. "Not oleander. It's poisonous but doesn't produce nectar."

"But rhododendron—"

"Yeah, rhododendron. And swamp laurels, buttercups, azalea—"

"All of those are near Graces's hives."

"And there are several other noxious plants there, too."

"Is that why you put your Bee Yard so far away?"

"Yes. To be near the neighboring fields and away from the poisonous plants."

"And you added good flowers, like Black-Eyed Susans."

"Yeah. Your favorites, right?"

Riley nodded. As if Nancy Drew were there whispering in her ear, Riley knew what to ask next. But her heart resisted. What if she couldn't handle the answer?

"Connie, did you use honey from Grace's hives to make the pie Mayor Stubbins ate?"

Connie closed her eyes and pursed her lips. She opened her eyes and exhaled a loud sigh.

"So, what if I did?" Connie seemed angry, no longer the with-it Grandma. "Mad Honey just makes people sick."

"But Mayor Stubbins was old and fat. You said his time had come."

"Well..." Connie's lips moved, but no other words came out.

"If nectar from rhododendron is poisonous, wouldn't spraying the plants with the Essence of Rhododendron make it worse? Wouldn't that make the nectar more poisonous?"

Connie's eyes narrowed. "So, you're an expert botanist and toxicologist now, are you?"

"Why else would you spray plants with the stuff that makes them deadly?" Riley's face flushed. "And why...why the Oleander Oil?" Riley looked at the bowl containing the glob of bee-patty mix and then back at

Connie. "Do you just add the Oleander Oil to the bee-patty and bee-candy? OMG, Connie, I mean—"

"You tell me. You seem to know everything else."

Riley's stomach churned as if a dozen butterflies were flapping their wings inside her. No turning back now. She swallowed hard. "Connie, did Mayor Stubbins eat pie sweetened with poison honey from Grace's hives? Poisonous enough to make him have a heart attack?"

Connie didn't answer immediately. But her face changed somehow, darker, and more serious. Her eyes narrowed. She pursed her lips. "Riley, have you ever heard of environmental justice?"

"Environmental what?"

"Stubbins has been trying to ruin Pungo for years. All to line his pockets with cash and enrich his greedy investors."

"But killing someone to—"

"To protect nature? And history? And this farm? If that selfish son of a…" Connie paused. "If…Stubbins…had his way, there'd be nothing left of how Pungo used to be." Connie's jaw tensed. "How Pungo's meant to be." She exhaled a loud sigh. "Maybe his death was Grace Sherwood's way of defending her bees and—"

"From beyond the grave? She's dead, you know."

"Is she, really?" Connie's voice sounded distant, weak. Her eyes were different, too. She looked ahead, straight at Riley. But it was a blank stare, as if Connie's mind had somehow become disconnected from her body. "Maybe she's—"

"A ghost?" Riley rolled her eyes. "I know I'm only thirteen, but do you expect me to believe—?

"So, you think I murdered Mayor Stubbins?" Connie's voice was strong again, determined. Her eyes reflected the same strength and determination.

"Well…no… I mean… At least I hope not." Riley paused and shook her head as if trying to convince herself of Connie's innocence. She didn't want to believe her grandmother could take someone's life. "But everything's so suspicious. And the timing—"

"I'm sure the police will be very interested in your death-by-honey theory." Connie moved swiftly to the shelf with the bottles and jars. "And what exactly do you plan to offer them as evidence?" Connie poured the remaining Oleander Oil and Essence of Rhododendron into the sink and turned on the water to wash the substances down the drain. Then she removed the other bottles on the shelf and did the same with them. "You can tell them all about it and give them the scout salute. Maybe they'll exhume the Mayor's body and test for what, honey residue?"

The remaining hours passed slowly as Riley waited for her mom to arrive. Connie left to deliver the homemade bee-patty to the yellow hive and tend to Grace's bees, while Riley stayed behind to pack. When together, they mostly sat in silence, avoiding the obvious. Mayor Stubbins and the strawberry pie—and assertions of so-called environmental justice—lingered in the background like an invisible eight-hundred-pound gorilla waiting to pounce. The clock on Connie's mantle seemed to tick louder, as nine o'clock and Riley's pending emancipation approached. Would she…should she…tell her mom?

Riley's mom arrived about eight-forty-five. Connie was her old self again, the with-it grandparent who played guitar, sang about strange creatures, and dropped F-Bombs when she didn't think anyone could hear. No mention of Grace Sherwood, Mad Honey, Mayor Stubbins, or rationalizing murder to protect Pungo's rural heritage. Nothing but praise for what a wonderful guest Riley had been. How easy it seemed for Connie to rewrite history without batting an eye.

As Riley got into her mom's car, Connie blew her a kiss. "I'm going to miss you, dear. Maybe you can come back this winter and help me make bee candy."

"Goodbye Grandma Connie." Riley pressed the button to close the car window. "Watch out for magic dragons."

Several minutes passed in silence, as Riley's mom drove north up Princess Anne Road.

"Magic dragons?" Her mom said. "Not much for old Puff, huh?" She chuckled, then frowned. "Didn't you have a good time with Grandma?"

"I guess it could have been better."

"Oh?"

"Did you know that Mayor Stubbins died a couple of weeks ago?"

"Yeah. I heard about it. He had a heart attack."

"The police came to talk with Grandma."

"You don't think she had anything to do with it, do you?"

Riley's heart raced and her temples pounded as she debated what to say. "Well…no… I guess not… I mean—"

"Did the police find anything suspicious?"

"No. Not really."

"It was probably natural causes, like the news said. A heart attack. Although…" Riley's mom paused. "Although, there wasn't much love lost between your Grandma and the Mayor."

"What does that mean?"

"Well, Mayor Stubbins was in favor of developing this part of Virginia Beach into residential homes and condos."

"And take away the farms?"

"Yeah."

"Grandma Connie's, too?"

"Right. He's been trying to buy the farm for years, even before he was Mayor."

"Really?"

"He almost convinced my dad—your Grandpa Walt—to sell just before he died."

"Mom. I don't remember much about Grandpa Walt."

"Not surprising. He passed away twelve years ago. You were so young."

"Has Grandma been living alone that whole time?"

"Mostly. Your Uncle Roy was there for a couple of years before he went to Virginia Tech. I'd been out of the house a while." She smiled. "Seeing the world in the Navy and having a kid."

"How did Grandpa die?"

"Well, it was very sudden. One summer evening, your Grandma and Grandpa were sitting on the screen porch eating pie. They'd been discussing the Mayor's offer to buy the farm. Your Grandpa wanted to take the offer. Your Grandma didn't. Your Grandpa said he was tired and was going to lie down on the couch to rest. He never woke up. Heart attack they say. Well, he'd had some issues, so it made sense."

Riley's face went numb, and her ears echoed with a metallic ringing sound. "Did…did you say pie?"

"That's right, Grandma Connie's strawberry pie."

Riley stared out the car window. The ringing subsided. Maybe the Mayor wasn't Connie's first victim. Maybe the deaths weren't accidents. Her face warmed at the thought. Didn't that mean Connie was a serial killer? What should Riley do? What would Nancy Drew do?

A grandmother—an environmental avenger—poisoning strawberry pie with honey to save the land and her way of life. Who would believe such a story, especially coming from a thirteen-year-old? And what proof did she have? Connie hadn't actually confessed. And what about the stuff Connie poured down the drain? It would be her word against Connie's. Riley pursed her lips and looked at her mother.

"Mom, can you keep a secret?"

"That depends, honey. What's the secret?"

NOTHING QUICK ABOUT IT

DAWN BROTHERTON

THE SQUAWKS OF SEAGULLS pierce my skull. Flinging an arm up to cover my eyes results in sand flying through the air and into my mouth. When I try to spit it out, I can't produce enough saliva. I crack open first one eye, then the other. The sunlight coming through the open bay doors sends another dagger through my brain. I haven't been this messed up in years. What did I drink last night?

Cautiously, I sit up, getting tangled in the tubes connecting me to a machine attached to the white wall. What the hell? I've done a lot of crazy things in the past but had never gone hard enough to end up in an ambulance.

Where is everybody? "Hey!"

Nothing.

Brushing more sand from my clothes, I unfasten the binding around my bicep, then carefully tug the needle from the crook of my left arm. The back doors to the ambulance swing with a gust of wind. Walking in a crouch, I make my way to the doors and jump to the sandy parking lot. A cell phone crunches under my boot. It takes a moment for me to regain my balance. The phone isn't mine, but it isn't going to do anyone else any good either. I pat my pockets, looking for the phone that should be there but is not. Leaning into the back of the ambulance, I do a quick visual check but don't see anything but medical equipment.

The beach is empty except for the raucous birds. My head pounds, so I edge around the side of the ambulance to find help.

Steam rises from under the hood from where the vehicle lost its fight with a light pole.

"Damn!" Immediately, my eyes search for the driver. A small hole surrounded by splintered glass in the driver's side window makes my gut lurch.

I hate to admit this isn't my first rodeo. I use my shirttail to cover my hand as I open the driver's door. "Band on the Run" by Paul McCartney and Wings plays softly on the radio. A man dressed in a dark blue uniform with a Virginia Beach Medical Center patch on his shoulder is slumped sideways in the seat. One look at the brain matter and blood covering the dash tells me the driver is dead.

Sirens sound in the distance and are getting louder. Self-preservation kicks in, and I break into a run.

* * * *

When I reach the relative security of the tourist shop-lined streets, I slow my pace and blend in with the early risers out for a morning stroll. Muttering curses under my breath, I glance around, trying to spot something familiar. The colorful window full of stuffed animals, moving trains, and Lego spaceships catches my attention. That's the shop where I bought the puzzle for Nathaniel. Was that yesterday? My head is still a little woozy, but things are coming back to me.

I recognize the cafe where I had lunch but not the waitress who smiles broadly at me now as she wipes down the patio tables.

"Late night or early morning?" she asks.

"Huh?"

She sets the tables as she speaks. "Are you up early or just getting home from a late night of partying? That happens on vacation, so I hear."

When I look at her blankly, her smiles slips. "Are you okay?"

I paste on a grin that feels fake. "I'm fine. Thanks. Can I get a cup of coffee?" When I reach for my wallet, I realize that's gone too. "On second thought, forget it."

She gives me a sympathetic look. I try my best to saunter away casually.

A police car streaks by, sirens blaring. It takes all my self-control to act curious rather than scared.

Having figured out where I am, I point myself in the direction of the motel. My best bet is probably to get in my car and get out of here. But what about Nathaniel?

I wanted to be there for his eighth birthday. A quick stop. My plan was to be back before my next check in with my parole officer. I don't even know what day it is. Maybe I missed his birthday altogether.

After a few more turns, the drooping sign of the shabby motel—the only one I could afford—comes into view. At least they took cash without asking any questions.

No one moves outside the motel this early in the morning. It doesn't take a rocket scientist to see my car is not in the lot. My heart sinks. I scan the door numbers as I pass, looking for room 106. When I get to it, I'm surprised the door is ajar. Shielding my body behind the outside wall, I gently push the door open with my elbow. Like I said, this isn't my first rodeo. All is quiet, so I risk a quick peek around the frame. It's empty. I slip inside.

The room has been tossed, and window glass crunches under my feet against the threadbare, industrial carpet. I spin in a circle, looking for the bag from the toy store. Neither it nor my overnight bag are in sight. I drop to my knees in between the double beds, searching underneath, coming up with a lone paper resting there.

Leaning on the mattress, I smooth out the drawing of a little boy holding hands with two adults. I've carried this picture of the bald man and the woman with crayon curls since Nathaniel drew it three years ago. I gently stroke a scarred finger across the smiling face of my son.

What am I going to do? I don't have a car or a present. Or money to get another one. Just one more time where Dad is a disappointment.

What if I at least show up? Would Nathaniel be happy to see me? Even empty handed? I inwardly scream in frustration. I don't have a car to get there!

Guilt from another angle rushes me. I'm stressing over a car when a guy on the beach just had his brains blown out. But I push that thought aside. Getting caught busting parole isn't going to bring the guy back. It'll only land me in jail for a crime I had nothing to do with.

I have no idea what happened, and I didn't see anything. I wouldn't be any help. The cops would only see a parole-breaker and stop looking for the real killer. At least this way, the cops will have to do their job.

I can't go back to jail.

* * * *

With the broken window and trashed room, asking about my car at the front desk is out of the question. Flashing lights across the street catch my eye. Not the blue and white of a police car. These are more inviting neon signs, promising cold beer and pool tables. It's as good a place as any to start my search.

Pushing through the grimy glass door, the odor of frying bacon and greasy biscuits assaults my nostrils, reminding me that my stomach isn't ready to forgive me for whatever I did the night before.

"Hey, Sam! Back already?" the bartender calls from behind the bar.

I don't remember the lanky man with a scruffy beard. "Was I here last night?"

The bartender laughs. When I don't join in, he says, "Dude, I didn't think you had that much to drink. Did you at least get lucky?"

Well, that answers one question. I haven't missed Nathaniel's birthday.

"What do you mean? Who was I with?" I perch on a barstool.

"Damn, you really can't remember that leggy, bleached blonde? She was all over you." A bell chimes, and the bartender grabs a plate of food from the kitchen window and slides it in front of a customer seated at the bar.

Catching the reflection of myself in the mirror behind the glass bottles, I decide to take the opportunity to make myself presentable. While the bartender is busy taking the order of a couple who entered after me, I amble to the bathroom.

The door's locked. As I wait my turn, I peruse the pictures tacked to the bulletin board. Obviously taken inside this bar, the pictures showed people packed in and having a great time. Every holiday and more than a few sporting events are represented. The different shades of face paint probably announced the wearer's team preference. This must be a hopping bar in the evenings.

My eye catches on a particular shot of a beautiful blonde with a magnificent smile. Her arms were draped over the shoulders of two men, equally intoxicated by their goofy smiles. But it's her gaze, focused directly into the camera, that stirs recognition.

I remove the picture from the board just as a man comes out of the bathroom, wiping his hands on his pants.

"Do you know these people?" I ask.

He gives me a strange look.

"Sorry. It's just, this guy," I point to the one on the right, "looks a lot like my college roommate, but I can't be sure."

The man squints at the photo. "Looks like those paramedics who are in here all the time. Don't know their names."

I thank him and duck into the bathroom.

Shit! Shit! Shit! I splash water on my face and put my mouth under the faucet, gulping down tepid water.

When I emerge, the television above the bar flashes with a special news bulletin. The lanky man turns it up, leaning against the bar to watch.

"An ambulance has been found abandoned in the parking lot of North End Beach," the newscaster reports. In the background, a police cordon is keeping people away from the accident scene. "One medic has been seriously injured. The other is unaccounted for, along with the patient the ambulance reported picking up."

Injured, my ass. That guy was dead.

Something niggles at the back of my brain, but I can't pin it down. I vaguely recall a struggle. Did I fight with the paramedic? Did I hurt him? No way. I was hooked up in the back. I squeeze my eyes shut tight and rub my temples. So who did I fight with?

Images from my motel room flash across my vision. She was there! The blonde! Her hands were pulling at me. Was she a hustler? Maybe she stole my phone and wallet. Does she have my car too?

I open my eyes to catch the bartender looking from the TV to me then back again before leaning in close and whispering to the old man eating his breakfast. They both turn their eyes on me.

It's time to go. I wave at the gentlemen and depart before they can ask questions I can't answer.

* * * *

I blink at the brightness when I exit the bar. The street is busier now, and many more tourists crowd the street, complete with floppy straw hats and the smell of coconut suntan lotion. The alarm bell sounds nearby, and I turn in time to see an ambulance turn at the street corner ahead of me. Virginia Beach Medical Center is stenciled across its side.

I head in the direction it came from. Maybe someone at the center can tell me who the woman in the photo is.

The medical center resembles a fire station more than a hospital. The large brick building with three oversized garage doors looks out of place among the rundown businesses across the street and the small houses on either side.

I'm still trying to think of a good cover story when a police cruiser passes me from behind. Heart racing, I assess escape routes in case I have to run. When it stops four houses past the medical center, I almost bolt, but the cops aren't looking at me when they get out of the car.

They walk somberly up the walk and ring the bell. The door opens, and my steps falter when it's opened by the woman in the photo. The woman from my room.

I quicken my pace, breaking into a jog as soon as the cops step inside and the door closes, not slowing until I'm one house away. I glance around, but the street is empty. As casually as I can, I walk between the two houses as if I belong there.

Out of sight of the street, I slip between a wall of bushes and a head-high window. It's closed, so I can't make out their words, but by peering over the sill, I see the woman sag onto the couch, obviously distressed. One cop pats her shoulder. They exchange a few more words, the woman shaking her head in response to many of the officers' comments.

Finally, they move to leave, and the woman escorts them to the front door. I stay put, not willing to risk being seen. The door closes.

"Did she seem off to you?" The voice of an officer drifts my way.

"Well, her husband's partner was killed. You'd expect that to shake her," the other answers.

"But more than her husband's disappearance?" The rest of their conversation is lost as they get into their car.

I'm so focused on their comments, the crash of breaking glass catches me off guard. I crouch low and try to slow my racing heart. A few more bangs and thumps, and I have to see what's going on. I resume my spot at the window as the blonde throws things about the room. Then she collapses into a heap on the floor, bawling.

This doesn't seem like the right time to approach her about my stolen items. I'm torn between wanting to comfort her and wanting to get as far away as possible. While I contemplate my options, she stands, pulls out a cell phone, and punches in a number. Wiping away her tears, she's all business now, and she's pissed.

Tucking the phone into the back pocket of her skintight jeans, she walks to an old rolltop desk that has seen better days. Raising the cover, she pushes on the back panel, where a small door pops open. After grabbing an envelope from the hidden compartment, she closes the panel. Without looking back, she races out the front door.

I hold my breath until she drives away in a red CR-V. I count to thirty. Then sixty before making my way to the backyard and up to the door. The lock is surprisingly easy to pick, and I'm inside in no time. Not knowing how long I have, I beeline for the secret compartment, figuring anything worth stealing is probably worth hiding.

My wallet isn't there. All I find is a stack of letters. Curiosity gets to me. I mean, if they were from her husband, why would she hide them?

Score one for me. Definitely not from her husband.

It's too much. If anyone finds out, it'll mean my career. I care for you, but we have to be done. Don't contact me again unless things change.

I glance back through a few older letters. They're pretty racy but no mention of undying love or promises. Sounds like his interest waned. Worth killing over?

From framed photos on the wall, I can now guess which of the two paramedics in the picture I have is her husband. Most of the pictures are taken in the woods. A playground built from wooden beams and posts, not the typical plastic and metal of a modern playground, is featured in many of the early photos. I don't see any as recent as the photo from the bar.

The house is a small one bedroom with a galley kitchen. The dishes in the sink give off a nasty stench, so I hold my breath as I open drawers, looking for where else she might have hidden my belongings. It doesn't take long for me to sweep all the rooms in the same fashion.

Once I exhaust every hiding place I can think of, I give up in frustration. She must still have my things on her, or she ditched them already.

* * * *

Not sure where to turn next, I walk toward the beach by a different route, hoping to spot my car on one of the side streets. Since I woke up on the beach, maybe my car is around here. I need to get to it before the cops find it near the incident scene and run my plates. That would alert my parole officer for sure.

As I get closer to the accident, crowds are stopping traffic to gawk. Even the honking horns don't move the pedestrians along. I circle around the bystanders, tossing an occasional glance toward the scene and the rows of news vans.

All the while, my mind keeps repeating the same questions: why was she pissed? Does she think her husband killed his partner and is on the run? If so, why not tell the cops?

I smack myself in the forehead. When did my focus switch from getting out of the state to solving a murder? Guess it makes sense. Afterall, I was plugged in to their machines. That means they have my DNA, and I'm in the system. I don't want to go down for a murder wrap. Breaking parole is a slap on the wrist compared to that.

I need to figure out who killed the driver.

First things first. How was I connected to the blonde? Was she looking for a hook-up after her lover broke her heart? That doesn't explain how I ended up in the back of an ambulance. I wouldn't have had that much to drink, knowing I was going to see Nathaniel on his birthday.

She had to have slipped me something. But why?

Five blocks away, I still haven't spotted my sedan, and I'm zigzagging my way away from the ocean. If it's close to the beach, I'm screwed anyway. The cops have probably set up a search area, not letting any vehicles leave. They wouldn't want the killer to drive away.

If blondie's husband is the killer, why would he shoot his partner when I was in the back of the ambulance? Surely he had a better opportunity. But if he isn't the killer, why is he running? Why not call the cops himself?

Ah, the cell phone I stepped on. But still, there are plenty of cops milling about.

The questions plague me as I wander the streets, getting farther and farther from the ambulance. When I finally take notice of my surroundings, I realize I've wandered close to the state park. Hardly anyone is walking these streets. The shops and restaurants are blocks closer to the beach.

An idea hits me. What if the paramedic saw the shooter and was running away? He could have easily run into the park, away from the shooter but also away from the throngs of people who could have provided protection. Without a cell phone, he was essentially cut off until he stumbled across someone, or someone found him.

I'm taking a big chance. But I still haven't found my car, so I can't go anywhere anyway. What the hell.

I leap over the waist-height stone wall, meant more for decorative purposes than a deterrent. Eventually I chance upon a trail cutting through thick live oaks, waxed myrtles, and gnarled loblolly pines native to this area. I randomly pick a direction, looking for a sign to guide me.

My thoughts return to my other problem of what I'm going to tell my ex when I don't show up at Nathaniel's party. Eight-year-olds aren't likely to understand the nuances of being accused of murder.

I shake my head clear of the nagging when I approach an intersection to the trail and a ranger sign with arrows pointing out key parts of the park. Exit to the left or playground and boat ramp to the right.

To the right it is.

No one was on the playground this early in the morning, but there are two cars in the parking lot. Halleluia! Relief floods me when I see my beat-up sedan, in all its rusted-out glory. This is my chance to get away...if I can find the keys.

My heart drops when I notice the red CR-V. What's she doing here?

I shake my head. It's a coincidence; that can't be hers. As I pass it, I rest my hand on the hood. Still warm. What are the chances? I look around for other visitors, but no one is within range.

Maybe the blonde is looking for her husband. But why not tell the cops where he might be and let them look?

Ugh! I have a bad feeling about this.

A sound freezes me in place. My fight or flight reflexes tense my muscles. I strain to hear. It isn't loud, and I can't make out words. The man could be out there hurt or in trouble. Or he could be a killer. The blonde could be there to help him or hurt him. Either way, I can't run away. With one more longing glance at my car, I move closer.

I leave the playground area, following a path downhill toward the boat ramp. Signs warning hikers to stay on the trail line the walkway. The ground on either side gives way to marsh.

When a voice gets louder, I creep quietly closer, staying out of sight behind a copse of bald cypress trees.

"You!" The blonde flings the word at the prone man like an accusation. "You're supposed to be dead!"

* * * *

That voice hits me like an anvil, stirring the nausea that threatens to give away my hiding spot. With her pitch, more memories return.

She had been in my room. She wanted to go somewhere, but I didn't want to. I only wanted to sleep, but she wouldn't let me. She needed a favor first. She grabbed Nathaniel's present and my still-packed overnight bag. I fought with her but couldn't coordinate my arms and legs enough to be effective.

"You want your things? Come get them!" She tossed them into the backseat of my car. When I crawled in after them, she slammed the door closed.

That same demanding voice is now directed at the man in a dark blue uniform struggling to lift his head. "You were supposed to drive the ambulance this shift. You'd been bitching about it all day."

He's keeled over in the marsh, bleeding profusely from a gash on his cheek. Cradling his right arm, he tries to get to his feet. He slides in the muck and falls facedown again, crying out in pain.

She shoves her knee into the middle of the man's back, forcing his head down. "You can't even die when you're supposed to."

He thrashes, coming up for air briefly before she thrusts his head down forcefully. She's still brandishing a thick branch in her right hand, and he can't seem to get traction in the mud.

Dammit! If I do this, I'm all in…and on my way back to jail for busting my parole. If I don't, that man's going to die. Maybe Nathaniel will forgive me because I did the right thing when it counted.

I lose my internal battle for self-preservation. Stepping from behind the trees as quietly as I can, I inch up behind the woman whose full focus is on her intended quarry.

"I killed you, not him." Her crying declaration certainly doesn't spur any sympathy from me.

The man's feeble splashes are louder than any noise I make as I bound the last few steps and leap at the woman, knocking her aside from the downed man in blue. Now it's her turn to swallow salt water as my weight shoves her into a deeper pool. The freed man splutters and flops onto his back, gasping for air.

I push away from the blonde and scramble to my feet. She rolls over to face me but doesn't get up. Now I clutch a fallen tree branch the size of my arm and almost as thick. "Why did you have to drag me into this?"

Blinking in sudden comprehension, the blonde laughs manically. "Are you kidding me?"

From her seated position, she reaches into her inside jacket pocket and pulls out a pistol. She points the gun at my chest, and my world drops into slow motion.

"Men. None of you do what you're supposed to." She pulls the trigger.

When I hear the click, I sigh in relief and things start to move at normal speed again. But when she makes to pull the trigger again, I swing my stick with all my might. The wood connects just as a bullet rips through my left shoulder.

* * * *

Memories flash through my head as I struggle my way back to consciousness.

I'm in the back seat of my car. How did I get here?

The door opens, and my body flops through the gap. I can't catch myself. The blonde has ahold of the back of my jacket. None too gently, she's dragging me from the car. My butt hits packed sand moments before my feet follow. Unceremoniously, she drops my head. Dammit! The sharp smack hurts like hell, however, I can't do anything about it.

My eyes are only open slits, but there's not enough light to see detail anyway.

When she opens the driver's door again, the overhead light comes on. She flops in behind the wheel and picks up a cell phone. It must be on speaker because I hear both sides of the conversation.

"Nine-one-one. What's your emergency?"

"There's a man passed out cold on North Beach. I'm not sure if he's breathing." The blonde is doing a pretty good imitation of someone who gives a shit.

"Ma'am, what's—" The line goes dead.

She's looking at me now. "Don't worry. They'll be here soon, and it'll be over quickly. According to the scanner, they're just coming off their break around the corner."

I can't read her expression as she closes the door and drives away. I try to call out, but it's useless. I give up and close my eyes.

When I open them again, two men are hovering over me; both are dressed in dark blue uniforms. One is going through my pockets. I close my eyes again.

The beeping of the monitors wakes me. I listen intently.

When I gather enough nerve, I open my eyes. I'm in an ambulance… alone. Tubes contact me to a bag of clear fluid hanging above my head. I sit up carefully, not sure if the vehicle is moving or if it's just me.

After another minute, the spinning stops.

I have to get out of here. I rip the needle from my arm, then unfasten the blood pressure cuff and toss it aside. Taking a deep breath to steady my nerves, I push the back doors open. My left shoulder cries out in protest.

The area is crammed with people. Every cruiser in town must have shown up.

A police officer approaches me. "Sir, are you all right? Let me get the medic."

I wave him closer and slide down to sit heavily on the bumper. "I'm fine. What's happening?"

The cop smiles broadly. "You're a hero! That paramedic says you saved his life. Came flying out of nowhere and took down that mad woman."

The mention of the woman reminds me of the gun. I lift my right hand to cover my heavily bandaged left shoulder and wince.

"You were shot. But it just grazed you. Nothing to be concerned about. A paramedic cleaned it up. They'll be taking you to the hospital to get it looked at as soon as we can clear away these looky-loos. Luckily, the gunshot brought everyone running. That's how we found you. You must have clubbed her hard before passing out. She was down for the count when we showed up."

The cop stops long enough to study my eyes. "You good? You'll need to give a statement. Let me get the lieutenant."

As soon as he turns his back, I grab a windbreaker left inside the ambulance. I pull the letter I found in the hidden compartment and the photo from the bar and toss them on the gurney. Slipping around the side of the vehicle, I force my arms into the sleeves, gasping slightly as I insert the left one. The pain is dull, so the painkillers must be pretty powerful, but I don't feel loopy.

The marshy area has forced all emergency vehicles and news vans into the boat launch parking area. Keeping my head down, I hasten for the path away from the reporters. My pants are covered in muck, but it blends into the brown denim, making it hardly noticeable. With the word PARAMEDIC plastered across my back, no one gives me a second look as I duck into the trees.

I see the sign for the playground and step up my pace. In my condition, running is out of the question. There are a few more cars in the lot but no one on the playground. They're probably trying to see what's happening near the police cars.

Thankfully my car door's unlocked, and I slide into the driver's seat, checking first the ignition, then the console for keys. Frantically I yank down the visor and am frustrated when nothing falls. Throwing my head back, I sigh heavily. I just need to catch a break.

My glance falls on my phone and wallet on the front passenger seat. At least I can call Nathaniel and wish him a happy birthday, so he knows I didn't forget.

I lean over to pick up the phone, and my foot detects an unusual bump on the floor. I whisk away the mat and pluck up the keys hidden there. Jamming the right one into the ignition, I say a silent prayer of thanks.

Slamming the car into gear, I remind myself to remain calm as I head for the state line. I'll call my son from there.

IT'S ALL IN THE FAMILY

MARIA HUDGINS

WILL GREENE checked the fridge to make sure his wife, Amanda, had made the burgers. His mom, Carol, stood at the kitchen sink of their Nags Head beach house rinsing the shrimp for their cookout. This year the family had rented two oceanfront houses because the kids were getting so big and rowdy the grown-ups decided this would be a good way to give themselves some peace at cocktail hour. The under-twenties could have the house at #2347 to themselves while the adults enjoyed drinks at #2345.

"When do we want to eat?" Will thought he would get the grill going about an hour before he put the burgers on so they could have their happy hour while the kids played video games next door.

"The shrimp will need an hour under the broiler so let's eat about, say, eight?"

Will was glad his mother said, "under the broiler," because it meant she was making his favorite kind of shrimp, and he would not have to deal with a tangle of skewered shrimp on his outdoor grill.

"Where's Amanda?" Carol asked, swiping a wisp of hair out of her face with her left arm.

"Next door talking to Sara. Girl talk."

"They've got a lot to talk about, I'm sure."

Sara was Amanda's sister and the widow of Tom Powell, former minor league baseball player who had been killed two years ago in a still-unsolved murder. Police had done their best but the proof they needed simply wasn't there. The family, the team, and their entire community was devastated, and Sara was left to struggle alone, raising two children, now 10 and 14 years old.

Will pulled a bag of charcoal briquettes out of the cupboard. "It's great that they have something good to talk about—for a change."

"So, is this a done deal or one of those squirrelly Hollywood things?"

Will laughed. "Squirrelly Hollywood things?"

"Oh, you know. Anyone who's ever got a book published gets hit up by some Hollywood fast-talker who gets the movie rights, but never comes through with an actual movie."

"I don't know," Will said. "But Amanda thinks it's a pretty sure thing."

The family had pulled together to help Sara make it through Tom's funeral, the kids dealing awkwardly and sometimes angrily with the loss of their dad, and Sara working full time while simultaneously burning the midnight oil to finish her book. Now the book was selling well, and Hollywood had come knocking with the promise of much more money.

Tom, in Will's opinion, had always been a jerk. A handsome, athletic guy who tended to be the life of the party but had never had an original thought in his life. He wondered what Sara had seen in him until he remembered that Sara was a woman and Tom was a handsome, athletic guy with the sort of little boy charm that women always fall for.

Tom was no better than his teammates, Will thought. *A bunch of mental midgets whose idea of a good time was an afternoon at the shooting range followed by too much beer, bragging contests, and the rehashing of every inning of every game they had ever played.*

"Anything new from the police?" Carol asked.

"Nada. No help. Amanda thinks they're giving up." Will pulled a Heineken from the fridge and twisted the cap off. "You know how many weapons they found in those guys' locker room? Twelve! That included guns, knives, and tasers in lockers, gym bags, wherever. Most of them were locked up in the safe in the coach's office but still …"

"But they don't know if any of them is the one that killed Tom?"

"The ballistics report cleared that up. Sort of."

"And?" Carol was aware that Will and Amanda did not tell her everything. They phoned and visited often at home, but they tended to leave out some things, saving Mom the gory details. "What do you mean, sort of?"

"They did find the gun, but it was under a bench in the locker room." Will took a long pull from his beer. "And the serial number was filed off."

"How convenient," Carol said.

"Right. But this was the only gun with a filed-off serial number. So, it kind of looks like it was intended for nefarious purposes."

"In other words, if you know you're going to kill someone, use a gun that can't be traced." Carol poured her five pounds of large shrimp into a broiler pan and turned to see Will and Amanda's daughter, twelve-year-old Olivia.

"Gram? When are we going to eat?"

Carol handed her a celery stalk and told the child to go next door. "We will eat at eight. Until then, make do with celery."

Olivia groaned, but she did as her grandmother told her.

Carol winced at the slamming of the screen door and turned back to Will. "No fingerprints?"

"On the gun?" Will recalled their interrupted conversation. "No. Doesn't that seem odd? Whoever dropped the gun under that bench would have had to deliberately wipe off the fingerprints before dropping it. They meant for it to be found there."

"Where anyone on the team might have dropped it."

"Or anyone on the coaching staff, or one of the janitors, or the grounds crew, or practically anyone."

"But does it eliminate the owners of the guns *with* serial numbers?" Carol waved her paring knife at her son. "Having a properly registered gun in your locker might make the one on the floor seem less likely to be yours."

"There's no law that says you can't have *two* guns. Having a gun that's registered to you doesn't mean you didn't also drop the gun that killed Tom." Will swigged his beer and wiped his mouth with the back of his hand. "It could have been anybody in the whole world."

"Most likely, someone who could be in the players' locker room without raising eyebrows."

Will paused before bringing up the theory most people considered quite possible. Tom was a playboy, and everybody knew it. His affairs were well known to everyone, including Sara. Will and Amanda had talked about it and about the fact that Sara accepted it as something she had no control over. She had her children and her writing. "You can't have everything, can you?" she had told Amanda more than once. Amanda didn't understand, but she knew she couldn't change her sister, and if she tried, she might lose her sister's love.

Will pulled the platter of burgers covered with wax paper from the fridge and began searching for the long-handled grill tools. "Amanda says Sara is already working on another book."

"It's a good book—the first one, I mean," Carol said. "I'm reading it for the second time."

"Maybe writing keeps her mind off of her troubles."

"I don't think it's that at all." Carol looked out the window. "Time to start the charcoal."

* * * *

While the grown-ups enjoyed their drinks in #2345, they could hear shouts and laughter wafting up from the beach. The four cousins plus two more teens that Bree, Sara's daughter, had met at Kitty Hawk Kites had joined them. They had been together and unsupervised now for quite a few hours.

"I keep wondering when we'll hear the first argument," Amanda said.

"Don't jinx it," Carol called in from the kitchen. "Hearing them laughing like this is music to my ears."

"Mine too," Sara said, glancing out at one of the big ocean-facing windows. "Poor Simon. He still has days when he misses his dad so much, he can hardly bear it."

And you too? Will thought but didn't say it. *The fact is, Tom's murder was a stroke of good luck for you, Sara.* "Are the police making any progress? Have they interviewed all of Tom's teammates?"

"Oh, they finished that long ago," Sara said. "And the coaches and everyone connected with the team."

"Who else are they looking at?" Amanda asked.

"Tom had enemies; you know," Sara said, very softly. "There's the wives and girlfriends of his teammates. Seems like every player had at least one of each."

Amanda laughed, then threw her hand over her own mouth.

Carol came in from the kitchen and joined them. "I heard that."

"Just telling it like it is," Amanda said, knowing her mother-in-law was definitely not naïve.

Carol put a hand on Sara's arm. "I wasn't born yesterday, but since you brought it up, are you having any fun, Sara? It's been two years."

Sara turned bright red. "I have my children and my job and my writing. I don't have the time or the inclination for anything else."

Carol looked from Will to Amanda and back to Will. All three faces said, *I don't believe that for a minute.*

Amanda had told Carol a lot about Sara's problems. Tom had kept them teetering on the edge of bankruptcy throughout the fifteen years of their marriage. The minors didn't pay that much, and the family depended on Sara's salary as a bookkeeper to make ends meet. Every time they almost got solvent, Tom would go out and buy a motorcycle or a new sound system or something that would put them right back in debt. Sara sometimes got strange calls at home. Tom spent money on girlfriends and tried to cover it up, but not cleverly enough to fool Sara.

Through it all, Sara put on a brave face as if nothing was wrong, but Amanda knew better. After Tom was killed, she and Will had a long talk about it. They didn't mind upholding the fiction that everything was fine between Sara and Tom, but wouldn't the police put two and two together? Wouldn't they suspect her? Didn't she have a better motive than anyone?

Carol left the room to check on her shrimp, and Will followed her with two glasses to fill from the pitcher of Margaritas on the kitchen counter.

In the kitchen, Will sidled up to his mother. "The police have managed to raise the filed-off serial number on that gun."

Carol dropped one of her kitchen mitts on the open oven door. She quickly retrieved it, slapped off a couple of smoldering spots on the mitt, then turned to Will. "I didn't know they could even do that!"

"Apparently they can, sometimes." He put down the glasses and turned, resting his back side on the edge of the counter. "Sometimes the metal underneath retains a memory of the pressure that was applied when the numbers were stamped on it."

"Have they identified the serial number? Do they know whose gun it is?"

"It was Tom's gun."

* * * *

Will and Carol stood stock still in the middle of the kitchen, neither one knowing where to go with that line of thought. Carol closed the oven door.

Sara Powell walked in and said, "That's right. Sort of makes me look bad, doesn't it?"

Sara had changed from her bathing suit to a knee-length tank dress but, as always, no makeup, no jewelry.

"Did you know Tom had a gun?" Carol asked.

"Of course. He kept it in his sock drawer. But it wasn't loaded."

"Had you ever checked that sock drawer in the last two years?" Carol's eyes grew large.

"No. Why would I do that?"

"Haven't you given away any of Tom's socks? His other clothes? Have you even looked in that drawer since Tom was killed?" Carol, with her spotless house, couldn't imagine taking such a casual attitude toward housekeeping.

"I've been very busy." Sara's voice sounded edgy. Defensive.

Amanda walked in and refilled her glass from the Margarita pitcher. "I take it the police have talked to you about this."

"When did they talk to you?" Will asked.

"Yesterday," Sara said.

All three just stared at her, open-mouthed.

"What's the story on the gun? Where did he get it and why was the serial number filed off?" Will was trying to make sense of this.

"I don't know, but I suspect he got it from one of his sketchy friends. Tom knew some people who didn't necessarily do everything legally," Sara said.

Another woman walked in from the front room. She carried an amber-colored drink in an old-fashioned glass. She had dark, curly hair and big hoop earrings. Will and Amanda greeted her, and Sara introduced her to Carol.

She said, "This is Megan Beri. We've been friends since college, and she's staying with me next door for a couple of days."

They all nodded. Since Sara and her two children were the only ones sleeping next door at #2347, there was no problem with Sara having a friend staying over. Carol was paying the rental fees for both houses, but she didn't mind the extra guest. In fact, she had told Sara she could invite someone else if she wanted to.

In the front room were a dozen or so people, mostly other vacationers one of them had met in the last week or so. These vacationers tended to meet and form casual acquaintances that only rarely lasted past the summer season. A few of them may have been permanent residents of the Outer Banks. Sara and Megan left Carol, Amanda, and Will still waiting to hear more about what the police had said. They slipped back into the front room.

Will ran his fingers through his curly hair. In a sarcastic, high-pitched voice, he said, "Oh, never mind, officer. You say my husband was killed with his own gun? How interesting! No, I have no idea how that could have happened!"

Amanda's eyes welled up. "I don't know what to think. This is horrible! Did she really do it? I haven't let myself think it, but it's starting to sound like she did it!"

Will laid a hand on his wife's shoulder. "I'm sure she wouldn't be here now if the police have confronted her with the situation. She must have had an explanation, or she'd be in jail now. They wouldn't have let her go, otherwise."

"Like what?" Amanda sobbed.

Will was fighting with his own thoughts. He couldn't let himself think this way. But the thought crept in again: Sara bravely puts up with a philandering husband for years. Even though he makes her look like a fool in front of all their friends, she doesn't complain. He dies, but she doesn't give his clothes away. She's living a lie. She's always been living a lie. Now that she's free, she doesn't date anyone new. She's sharing her summer home with her dear friend from college. Has Sara talked to—what is her name—Megan?

Will decided he would say nothing to anyone else until he and Amanda had a chance to talk it over.

And what about the threatening phone calls? Will recalled that Amanda hadn't wanted to talk about it, even to him, but he knew Sara had received phone calls that scared her shortly after Tom's death. They had come from area codes in the Midwest. Until this thing with Tom's gun came up, Will thought the most likely killer was one of the shady characters Tom dealt with when he needed fast cash. Will had done a bit of snooping on his own without telling the police and had discovered a real estate scam in

Florida that was ripping off potential buyers. But how was Tom involved? He hadn't got that far yet. Will looked out the window. He saw Sara and her friend, Megan, crossing the dune that led to the beach.

* * * *

"What did the detective want?" Megan asked.

"He needs to talk to me again," Sara said.

The two women took advantage of beach chairs someone had left. Two of the kids were skimboarding in the shallow water. Three others kept a pickleball aloft with paddles, and a couple of teenage girls stood talking in waist-deep water.

"It's all so hopeless. Ridiculous." Sara dug her toes into the dry sand.

Megan went silent for a long time, then squinted out to the water with its wave crests reflecting the rays of the setting sun. "It's not as if they can learn anything by visiting your house now. After two years, what could they find?"

"Right. I may be a lousy housekeeper, but even I have cleaned up a few times since then."

"He's already interviewed everyone Tom knew, but he can go back and interview them all again. This time, he won't bother with the players and coaches and such." Megan dodged a loose pickleball.

"I won't be surprised if he doesn't start with my sister."

"Amanda? Why her?"

"Because he knows Amanda and I talk about everything. What he needs to know now is what my marriage was like. Were Tom and I getting along as well as it seemed?"

"Did someone speak my name in vain?" Amanda had walked up behind them. "Time to eat," she said, and then louder, to the kids, "Go to the house. It's time to eat!"

Before Amanda reached the house, her cell phone rang. She paused on the slanted dune and answered it.

"Amanda Greene? This is Detective Rodrigues, Durham Police."

Amanda couldn't say she wasn't expecting this. After talking to Sara about the fact that the gun was apparently Tom's, and until the forensic report came back, the police had no way of determining its owner, she knew the police would be zeroing in on the domestic scene. Barring another strange development, it now seemed as if the baseball team had nothing to do with the murder. The locker room too, was nothing more than the place the gun was dropped.

"Sorry to call you so late, Mrs. Greene, but it's important that I talk to you—and soon."

"Is this about my sister?"

"It's about some new evidence that we have in the murder of your former brother-in-law."

Of course. The police never answer your questions, and he hadn't answered hers. "When do you want to talk? Do I have to drive to Durham?"

"Where are you now?"

"I'm in Nags Head. The family is vacationing here."

"It's eight o'clock now." Rodrigues said. "I could be in Nags Head by eleven, no, no, that's too late." He paused a minute.

Amanda's heart leaped. *He actually wants to come here tonight!* She knew this was important. She waited for Detective Rodrigues to go on.

"Could you possibly meet me at the Nags Head Police Station tomorrow morning about nine?"

"Well…sure. I guess so. But I don't know where it is."

"Could you give me your email? I'll send you the address."

Amanda gave him her email address.

"And also, Mrs. Greene, it would be nice if you didn't tell the rest of the family about this meeting. Not permanently. Just until we've had a chance to talk."

Amanda rang off, shaking. She wasn't sure that police were allowed to tell you not to tell your family where you are going. Why did he say that?

* * * *

Will was running down the beach the next morning when he glanced between the houses that lined the waterfront like an advancing army threatening to overtake the Atlantic when he saw, through a gap in the dunes, their red SUV coming up their driveway. He turned and ran up the steep slope to meet Amanda before she made it to the kitchen where Carol was making sandwiches. He wanted to find out what Detective Rodrigues had said.

"Let's take a walk," Amanda said.

Will was glad she said that. Now they could talk privately before they had to tell everyone why she had left the house so early.

Amanda kicked off her shoes so she could walk in the sand. "I feel like I've been through a wringer. He asked me a thousand questions." She leaned into her husband's side as he gave her a kiss on the forehead. "You know what? I wondered how he could get here so early all the way from Durham, so I asked, and he said he left home at five-thirty in the morning. I thought, wow, this must be important."

"Get on with it! Tell me."

"He told me they had identified the gun that killed Tom, but we already knew that. He said they knew the bullet that killed him was definitely fired by Tom's gun. The gun was found under a bench in the players' dressing room."

"We already knew that," Will said.

"And Tom's body was found in the players' lounge about fifty feet from the dressing room. Two doors between the lounge and the dressing room."

"We already knew that, too. So, it was impossible for Tom to have killed himself. There would have been a trail of blood all down the hall."

Will wished she would get on with it. As soon as they identified the gun under the bench as Tom's they knew it couldn't have been suicide. Will frowned. "Why did Detective Rodrigues need to talk to you?"

"Because he now knew it wasn't likely to have been any of the players or the staff. What about someone from outside? Tom had plenty of other people who might have wanted to kill him, but who would have been able to get the gun from Tom's sock drawer in their bedroom?"

"I guess a break-in would have been possible, but not likely. Risky."

"So obviously, they are now concentrating on Sara herself."

"Right. And that's why Detective Rodrigues doesn't want me to tell Sara about our meeting this morning."

Will walked along, his face to the sky. How long can she possibly deny the meeting? Sara is going to know she's now the prime suspect. She's not dumb. I'll bet she's been looking out the window this morning. She may have seen our car driving in. This is not a secret they can keep very long. In fact, it's rather unreasonable for Detective Rodrigues to ask her to keep it from her own sister. "Amanda?"

She wasn't listening to him.

"Amanda?"

"Ohmigod!" Amanda threw her hands to her head. "Ohmigod? SHE did it!"

"Sara?"

"No! Listen! I just remembered something. Two years ago, around the time Tom got killed, I was at their house, helping Sara clean up. She's so unorganized, you know. I just remembered finding a big hoop earring on the floor beside their bed. I put it on top of their dresser, and I didn't mention it to Sara because I knew she would find it on the dresser."

"Apparently you think it wasn't Sara's."

"I KNOW it wasn't Sara's. This was a big, silver, hoop earring. Sara is allergic to almost any metal but gold. Fourteen karat or better."

"So, it wasn't Sara's."

"No. And who else could it belong to?" Amanda was so excited, she ran out in front of her husband, turned, and began walking backward.

"Who else comes to their house often? Into their bedroom? I mean besides me."

"Megan? The girl we met last night?"

"Exactly. But I've met her before. Sara has told me about her, and I know she's visited them, but I don't know how often."

Will stopped, freezing in his tracks. It did make sense. Too much sense. He dropped to the sand, rested his elbows on his knees and lowered his head. "We must be careful here. We can't go accusing Megan of murder just because she isn't allergic to silver."

"At any other time, I would say that the owner of that earring could be anyone in the world, as much as Tom fooled around, but I can't imagine him having a woman into their bedroom. That would be too risky," Amanda mused. "But your wife's college roommate? Megan could probably explain that away with something like, 'Oh hi! I was looking for that blouse you said I could borrow.' Or something like that."

"We shouldn't deal with this, Amanda. This is for the police to handle. Call Rodrigues back and tell him about this earring."

Amanda pulled her phone from her bag.

SILVER BELLS AND BULLET SHELLS
(PRETTY MAIDS ALL IN A ROW)

ALLIE MARIE

TIME TO GO. While he preferred his solitude when he was on vacation, he found the need to be around people had increased a little more these last few days. He shut down his computer and closed the top.

The isolated cottage he had rented from a friend was located a few miles southwest of Jockey's Ridge State Park in the Outer Banks, a major tourist destination on North Carolina's east coast. Made of much smaller sand dunes than the state park and dotted with small ponds, marshy areas, and patchy forests, Marshall Beach was private property owned by a few old families. He was the only soul for miles around, unless one counted the joggers, walkers, and bird watchers who traipsed the nearby trails.

The hot shower refreshed him. He wiped steam from the mirror to prepare to shave away the three-day growth, but instead frowned and leaned closer to study his reflection.

A lot more salt seemed to show up in the pepper of his once all-black beard. He angled his head to the side. Yep, a few more silver threads rippled through the dark at his temples.

Not too shabby for a man turning fifty, however. He finished dressing, ready to enjoy his self-gifted birthday present today, just like his past presents for Christmas, Valentine's Day, and Easter. Maybe he'd add July 4th to collect his next reward, but he could decide later. He didn't always celebrate on the actual holiday, but at some point during the week of the festivities, he managed to have his own celebrations—when the mood struck him.

That's what loners do. Like too many others, he had withdrawn from society. Politics had gotten crazy, political correctness even crazier. The bureaucratic red tape and other idiotic formalities he had to go through just to get his medication was enough to aggravate even the staunchest citizen trying to survive. His choice was to remain alone and away—as far away as he could get—from all the bullshit.

But he still needed occasional human interaction.

First, he would stop at the fast-food joint, grab a hot coffee and a cardboard breakfast of scrambled eggs on a biscuit, and skim through the free newspaper they provided.

Then he would zip out on the beach highway on his motorcycle and enjoy the early spring air. Winter still clung to life, sending a last-ditch effort to linger with a chilly wind. The sun would make short work of that by the time he reached his hiking area. Dunes surrounded the trail, blocking the view of the beach. Or blocking the view of the park from beachgoers—depending on the point of view of the visitor.

He parked his motorcycle and walked into the small establishment. The teeny bopper behind the counter greeted him with the effervescence of someone who had just started working at the Smile and Go Restaurant and Convenience Store. He placed his order and she scooted away to fill it.

Give her a few more days and she'll be as grumpy as the rest of the overworked, underpaid staff at this bustling restaurant. With Memorial Day bringing the start of the summer season, the swell of tourists would only add to the overload of the small staff later this season.

No skin off his nose. He was just a beach tourist today. He had a mountain retreat in mind for the 4th of July. A mid-summer gift to himself might be fun, away from sand and ocean—and even more isolated.

"Number thirty," the clerk called a few minutes later.

"Me," he answered and stepped up to pay. He nodded, took his change, then winked at the girl, laughing inwardly at the warm blush creeping up her neck.

His next stop was at the condiment counter, where he added creamer and two sugars to the coffee. He grabbed some salt and scrutinized the room, looking for the most secluded spot he could find. Three empty tables near one corner caught his eye, and he headed for the center table of the trio. The other two were too close to occupied tables. He'd rather sit at an isolated island than crammed beside chattering vacationers.

A quick perusal of the newspaper reminded him of why he had withdrawn from society: the Dems and 'Pubs were slinging insults at each other instead of dealing with the current issues.

All the while, new tensions flared in the Middle East, healthcare was in disarray—*yeah, they should talk to me about that*—border and immigration issues were pitting sensibilities against compassion, race-baiting occurred on all sides. These days, you could not even open your mouth for fear of someone feeling disrespected.

The country was going to hell in a handbasket.

The local news wasn't much better. Taxes increased while services declined. Some mother was so proud of her son for refusing to stand for the national anthem, while a veteran of the war in Iraq, who could no longer stand, fought eviction from his home because he couldn't pay the bills. His disability checks were being held up by red tape.

The local crime news only emphasized the gloom. The usual litany of car thefts, break-ins, and thefts filled the columns. One article indicated that the police still had not found the killer of several women whose bodies had been found along various jogging trails around the state. Investigators had few clues, other than some evidentiary items left at each crime scene. The report indicated the police declined to identify specifics.

A noisy family of four took over the table to his left. An older couple took over the one to his right. He gathered his trash and placed it on the tray.

Time to go. His birthday present awaited.

He dumped his trash and by accident, the tray. He shrugged, not about to dig through the bin to salvage the cheap red plastic server.

Finally, he roared away on his motorcycle and drove to the perfect spot. He hiked to the tree he had long ago selected, leaned against it, and checked his watch.

Waiting. The anticipation made him giddy, as if a thousand ants crawled across his skin.

It took about ten minutes for everything to fall in place. Finally. *Happy birthday to me*!

He smelled her scent long before he heard her. *Why do women wear perfume when they jog?*

He heard her long before he saw her. Thumping footsteps, leaves and twigs snapping under her shoes, gave him ample warning. She was right on time, just like she'd been the previous five days he had watched and sur- veilled. With his right hand, he withdrew the 9mm from the special holster he'd sewn inside his cargo pants pocket to handle the extra length of the suppressor.

Sunlight streamed through the forest. Her shadow flickered as she passed by a row of oaks, causing a strange choppiness to her movements as she passed by the trees. It reminded him of the old-time stick figures he and his friends used to draw on the bottom of a notepad. When they flipped through the pages, the stick figure became an animated cartoon, doing flips, running, or batting a ball. A moment later she appeared on the short stretch of straight trail.

Happy birthday to me. Rotating on one foot, he stepped onto the path, filling the passage narrowed by fallen tree trunks. His left hand tightened to muffle the jingle of the little silver bell encased in a plastic baggy. When he was finished, he would shake it out of the bag and leave it behind as his calling card.

Startled, the runner stopped short, and bent forward, hands braced on her knees as she gasped. He'd chosen his gift well. She'd been running a long time already, and he had broken her rhythm. Despite the chilly weather, she wore a black tank top and maroon leggings that showcased her perfectly formed figure. The tall willowy blonde wore her perfect platinum hair in a ponytail high atop her head, framing her face painted with the perfectly applied makeup.

Makeup to jog? Excellent. He raised the gun.

The runner looked up again from her panting position, slanting her eyes in anger. When her gaze fell on the barrel, the alarm glazing in her bright blue eyes sent a shiver of satisfaction coursing through his body. The gun would look like a cannon to her at this distance.

She opened her mouth but before she could utter a sound, he pulled the trigger. *Ping.* The silencer did its job as the hushed bullet struck her forehead.

Only he heard the little click as the slide snapped back, ejecting the single shell.

No worries about fingerprints. The cops would have to obtain the gun to match the rifling to the spent shell. He'd make sure that would never happen. Since he never touched the bullets with his bare hands, any fingerprints that might have been permanently etched in the casing would not have come from him. Maybe the manufacturer. But he always wiped his bullets clean anyhow before loading the magazine with gloved hands.

He left the casing and his calling card…the silver bell. He had no intention of getting arrested, but when and if the police caught on to him, he wondered how long it would be before they noticed a very distinct pattern of where he left his victims.

Pretty maids all in a row.

As the shooter headed back to his motorcycle, he pondered the same thought that he'd had earlier.

Why *do* women wear perfume when they jog?

It only attracts insects…and killers.

HAPPY DAYS AT THE HALLVIEW CEMETERY

MAX JASON PETERSON

IT WOULD NOT be a cemetery visit without the picnic.

Mirabelle loved going to the Hallview Cemetery with her family every Sunday. Once a part of Denbigh Plantation in Newport News, Virginia, it had been in their family for 150 years.

Cemetery visits were her idea of a vacation. All the best people were here. Her grandparents, to start with. And her mother. Her little brother, two years younger, who'd died when he was only five. Her Uncle Cedric, whose sweet tooth had brought a not-so-sweet end. Her Aunt Ethyl, whose passion for independence had given her one final chance to trip lightly down the stairs.

The family traveled from miles and states around to join these regular reunions with their festival air, spreading out checkered blankets near family graves. Cousins passed bread and cheese, singing songs from their youth. The living and the dead seemed to lift their voices in harmony in those moments.

As the family grew and grew—cousins and greats, in-laws and the kin they brought with them —so did the vociferous family battles, with some running after one another in a vicious game of flag football, claws extended. If they caught you, there would be rending and tearing of flesh. The high-pitch shrieks weren't all for fun. Except that they all had so much fun coming here together. Even when black eyes or pulled-out hair or missing teeth got in the way of enjoying the family meal.

But Mirabelle found as the family grew, the in-laws did not seem to view the picnics the same way. The women whom her brothers had married sat quiet and prim, eying the family with narrowed eyes and pursed lips that seemed to say, *What an uncouth lot you are.*

She noticed that her younger cousins and their mothers had begun to stay away. It was all reasonable, she supposed. You couldn't exactly argue with church work: it was always about their volunteer missions to bring pantry food to the poor or carry the tapes of church services to the nursing homes. Yet she had to wonder: Would she ever see them again?

Her family only ever got together for these Sunday picnics at the grave-yard. And these were Mirabelle's most favorite times. Where else would she see so many flowers, or walk amongst the trees arm-in-arm with a cousin her exact same age, who might have been her sister, both skipping across the graves, their twin braids bobbing in time like four horse tails?

Yes, this was the life. Finding a raven's feather and planting it in her father's grave so he could write to his heart's content, along with Mr. Poe, one of his favorite authors. Planting a pinwheel whose arms held the precious compliments they wished to share with the parents and grandparents they loved. These were only things Mirabelle and her siblings agreed on anymore.

But fewer and fewer came, until one Sunday, Mirabelle found herself sitting there in the graveyard all alone. She waited and waited. She populated it in her mind with those she'd loved. But these smiling faces—she missed them so. Her grandfather with his rancher's ruddy cheeks and fish-bowl lenses. Her grandmother with the plump, flowered dress covered by an apron, white with flour fresh from baking a lemon cake to serve them all here on the grass like an icy treat in the heat of summer. That frosting was so delicious Mirabelle could still taste it every time she thought of Grandma, even though it had been almost twenty years now.

Mirabelle found herself wondering whether she had run out of time to change things, now that she was fifty-two. She'd certainly left herself no time to go out and find a family of her own. Those days had long since passed while she devoted all her time to gathering the family history, to organizing their family photos, to archiving their reel-to-reel tapes and cassettes, and even their DVD, VHS, and Super 8 family movies. Each Christmas, she meticulously packed up more archival treasures, organized and presented in the most entertaining fashion, and mailed them out to her silent kin. But these never elicited the enthusiastic response she expected—nay, deserved.

But she could not fault them. Where were the fights, the knockdown drag-outs, the bloody noses, the black eyes? Where were the vicious verbal tirades of Uncle Spruce, which had driven Aunt Isme to tears and suicide? Where was Cousin Tilda's attempt to poison them all with arsenic one summer, when she'd had enough after working her fingers to the bone for her father and his two wives and their fifteen children during the fifteen years since her own mother had died? All these wonderful memories.

The graveyard was getting ragged. The branches of the Hallview family still had plenty of leaves, but those were mostly young and vibrant. Fall was a long way off. With only Mirabelle to tend all these graves, the grass clippings alone were covering up the names of those she loved. With a soft-haired brush, she cleaned out the crooks in the g's and o's. She brought grass scissors and detailed the edges till they were crisp and clear.

When would she see her cousins? They didn't even return her Christmas cards anymore. She missed their brawling. Even their sobbing was better than silence.

The time had come for drastic measures.

She pulled out all her old recipes, family lore kept in an old metal bread box, these creased pages soft with time, the looping handwriting faint, often written in pencil by women in her family who had scarcely been allowed to attend school beyond the second grade. Back then, they were too much use as workers and housewives. But they had a genius for cooking and baking, not to mention household remedies.

Mirabelle gathered the best of these. She thought and she thought. She jotted notes and remembered. And she looked through her letters over the years and determined what were the favorite treats and dishes of the remaining cousins, far-flung through the world.

And she rented an RV, creating an itinerary in which she'd visit each one in turn, bringing their favorites. The deep freezer, backed up by the generator, would keep her creations safe. Plus, she could bake more in the RV's kitchen once she got on the road. She packed up her cats, bundled up her purse, and carried a bit of soil from each beloved grave marked in a jar with the name of the family member to whom it belonged.

Now was the time to act. Now, before it was too late. Before the family scattered to the four winds and forgot its roots altogether.

She started first with Second Cousin Charlie. He'd always had a sweet tooth. He loved angel food cake with the open center filled with devil's food cake. Topped by cherries and homemade whipped cream. She whisked it up the way her great-grandmother had taught her, then knocked on his back door, just as she used to do when she was a girl.

"Charlie," she sang out. "Charlie!"

The door creaked open just an inch. A bulbous red nose poked through the crack in the curtain over the back door windows.

She held up the presentation plate and lifted the cover so he could see the confection. "I brought your favorite."

The door opened a few inches wider.

"Charlie," she said coaxingly, "I've been combing through all the records, as you know. And I found a bequest that they missed giving you. It's from Great Aunt Florence. You remember, you always were her favorite. She wanted you to have that harpsichord you loved playing when you were a boy."

The door swung wide. His face lit up like a little boy's at Christmas. "Mirabelle," he said reverently. "Mirabelle, thank you, thank you!" He held out his arms. She came in for a hug. She put her plate of angel food/devil's food on the little shelf just inside the door.

They stood for a few moments reminiscing about old times, then took a walk in the herb garden, before she affectionately kissed his cheek and told him she must be off. "See you in the cemetery this Sunday," she said casually.

And he nodded and said happily, "Yes, yes, of course I'll be there. And you say the harpsichord will be delivered on Saturday?"

"Yes, there's no question of that," Mirabelle said, and winked at him. "You'll hear the heavenly music. And you will play your heart out in that lovely wooden frame."

And she walked away, light as a cloud, knowing for sure that Charlie would drop dead within a few hours after gobbling up the poisoned angel's food. And that his coffin would be sure to arrive on Friday. And he'd roll out in that old pine box on Saturday. And, with her expeditious arrangements, he'd make it to the cemetery in time for their Sunday gathering.

* * * *

Charlie's funeral was such a happy event.

All the family remarked on it, shedding a tear as they planted a kiss or some sheet music or a poisonous orchid on the casket. The cousins, aunts, and half-siblings walked arm-in-arm, catching butterflies, singing hymns and family favorites from the crooner era. The picnic lunch. Oh, those picnics! With reawakened zest, the Hallviews started visiting the cemetery again—not because they'd loved Charlie so much, but because his funeral reminded them they missed each other. For three months straight, they held those legendary Sunday picnics, all the family reminiscing, different out-of-towners returning every week, a few even moving closer to town.

It truly was wonderful.

If only it could have lasted.

The falloff didn't happen all at once. People still loved the reunions, even got teary-eyed in between the pranks and crimes, the tires slashed with glee at the opportunity to finally settle an old score. But gradually— "real life" got in the way. Fewer came. Those who returned missed those who'd gone. And, gradually, the stream dwindled to a trickle.

And one Sunday, it was just Mirabelle all over again. Singing by herself to scores of graves. Dancing among them, scattering flowers. Planting cookies from Grandma's ice box recipe on each one. Trying desperately to make up for the silence, the absence. Feeling the interest from all their dear ones in the ground, the great loving weight of them listening for more.

Mirabelle decided to take her show on the road again.

First up was Great Aunt Bernadette in the nursing home. At ninety-three, she hadn't been up to attending Charlie's funeral, though Mirabelle had stopped by with the memorial bulletin and some candy flowers.

"Auntie, I'm so sad. They've already stopped coming to the cemetery," Mirabelle lamented. And she and tiny Aunt Bernadette leaned their shoulders together and warbled "On a Hill Far Away," a family favorite, Bernadette's sweet, vibrating soprano making Mirabelle shiver with the eerie sense that her favorite aunt wasn't long for this world.

"I'm worried, Auntie. The younger generation—they're just not invested the way we were. They don't have enough context to understand, probably because for much of their lives, attendance at the cemetery has been optional."

"Whereas for us, we treated it as de rigueur," Bernadette said, nodding, her perfectly shaped, dyed-auburn curls bouncing.

"The thing is, who's going to keep the family going when I'm gone?"

"Who says you're going anywhere, Mirabelle?" Bernadette's fond eyes twinkled.

"Well—I'm not getting any younger."

"Neither am I," Bernadette cackled.

Mirabelle's heart warmed. "Between you and me, I have the feeling I'm on the verge of a breakthrough. More and more, the dead speak to me. They say we love to hate each other, in the most convivial way. We only show up for funerals or cemetery visits, and then we show up in abundance."

Bernadette put a hand over hers. The swollen knuckles and age spots only made that tiny hand more beautiful. "I know, honey. It's been that way from the beginning. Only some of us try to pretend it doesn't affect us. Because it's just so damned disconcerting in daily life."

Mirabelle swallowed hard, her eyes wandering across the mantelpiece array with its photos of family men and women who'd flown in World War II, Korea, Vietnam, Desert Storm, and yet who—or whose bodies—had always, always come home.

Her eyes fastened on Uncle Wilmer, who'd saved his squadron but gone down anyway. "Mama said they sent—dispatches—"

"That's right, dear." Bernadette patted her hand, then reached for the portrait on the end table next to her, in which her husband Trevor wore his original blue wedding suit on their seventieth anniversary, and she, her robin's egg wedding dress, all wrapped in lace. "They always do," she murmured, tapping the dimple in his cheek as they smiled at each other, as if no one else existed in the world. She looked up at Mirabelle. "You know the ones who've gone before aren't as happy as you might think, having Charlie join the heavenly choir so soon. Even if he does play that harpsichord like an angel."

"I had good reasons."

"I know you did, dear." Bernadette patted her knee fondly. "Have a cookie?" She passed the tin.

Mirabelle smiled fondly, recognizing the tactic. She opened the lid, inhaling the delicious aroma of gingerbread, an old family recipe equal to none.

She decided to take a risk, selected a fat gingerbread person, and bit off the head with a nod to her great aunt. "Divine," she proclaimed around a mouthful, then carefully released the sticky head into a delicately held napkin.

Bernadette beamed as though Mirabelle had passed a test. She nodded decisively. "All right, dear. You have work to do. You don't want to be spending all your time hanging around here. Although there might be a few—new family members to tend to," she said with a wink. "That is, if you're interested."

Mirabelle perked right up. "Oh? Will we be adopting some orphans?" She meant it in the way she'd heard Bernadette's husband Great Uncle Trevor talk about the soldiers under his command who'd died without any family to bury them—whom he'd adopted as his family, taking care of all their funeral arrangements. Most rested in the Hallview Cemetery right now.

Bernadette shrugged her bony shoulders as though stretching invisible wings. "There's no one to object. They're ready to be planted, and none to claim them from this mausoleum of a rest home but the county morgue. But I have a feeling if you dig deep enough into the family tree, you'll find they're long-lost cousins of ours. I have some money set by for unexpected funeral expenses. But enough about that. I think it's time to put you in touch with that brother of mine."

"Uncle Eustace? Oh, I'd love to see him again. We had the best times when I was a tot."

"Stace always did have a soft spot for you. Now buck up, buckaroo. We'll get that cemetery bouncing yet." She gestured, and Mirabelle bent obediently for a hug and kiss. Bernadette pinched her cheek, and Mirabelle yelped, then laughed at the pain as Bernadette used her hold to pull Mirabelle's ear to her mouth to say conspiratorially, "Just remember, we have a lot of family. Enough to spare a few. But don't go too quickly. We don't want you getting caught."

* * * *

Decades younger than his oldest sister, Uncle Stace had to be at least sixty-seven, but as Mirabelle hugged him, she told him honestly, "You don't look a day over forty-five!"

Uncle Stace was like no one else Mirabelle had ever known. He looked like a modern version of a fashion plate from the turn of the 20th century, with his peacock ascot and a silver-and-black waistcoat with velvet collars. A rock musician with a sense of style that included silk paisley shirts with mother-of-pearl buttons, black jacquard pants that buttoned up Edwardian fashion, and form-fitting black riding boots, he looked like he'd stepped on stage at the height of the 1980s as one of the New Romantics. This was only accentuated by his mop of black curls and the eyeshadow, eyeliner, and lipstick that cemented his identity as a rock-and-roll dandy.

"Neither do you, darling," he said, laughing.

"Flatterer," Mirabelle grinned. "But I needed that extra seven years for wisdom."

He nodded, hazel eyes twinkling. "That's what I hear. Welcome to the inner circle, Mir. I've been waiting for you. Can't say I thought much of Charlie as a celebrant of the great cemetery, but you pulled off that stunt with style."

Stace had regular gigs as the frontman of a band that had been popular for forty years. For the same length of time, he'd toured with his partner, Nico, who played keys.

For their next reunion concert at an old, gilded theatre in D.C., Stace placed Mirabelle in the guest box. She cheered as loudly as anyone in the crowd, while Stace strutted with his lyre like some hero from Greek mythology. Nico stepped out from behind his bank of tiered Roland keyboards. Grabbing a portable instrument, he slung the smaller keyboard across his chest, standing back-to-back with Stace. The two of them danced in a dirty synch as close as the tango, getting funky, their joy radiating out from that stage and into the audience like a nuclear explosion. Afterwards, Nico and Stace, longtime lovers and recent husbands, welcomed Mirabelle to their townhouse with open arms.

* * * *

"I'm lucky you came along," Stace said one day. "I can only create so many more family plantings. Honestly, I shouldn't have done this many. It puts a mark on me, and I have Nico to think about."

"Yeah, not to mention how in demand your services are now. There aren't many rock stars who double as hitmen. Which is convenient, since you know everybody, and everybody wants to know you," Mirabelle said cheekily.

He smiled at her—the smile of an angel, really. "Yes, my dear," he said with a fond wink. "I admit, the thrill of celebrity does have its pull. And thanks to the necessities of the job, I can have a nice drink and get to know my long-time heroes before they expire."

He truly was the hitman to the stars. It was all so civilized.

And he'd learned from the best. Aunt Bernadette. Who knew?

Mirabelle wondered what she might've done with her life if she'd started her career as cemetery nurturer earlier than fifty-two. Still, there was no way to tell.

"I love you, Uncle Stace." She put her hand on his.

He hummed fondly and patted her cheek like he was petting a cat, and that was something, really—how comfortable they were with each other.

As the years rolled by, Mirabelle loved working with Uncle Stace but wearied of doing it for the sake of the cemetery.

It wasn't that she tired of the killing, per se. It was more that she no longer relished the aftermath quite so much. The relatives who'd been planted turned out to have been the best of the crop. Indeed, once a newly dead family member lay down under the earth, she promptly felt a swell of affection for them. Whereas she was heartily sick of all her living relatives.

All but Uncle Stace, Uncle Nico, and Aunt Bernadette.

In them, she found suddenly that she had a family she cared about. Unlike all the cousins of first, second, or third degrees, and the other aunts and uncles and faux parental figures. All of whom hated each other with a fervent, friendly hatred. Which was as it had always been. The hair-pulling, tackling, and grinding down into the graveyard dirt would not have been nearly so much fun otherwise.

"Uncle Stace," she said hesitantly, "what if I just—stop?"

He looked at her curiously, down his long, elegant nose from his great height. He may have been dyeing his hair, but it was a superb job, his curls dark and lush. "Stop what, dear child?" He picked up her hand, tracing her lifeline, raising an amused brow. "You're very talented at our work."

Mirabelle huffed out a pained sigh. Out the window, dust rose on the distant highway. So many lights. So many towns. So many cover stories. This time, it had amused Stace to name himself Charlemagne and describe himself as her chauffeur and butler. She was meant to be an eccentric heiress in command of a media conglomerate.

"I mean—" she waved at the world beyond their high-rise motel walls. "It's not the job. It's the other job."

He nodded knowingly. "The family. Keeping everyone together wearies you. Or is it the demand for your devotion, which is never returned?"

She nodded to the first part, frowned at the second. "I don't think about it that way."

"Maybe you should. After all, it's your choice."

"My choice?"

"To walk away." He let that hang in the air as he carefully removed his dapper fedora from his curls. "Whether or not they survive your departure, you've certainly earned the rest, and they have no right to demand more of you. You've already given them your entire life."

"Well, except for our jobs."

His smile curled up one side, leaving a thin, hard edge. "Our jobs are another matter. About which. I'd like to bring you onto the stage with me as well. I've heard you singing in the shower and the cemetery. Your voice is phenomenal."

Taking the stage with Stace and Nico—took her breath away. It was a beautiful and passionate life—as much their triumph as hers. Their beautiful niece-successor.

Mir traveled with Stace and his husband across the country. Her own skills with guitar and harmonies were, they reassured her, enough to justify her place on stage. After a concert, Nico kissed Stace fondly, then retreated to their home of the moment.

Leaving them time to hit the stars…and tend the cemetery.

Mir knew the cemetery did need tending. And at her age, deserting her life's work might leave her floating off into the clouds like a lost helium balloon.

Stace tried to encourage her. "We have to look to the future." He showed her the room hidden behind the wall of guitars in the basement. There, an assassin's instruments awaited the family's need. Stace opened his heart and taught her everything. How the band he loved also helped with the family mission and his hits, providing the excuse for travel, for being out of touch, and for making so many friends on the road that he sometimes left for impromptu visits across the country.

"It's not a choice anyone would make lightly," Stace told her, as they pored over family albums and genealogies. They discussed which deaths would have the most impact, carrying the weight and tenderness needed to bring the family back to the graveyard again and again.

Doing their work—sometimes all three of their jobs in one evening— Stace let his hair down around Mirabelle. She saw a tired old man who looked perfectly ordinary in a short-sleeved shirt and slacks, not glamorous at all. One who blended into a crowd. He even told her how much he hated to be seen this way, as though part of him were stripped away. But looking so much unlike himself allowed him to go unnoticed despite his fame while carrying on his deathly duties. The great effort he put into looking like a dandy onstage and off wasn't just about being true to himself.

"We don't want to cut off anyone unduly before their time," Stace cautioned. "Sometimes we have to make a hard decision—one the family couldn't make on their own. But which ultimately is to their benefit. Not just in terms of the inheritance but cleaving together. That's what's so hard.

The deaths that have the impact to hold us together—are the ones that cost most dear."

And so Mirabelle learned to be sparing with her deathly ministerial attentions. She learned to be caring and kind and cut the deepest where it hurt the most, but then only when the family absolutely needed to plant this devotion in the ground to keep going.

Meanwhile as they toured the country, they took time out to visit family. It felt like a golden age. So many of them loved Stace, and he regaled everyone with tales. Each stop, Mirabelle met new additions, reconnected with lost cousins, and updated her records about who would like which plots. Along the way, she and Stace recruited new family members as necessary. It was easy to play matchmaker to their cousins, since there were plenty of friends and would-be lovers who were all too happy to belong.

It revived Mirabelle to find that most of the family actually viewed these happy days at the cemetery with the same love she felt. She grew adept at diverting conflict or reviving the will to live by reminding them of happy days at the Hallview Cemetery (no doubt the whiff of death also perked them up a bit). The family always had enjoyed singing together and telling stories of the past, especially big whoppers, tall tales, and the antics of anyone, especially themselves.

So Mirabelle would pull out her guitar, and soon they'd all be singing their favorite tunes, ones that often echoed through the cemetery—everything from hymns and old classics like "Daisy Bell (Bicycle Built for Two)" and "Tiptoe Through the Tulips," to the latest Billie Eilish and Taylor Swift—belting them out with gusto and great harmony, including Stace and Nico, who hammed it up with swooping solos and roaring duets.

"You're a natural," Stace told her fondly.

And Nico grinned and pressed a fist of solidarity to her shoulder.

They stopped by to visit Bernadette often, detouring any time their path didn't bring them close enough. Stace regaled her with tales of Mirabelle's skill, and Bernadette added pithy comments like "The dead need the living, and the living need the dead," and always ended with "You do a much better job than I ever did, my dear," which swelled Mirabelle's heart.

Whenever they left, Aunt Bernadette insisted they take along treats and leftovers: fellow compatriots at the nursing home who'd died without family, "orphans" to be retroactively adopted and buried in the family plot.

Even though no one knew who they were, the family played along, happy to have their cemetery traditions revived, even conducting séances when necessary to find out what the orphans wanted in their eulogies. And their cemetery dead welcomed the newbies with open arms.

As the concert circuit brought them to more family reunions, and Mirabelle listened fondly as Stace entertained their cousins, she realized that Bernadette, always so kind and dear to her, was like a queen to the family.

Leaning close as they walked out to the car, Stace told her how Bernadette had done her share of murders back in the day, when she was in "the prime of life," between about fifty and eighty. Stace sounded bittersweet about it.

Mirabelle commented, "You and I are both in that age-zone."

But as Stace, Nico, and Mirabelle slipped into a booth at the local tavern, Stace continued, "I may look young, but I'm on my way out."

Nico said, "Oh, no, love, I wouldn't say that." He brushed Stace's dark curls back from his eyes. "You have a world of living yet to do."

But Stace gave him a wolfish grin. "You're just being kind, sweetheart. I can count on you for that."

Nico scowled, as if resenting the implication that he was only being kind. "Sure, you can say that. You've got looks that last for eons, while the rest of us stress over every wrinkle and gray hair." He held out one of his straight brown locks to demonstrate gray roots.

But Stace smoothed his cheek fondly, his eyes smoky with desire. "Come on, Nico, tell it to someone who doesn't already know you're the sexiest man alive."

And Nico succumbed to the kiss with twinkling eyes.

Of course, all good things must come to an end. While Nico settled happily into snarking about their musical competitors, Stace leveled a significant look at Mirabelle over his head: a burning anger about their entire situation.

But he waited to tell her until later that night, after he and Nico had spent a few hours alone.

Mirabelle, already wearing black leather boots and an outfit that would have made Joan Jett proud, opened her hotel room at his first knock. He quickly closed the door behind him, even though they ought to be leaving for their most lucrative job.

She fixed cocktails while Stace loosened the tie he must have only just finished contorting into an Eldredge knot—because, of course, Nico—plus, he'd been wearing a purple silk tie at dinner, and this one was tan, green, and red paisley, a truly atrocious number that Stace once told her he kept because it was so good at disguising errant blood stains.

"That family cemetery is a sinkhole."

"I know, Stace. Maybe we should both quit."

"We can't quit. I can't, and you can't, Mirabelle. Not now that we're in this deep. And people are counting on us." His eyes looked wild, red-rimmed, as he stomped around the room, examining the paintings and fixtures with disgusted sounds despite the hotel's five-star status. "Where's that goddamned drink?"

"Who is it this time, Stace?"

He dragged a hand through his curls. "That's not the point. You know how this works, Mir. As soon as I retire, it'll be my head or Nico's on the chopping block. And whichever goes first, it'll be so bad for the one left behind that you might as well plant us both." His fierce, puffy eyes had an almost pleading look.

"What in hell are you asking of me, Stace?"

"Not that! Not now, anyway. Not if—" he hesitated, and then said, "You know you're going to have to pick someone someday and train them up…just like Bernadette trained me." He met her eyes. His intelligent, brutally honest look said he knew exactly what he was saying.

But what he actually said was, "You know I'm not a Hallview, right?"

She hadn't. What the fuck? Slowly, calmly: "I did not actually know that. But I'm not sure what difference it makes? You'll always be Uncle Stace to me."

"That's what Sis always said. Bernadette. We've been best friends since the day we met. I got folded into the family because we loved each other so much, and I didn't have any family, and she apparently didn't have enough. Or not ones she could trust, anyway. When she took to murdering, the family was in danger of faltering even worse than it was when you stepped up to the plate. But for a long time, she kept it from me. She protected me," he told Mirabelle with a haggard look.

That's when it dawned on Mirabelle. "Bernadette. God, no."

"She asked for us. She asked for—you."

"Tonight? That's what this is? Can't we just refuse?"

Slowly, he shook his head.

"But she's ninety-three. There's no need to cut things short; it'll happen naturally—"

"She asked for us," Stace repeated, his voice harsh. "And—she told me to bring Nico."

That—wasn't ominous in the slightest.

Without an instant's hesitation, Mir slipped the hotel key in her pocket. They left, pausing only at the next room to collect Nico, who was freshly coiffed and dressed to the nines. His dark eyes said he knew perfectly well how serious this was.

No one spoke on the drive to the home. It was after hours. But Stace and Mirabelle were old hands at getting past security systems.

Bernadette greeted them all with quiet cheer, then asked to speak to Mirabelle alone.

"Wouldn't you rather—Uncle Stace?"

Bernadette's eyes gleamed with tears as she smiled, but she shook her head. "Eustace and I said our goodbyes. This one is all for you, dear."

Mirabelle kissed her cheeks, her forehead. "Auntie, are you sure about this?"

"Of course not, dear. I was hoping you could come up with a better plan." She regarded Mirabelle serenely. "But you know how it works. Keeping the family together in the cemetery isn't for the faint of heart. Small losses are fine and help fill the gaps. But you must keep them caring. A big loss will keep them coming longer—with fewer deaths needed in between." She waggled her eyebrows and laughed. "I'm actually very popular. Everyone but you has to schedule time to see me. Even my grandchildren."

Mirabelle's heart ached. "I can't do this, Auntie. I just—can't." She sank her head down on the bed beside Bernadette, who rested a hand on her hair.

"You don't have to, sweetie," the lovely, thin soprano floated over her. "But you do have to decide. For all of us. You're the next generation. Our hopes and dreams. You've given more to this family than anyone else. Is it worth it? To continue? Or do we finally put this monster we've made to bed once and for all?"

* * * *

Mirabelle asked for time to think.

She went into the sitting room to talk it over with Stace, while Nico visited with their old dear.

She thought about everything. Her life. Her service to this family. "I'd rather die," she said in a strangled voice, "than kill you or Bernadette. Let alone Nico."

"That can be arranged," he said seriously, but his forehead puckered in the worst sort of anxiety.

Was it really worth that? Just to have the family reunited, coming consistently to the cemetery for their picnics? Singing songs and pulling hair? Tending the graves and sending one another into early ones?

Was it worth it to give up Stace? Or Bernadette? Or Nico?

Looking down, Stace regarded her with clear hazel eyes. He smiled slowly, planting a finger on her chin, tilting her face higher. "Chin up. Stay proud, buttercup. You're a Hallview, all right. Through and through. No one can take that away from you. You'll always have us."

"In the cemetery," she said with heavy irony. "Where I barely have time to sit and smell the roses any longer, if you recall. What with all our activities planting new ones."

He smiled fondly and circled her shoulders with an arm, pulling her into a side-hug. "Well, you'll find someone else to replace you one day. Then you can come and talk to me."

She shuddered. He must have felt it. He looked concerned at once. "Stace," she said. "That other life—with you and Nico on stage. Or just—the client list. I'd rather—"

"Not the family?"

"Too much of a burden—"

"You've devoted your life to it. Most of them are ungrateful shits. Of course, you'd like a break from devoting everything you have to it, but—"

"Too many skeletons. The family photo albums are a graveyard."

His smile carried so many ghosts. "Isn't that what we're aiming for?"

* * * *

Mirabelle wasn't just making up her own mind. She was feeling the others out. She headed back to talk to Bernadette again. A quick exchange with Nico in passing—he shook his head, dark eyes eloquent with grief. He pressed her hand. She kissed him on the lips. Family greetings.

Mirabelle held Bernadette's hand. "Keeping the family isn't worth losing Stace. They may think he's entertaining, but they'll never appreciate him the way we do."

"I agree with you, honey." Bernadette's watery blue eyes and kind smile faltered only a little. "It's time for all this to end. Not to take Stace, no matter what he says."

From countless funerals, Mirabelle could cry on command, but these tears came unbidden. "I don't think he'll listen to me. The way he talks, he's always known the way this would end, and he's honor-bound to follow through with it. Frankly, I don't think he wants to go on if you don't. But he worries about Nico…"

With conviction, Bernadette said firmly, "He'll listen to me."

Mirabelle ushered in Stace and Nico. They sat on either side of the bed, holding Bernadette's hands.

"It's time to retire," Bernadette proclaimed, looking from one of them to the other, squeezing their hands. "True love should never be ignored in service of duty. The family isn't what it used to be, and even what it used to be wasn't all that great."

From where she stood by the head of the bed, Mirabelle watched with so much pride and love in her family, her true family. Stace sat very still, back straight, head bowed over Bernadette's hand, the perfect picture of the dutiful knight he was. "But what of Mir? This is her life's work. Her legacy."

"Yes, honey. Mirabelle may even have been the first of us to do it for all the right reasons, to really care."

From Bernadette's other side, Nico chimed in. "Mir loved this family even when most of it didn't love her. Even when it was pretty awful most of the time."

"You're my family," Mir burst out, unintended. Loud over their voices. They all looked up at her. Her voice sank as she added, "My only one."

"And now, my dears," said Bernadette, sitting up, "it's time for the four of us to go riding off into the sunset."

* * * *

The happy days at the Hallview Cemetery were over. No more holiday picnics or vacations to the family graves.

Every last Hallview had been buried, in ostentatious mass ceremonies that filled every open plot.

But despite the lack of any living mourners to visit, the dead at Hallview would never be lonely. Now that celebrities had been buried here, Hallview became a gawking site. The graves of musicians Eustace, Nico, and Mirabelle Hallview were constantly decorated with the offerings of adoring fans: some obscene, some sublime, all left in thanks for the music.

While the graves of most of the Hallviews were real enough, the plots of Eustace, Nico, Mirabelle, and Bernadette were empty save for portions of ashes scooped up from the mansion fire. No one could be sure if those ashes related to any of the four, or just their furniture.

All anyone knew was that Stace, Nico, Mirabelle, and their beloved matriarch Bernadette must have been killed by a very skilled assassin, who'd been paid to leave a message. At the site of their incinerated mansion, a tombstone had been left like a calling card: "Family means survival. Never forget. We thrive as we strive to honor those we've left behind."

It sounded vaguely like a threat.

But who was there left to threaten?

The four swept through the country on a final concert tour, graciously presenting free concert tickets to every living Hallview. None could resist. Especially not with grand dame Bernadette making guest appearances. Soon enough, a special slow, untraceable poison first devised by the Borgias ate its way through the veins of all the family members in attendance, killing them all at random places, days after each show. All of which augmented the conspiracy theories about a celebrity assassin who'd wiped out the whole Hallview family.

They weren't entirely wrong.

Bernadette herself planned all the funerals.

From the safety of their Virginia Beach hotel room, the four watched the funeral livestreams, exclaiming fondly over the flower arrangements and fashionable, paid mourners.

Afterwards, they toasted one another with cocktails beside their hotel pool.

Mirabelle sighed romantically. "We had so many happy days at the Hallview Cemetery."

"Yes, dear. We'll always remember those days with fondness," Bernadette said.

Stace extended a gallant hand to Bernadette, helping his best friend rise from her chaise lounge. "I'm especially fond now that it's all over."

"You and me both, love." Nico slipped an arm about his waist and kissed his temple.

"I'm so glad we finally get to enjoy some 'us' time," Bernadette said, smiling. She held Mirabelle's hand all the way to the beautiful beach. It was an easy clasp, swinging their arms between them like girls. It turned out Bernadette had a surprising amount of life left in her.

All of them did. Now that they'd taken care of the rest of the Hallviews. Fulfilling every obligation, and thereby freeing themselves. Faking their own deaths? Chef's kiss.

With her toes in the soft, wet sand, Mirabelle remembered the feel of the cemetery under her feet. Even now, the deceased residents would be singing and pulling pranks—especially on the living. The best part was, the current mourners had come to gawk of their own free will. And thanks to the famed musicians "buried" at Hallview, there would always be music.

Mir would miss the cemetery, the Hallview happy place. The joyous, grateful corpses and their loving devotees. But it was truly time to let go. "We did our jobs well," she sighed, leaning her head on Stace's shoulder. "We deserve to enjoy our retirement."

He held her shoulders firmly. "Time to live our best lives. They'd want that for us."

Nico held Stace's hand. Bernadette did the same with Mirabelle. They watched the sunset together. As loving and happy a family as there might ever be.

COTTAGE FOR RENT

ALLIE MARIE

BECKY MCCURDY hummed a tune as she brushed her doll's hair. Though she seemed to mix two different songs into one, she tilted her head from side to side with the rhythm of her jumbled tune, her golden pigtails flopping and sweeping against her neck. She smiled as the brushing motions pulled the doll's head backwards, enough that its eyes began to close, almost as if falling asleep.

"My doll is the prettiest!" Becky said to her sister, her girlish voice rising with each syllable.

Lorrie McCurdy glanced over and grimaced at the tangled mess that her sister only made worse with each stroke. Being the elder of the two, she tried to hold her tongue. Their mother worked two jobs, so the two sisters depended on each other during the day. Choosing to keep the peace, Lorrie fiddled with her ponytail to see if her red hair resembled the nest on Becky's doll.

"Just try to slow your brush strokes," Lorrie instructed. "If you're not careful, you'll break her head off. Believe me, I've had that happen before…"

"You're not my mom." Becky stuck her tongue out. "I will do it how I want, or you can just go to your own room."

Lorrie rolled her eyes. "Okay, okay. Don't come crying to me when you break it."

The curtains billowed at the windows. Lorrie sniffed the air and sighed. "I just love the fresh breezes when the cottage is opened for the summer. I can smell the ocean coming through the windows. The sheets are clean and smell like sunshine."

"You can't smell sunshine," Becky said matter-of-factly. She was now attempting to weave the doll's mangled hair into braids. "The sun is too far away to smell it."

"True. But I can smell the ocean. I love how it smells, so salty and like seaweed sometimes. The Outer Banks is still the best vacation place ever.

We can swim in the ocean or the pool. And we can go to the Wright Brothers Memorial or go to Jockey Ridge and watch the hang gliders."

"Or play mini golf. When will Mama be home?"

"It won't be long now. She had to finish cleaning the other house to get it ready for the summer, then she has to do the second one. That's why we get to live here. She takes care of other people's houses all summer and we can live at the beach while she works."

"I'm hungry. I hope she brings us McDonald's. Or Dairy Queen."

A creak from the stairs below forced them both into silence. Staring into each other's widened eyes, they stopped in mid-movement, poised like statues. They sucked in their breaths and held until a second stair creaked. Tiptoeing toward the door, they pressed their ears against it. When another stair was breached, Lorrie held a finger to her mouth and her sister nodded in understanding. The older girl used both hands to grip the knob.

"Get out of my house," a hoarse voice rasped. The eerie voice seemed to float through the door and out the windows.

The sounds from the stairs paused. Lorrie dropped to her knees and peeked through the keyhole. She could see nothing in the limited view.

The familiar creak of the stairs faded away, signaling they were safe—for the moment.

The girls stood in place.

Becky whispered, "Do you think it was the Old Ghost Man?"

"Who else would it be?" Lorrie snapped. "He always appears first, before the others come. This is a haunted cottage, you know."

Tears welled in her little sister's eyes, but before Lorrie could apologize, a door slammed somewhere in the house. They were used to hearing footsteps and the gruff whispers, or doors opening and closing, but most times they never saw anything.

Both girls scuttled across the room and slid beneath Becky's bed, adjusting the skirt so no one could see into their favorite hiding space. They huddled together, hoping the entity would never find them.

The Old Ghost Man was not the only such being the sisters had encountered. Others came, too. Sometimes they arrived in groups and stayed for a while but, one by one, they would stop coming, to be replaced by another group.

"Mama never sees them, does she?" Becky whispered.

"Of course not," Lorrie scoffed. "If she saw them, she would never leave us alone to work her two jobs, would she?"

"What did Mama mean when she said that they were probably wayward spirits that were searching for the light? What light?"

"I don't know." Lorrie pressed her cheek to the cool floor. "I like it in the spring, when they are opening up the beach house for the season. When it gets hot in the summer, my skin sticks to the floor."

Becky giggled and rested her head against the wood plank. "And when you lay your skin too long on the floor, it makes a sucking sound when you lift your face." She made a slurping sound that sent the sisters into giggles.

It was Lorrie who woke up first. She didn't know how long they had been asleep, but the sun had drifted lower in the sky, casting long shadows in the room. She nudged her little sister.

"Is Mama here?" Becky asked, yawning.

"No, just us for now."

"I hate the Old Ghost Man," Becky said. "I wish he would disappear forever." She searched for her doll. It was not where she remembered leaving it. "I think the Old Ghost Man took my doll."

"Not this time. There it is on the window seat." Lorrie raised the bed skirt and pointed.

"His son Jimmy was fun. He loved to play with us. I wish he still came here," Becky said as she wiggled her way from under the bed.

"Maybe Jimmy found the light and is with God now." Lorrie's face beamed.

"He didn't die, remember? Mama said a ghost wanders the earth because it died and is looking for the light to cross over. Jimmy's not a ghost, but he doesn't come here anymore. Why?"

"I don't know."

"Well, I hope the Old Ghost Man goes to hell."

Lorrie shrieked in disbelief. "Becky!"

"What?" her sister asked. "They say it in church all the time."

Moving her hands in an excellent imitation of her mother, Lorrie said, "I should wash your mouth out with soap."

Becky stuck her tongue out. Then the sisters giggled.

"Do you remember what we always try to do on our first night here every summer?" Lorrie asked as she scooted from under the bed.

"Yes!" Becky scrabbled out on the other side and the sisters ran to the dormer window. "It's our tradition."

"Wait until I get to my room and when you see me stick my head out the window be ready, okay?" Lorrie ran out the door and scooted to her own room. She removed the screen and called to her sister to do the same at her window.

"Are you ready, Beck?" she asked, leaning out the window until she saw her sister's face. They waved.

"Yes."

The two sisters climbed from their respective dormer windows and tiptoed across the slanted roof, arms outstretched for stability. When they reached the halfway point, they patted hands in a high-five. Lorrie stayed on the outside, closest to the edge, making sure Becky kept her balance. Each girl continued on the path toward the opposite window to climb into the rooms when the crunch of gravel reached their ears. A car turned into the long driveway.

With a squeal, Becky stopped in her tracks. "Mama's home!"

"That's not her car. Go to the room, Becky."

"I'm afraid, Lorrie. Come get me."

The car backed out of the driveway and headed back in the direction from which it had come.

"Hurry, Becky, and get in my room. We have to do this. We try to do it every year but we never finish crossing over."

Arms sticking out for balance, Becky walked the few remaining feet to the opposite dormer and scurried over the sill. Lorrie did the same into Becky's bedroom and ran to the door. Becky emerged from the second bedroom and raced to hug her sister.

"We did it." They giggled. "We finally crossed over."

A door slammed downstairs, and the two girls froze. Lorrie leaned over the banister and her mouth formed an "O" as she pointed downward. Becky peeked around her and gasped, shocked to see the Old Ghost Man pacing angrily at the bottom of the stairs. He held one hand to his temple, yelling words neither girl understood.

Backing cautiously toward Becky's room, the girls stepped on a loose floorboard. The creaking wood sounded like a shrieking hawk, instantly catching the attention of the Old Ghost Man. He glared up at the stairwell. With a furled brow, his face distorted into a frightening grimace, accentuated by shaking the closed fist of his free hand. Racing to the bottom of the stairs he began to yell.

"This is my house! Get out of my house!"

Becky and Lorrie ran to Becky's bedroom and slammed the door. Sprinting across the room, they slid beneath the bed.

"We'll fool the ghosts again," Lorrie whispered. As before, they fluffed the bed skirt to avoid detection. The grating sound of the doorknob turning shocked them both as they realized they had not locked the door.

Just barely able to see through a small crack between the bed skirt and the floor upon which they rested their chins, Lorrie draped her arm protectively over Becky's shoulder. The shivers coming from her younger sister shook through her, though in truth, it could have been her own body shaking just as well.

Slow, heavy footfalls moved up the steps and stopped outside the room. Becky whimpered as the door opened and footsteps entered the room. Lorrie placed a hand over the younger girl's mouth to mute any noise.

The Old Ghost Man had entered the bedroom before. He usually spent a few moments walking around the room, examining everything from toys to hair ribbons, but never taking anything.

Lorrie had long assumed his obsession was with the sisters.

When the feet approached the bed, the sisters both froze. This time the Old Ghost Man wore beach shoes, and his toes poked under the ruffles of the bed skirt. His big hairy toes wiggled in the sandals, inches from their faces.

Becky held her nose and made a silly grimace. Lorrie tightened her clamp on her younger sister's mouth, but clasped her other hand over her own mouth to stifle the nervous giggle that bubbled at her throat.

The feet shifted on a loose floorboard. The moans of the hardwood terrorized the sisters. The old man walked toward the window. Lorrie peeked through the eyelets in the bed skirt ruffle.

"How did this happen?" he grumbled at the loose-hanging screen. He poked the frame back in place, and after a short time walking around the room the Old Ghost Man left, closing the door behind him.

"I hope he never comes back," Becky whispered. "He needs to find the light." She scooted from the bed and grabbed a coloring book and crayons. Lying on her stomach and kicking her crossed legs behind her, she snapped a crayon with a frustrated growl.

Attempting to use the broken edge to color, she added, "His feet stink."

Lorrie crawled beside her sister. "His stinky feet have big, hairy toes on them, too." The two sisters leaned close until their foreheads touched, and they burst into peals of laughter. Then Lorrie said, "He is trying to make us leave this house."

"Because he is an Old Ghost Man." Becky gave her pat answer with a shrug, which caused her to color outside of the lines of a nearly perfect picture.

"When Mama comes home, I am going to borrow her pepper spray, so if he comes back, we can make him go away forever."

"Can you scare ghosts away with pepper spray?"

"I don't know, but we can try."

A dog yapped in the distance. Both girls scrambled to their feet and peeked out of the dormer window. Within the fenced yard, the chocolate lab puppy pranced about the small enclosure, as if looking for an escape route. The sight of the puppy caused both of the bored girls to smile.

"Oh, look! A dog. How did it get in the yard? Can we keep it?" Becky asked, excitement dancing in her eyes.

Lorrie shook her head. "Mama would never let us. She has to work two jobs just to feed us. But we can watch it play," she said, then tapped the window to get the dog's attention.

"Hey, he is looking at us!" Becky said. She waved and rapped the window.

A loud bang came from their back door and rocked the house. The Old Ghost Man shouted something, but they could not make out the words. His presence seemed to agitate the dog, which scurried through a small hole it had apparently dug near the fence.

"Why won't that man go away?" Becky wondered.

Lorrie bit her lip, digesting it all, then said, "He's just trying to scare us into leaving this house. See, the dog doesn't like him either." She had seen other animals react the same way.

"Is Old Ghost Man finished with bothering us tonight?" Becky asked.

"I don't know. I never saw him act like this."

"I want Mama," Becky said, fetching her doll and working vigorously on the matted hair.

"She'll be home soon."

Footfalls clomped on the steps.

"Shh, he is coming up the stairs again," Lorrie warned.

Opening the door a crack, they saw the Old Ghost Man behave in a way they had never seen. He walked upstairs and disappeared into their mother's room.

"He can't go in there!" Becky fumed.

"She's not home yet, but she can't see him anyway."

"Let's go find the dog. Maybe Mama will let us keep him if we clean him up."

"No way, we would have to walk right past Mama's room," the older sister protested.

The door opened and the shadowy figure emerged. He ran his fingers through his hair and sniffled. Without a glance at the girls' room, he went back downstairs.

Becky rubbed her chin as she contemplated. "He's crying. Maybe he is finally going to go to the light."

When she was sure Old Ghost Man had disappeared, Lorrie said, "He is not our problem. We're going downstairs. That dog is waiting for us." Lorrie dragged a protesting Becky behind her.

Stepping at odd angles to avoid the boards they knew would squeak, they made their way into the kitchen.

"Listen," Lorrie said, cupping a hand over her ear to listen more intently.

The muffled sound of crying could be heard. The soulful keening wafted through the open window, past their ears.

"Ghosts are on the back porch!" Becky gasped. She froze in place.

"What in the hell is going on in our house? Why won't they leave?" Old Ghost Man wailed. "It's not fair. This is ruining us." His sobs sent shudders through Lorrie.

Lorrie inched closer to the window.

"What are you doing?" Becky pulled at her sleeve.

"Shh! I want to listen." Lorrie peeked over the sill. She could see Old Ghost Man in a rocker, leaning forward with his head in his hands, elbows resting on his knees. He pressed a phone to one ear.

"It is just not fair!" he said, turning slightly, as if he knew they were there but didn't seem to care any longer.

For the first time, she was not afraid of him. She felt sad for him.

Old Ghost Man spoke again. "It wasn't worth opening the cottage for the season. We can't pay for two houses, Liz. I know Jimmy is worried for us. But what can we do? It's unfair. The word is out that this place is haunted, and no one will rent this house anymore. We've been losing renters every year since it happened. We hardly had any rentals last year and have none reserved for this whole summer. We'll be bankrupt before long."

Another second of silence followed, then he spoke again. "It's still happening, Liz. I've seen and heard the apparitions several times today. If it drives me crazy, think how our guests felt. The realtors should have told us that the mother who owned this house was working two jobs to raise her kids when she died in a car wreck driving home. They should have told us the sisters were playing on the roof and fell to their deaths the same day."

In that moment, Lorrie and Becky looked at each other with wide eyes.

"We're dead?" Becky asked, her bottom lip quivering.

"We're the ghosts?" Lorrie replied as they both realized who they really were.

A golden glow filled the room and shined through the window. A warm wind blew over the Old Ghost Man. A sense of peace overwhelmed him.

"Hold on, Liz. I see a strange light, but I feel something good."

He got up and moved toward the house.

Inside the kitchen, the glow shimmered and enveloped the girls.

"Something is happening to us, Becky. I can see through you." Lorrie held her hand up and could see the refrigerator through it.

The glow moved upward. Lorrie and Becky followed the floating orb, leaving their cottage behind them.

They went into the light, where clouds whisked away and a figure appeared, with arms outstretched to welcome them—someone they had not seen in a very long time.

The girls squealed in delight.

Their mother, radiant in a shimmering white gown, stretched her arms wide to welcome her daughters home.

THE INFLUENCERS
JUDITH FOWLER

MAISIE SAT BEHIND the RV's steering wheel and looked at her phone while she and five vehicles in front of her waited to register at the campground's entrance. She couldn't post what she was thinking—that her dream of becoming an RV influencer was seriously off course.

Their water tank—empty for the last six days—had sabotaged basic hygiene. She and Jaxson could fill the tank inside the park, though if the line had a leak—neither of them possessed any repair skills—she'd have to coerce some willing RV enthusiast to help her.

The two thousand followers they'd acquired on #livingourbestlife, @ Maisie and Jaxson, and other platforms loved their first three weeks of content. Jaxson rock climbed, Maisie swam under a waterfall in Stowe, and selfies taken in scenic picnic areas from Maine to Delaware brought likes and retweets and thumbs ups.

She couldn't tell her followers that money had gotten tight and that gas had guzzled nearly all the waitressing money she'd earned over two summers serving lobster rolls and iced tea to tourists in Maine, with their campers and conversion vans. Maisie was envious, and when her boyfriend Jaxson said they could borrow his dad's camper to get on the road, her vision of becoming an influencer became a reality.

Without plumbing or cash, her dream of becoming an influencer had now become a nightmare. For the last two nights her videos were of the moon rising and setting over their camper in a Walmart's parking lot. Clicks, views, and likes stopped. Her goal of creating a website now seemed impossible.

Jaxson returned from the park's welcome station and Maisie pulled the RV door's lever to let him back in.

"You want the good or bad news?" he asked.

"Good," she said. "I need it."

"Okay. The park held our mail, and Mom sent twenty bucks in a letter with a P.S. from my father."

"Great. We can eat tonight. What's the bad news?"

"Dad canceled his RV insurance. He wants the camper back."

"You told me he said we could drive it as long as we wanted."

"I may have embellished that a little. Does it matter now? Mom thinks he'll still let me live in it in their driveway if I get a real job."

She handed him her phone. "Call him. Tell him we picked up nearly two thousand followers in only three weeks."

Maisie believed the universe still wanted her to live her best life on the road. They had a built-in audience of Gen Zs who had responded to her videos and who envied their freedom.

"We're filthy and tired," she said. "After we park the RV, we'll shower and ride our bikes to the beach and come back for some firepit content."

"How much is left on your debit card?" Jaxson asked.

"Let's just say I'm glad we pre-paid for the week."

"I only Zelled a deposit, and the guy at the gate needs the whole thing before we drive in."

"If not do we lose our deposit?"

Jaxson cracked his knuckles and tucked his arms behind his head. "That's gone."

"Gone? I need a shower!"

"They used the deposit to reserve the spot and hold our mail."

"Our tagline is that the universe will provide, Jax. What if we tell the manager we've got two thousand followers who'll see this RV park in our videos?"

"I tried that. No go."

She sighed. "Then we'll drive to the oceanfront and record some content with the sunset over the RV. We'll sleep there tonight."

"Trailers can't park at the oceanfront, the guy told me. Do we have any beer left in the cooler you bought when the fridge stopped working?"

"What we have are olives and moldy yogurt."

Gone were her hopes of sharing hotdogs and potato salad around a neighborly firepit.

The caravan line began to move.

"Go forward or turn around!" someone shouted.

"Switch seats. I'll drive," Jaxson said. "FYI, Maise, you're starting to smell."

"Look who's talking. Let me video you so you can see your nasty self." She raised her phone.

"You'll depress the followers we have left." He jerked the RV forward and back to inch it out of the line.

"We may end up sharing a video from a homeless shelter tomorrow. I can't believe the universe is letting me down like this."

"You used to be so upbeat," Jaxson said. "That's what made me think we had a shot at becoming influencers."

His challenge led her to scroll through her past week's texts. "Mom texted the address of an uncle of hers who lives near here in a senior residence. Maybe we can park the RV at his place tonight. I'll ask her to call him."

"Great," Jaxson said. "Some old geyser's place. I'm starting to hate living our best life."

* * * *

Benjamin Shandi, a retired surgeon, had opinions people valued—or so he told the residents of Marina Village who found themselves trapped with him in the dining room or on the facility's elevator. They'd learned to move on before he began one of his self-promoting lectures.

None of Dr. Shandi's grown children or ex-wives had visited him since he moved into the residence, but he hadn't chosen Marina Village to make friends. When he'd reluctantly sold his East Beach mansion—with its private dock—he needed somewhere to tie up his boat. The building's hallways accommodated his new motorized wheelchair, and since the doctor had never cooked for himself, he also needed its excellent dining room.

"Wow," Jaxson said as he entered the doctor's spacious fourth-floor apartment. "Is this the penthouse?"

Maisie gently hugged the man in the wheelchair. "I'm glad to meet you, Uncle."

He patted her shoulder. "I last saw you the day you were born," he said. "The dining room downstairs isn't open yet, but I had them send up refreshments for you. Your mother didn't say if you'd be spending the night. If you'd like to, I've got a guest room I use as an office. The maids made up the bed."

Maisie's shoulders relaxed. "We'd love to stay with you. That would be wonderful. Would it inconvenience you if we showered before we sat down to chat? Jaxson and I spent all day on the road."

"Fine. The guest bathroom is on the right."

* * * *

"It's like Shangri La in here," Maisie called to Jaxson from the shower. "I never want to leave."

She lathered a third squirt of fragrant shampoo into her hair.

Jaxson finished shaving at the sink. "Wait till you feel these towels, babe."

"My clothes are so dirty I may wear one of those towels to dinner."

Later, on her uncle's balcony, they took selfies with a picturesque Coast Guard station and a marina full of expensive toys—sailboats and yachts—as a backdrop.

"Is one of those boats yours?" Jaxson asked. He took a swig from the beer the doctor offered.

"That forty-foot cabin cruiser's mine," the doctor said. "I had her outfitted with a disability ramp when my legs weakened, but I may sell her soon. Fishing parties bore me now."

"What did that baby cost?" Jaxson asked.

"My career in heart surgery was lucrative. What is it you do for a living?"

"We're influencers," Jaxson said.

"As am I," the doctor said. "I've retained tremendous influence in retirement. Patients and their families still call to thank me for their surgeries. Southeastern Virginia magazine interviewed me only last year."

"That's impressive, Uncle," Maisie said. "RV influencers are what we aspire to be. At the moment we're travel bloggers."

"With two thousand followers," Jaxson said.

"I'm unfamiliar with those occupations."

"On social media," Maisie said. "The universe got us off to a good start, but—"

"We're #livingourbestlife," Jaxson said. "Look us up. I'm going to grab another beer."

"Wheelhouses," Dr. Shandi said. "That's what they called recreational vehicles in ancient times."

"Really?" Maisie said. "That's good content. How about letting me record an interview with you before we leave?"

"Content?"

"What we post online. The camper's always in the shot. Jaxson does backflips, and I run through meadows or do yoga in beautiful places. So far that's all we have to promote."

"Maybe your uncle wants to be our first patron," Jaxson said.

"We're guests here," Maisie said. "No business."

"The doc seems pretty well off."

"I made more money than I knew what to do with," the doctor said. "Bypasses were goldmines before stents."

Maisie wore her cleanest dress to dinner downstairs and a smile as broad as one she'd posted from a mountain peak their first day on the road. Squeaky-clean fingernails had lifted her mood.

Few but the waiter showed interest in her uncle or their table, and only one other senior had a guest younger than fifty. Maisie felt the guest's eyes on her until she glanced his way.

As they ate, Dr. Shandi held forth about his ungrateful children, his luck buying real estate, and his years of surgical victories.

"I invite you to a cruise tomorrow," he said over dessert. "Might be my last opportunity to take the boat out before I sell it. Just a few hours on Chesapeake Bay, but you wouldn't have much time to get on the road when we get back. Could you stay another night?"

"Yes!" Maisie said.

Upstairs in her uncle's guest bedroom, his niece slipped between clean, silky sheets. "What are you looking for in that desk, Jax? Come to bed."

"Your uncle's loaded," Jaxson said. "He brags about the two million he got for his house, but that boat cost plenty, too, and he's got other investments."

"Those are his private papers."

"I'll bet there's cash or checks in one of these drawers. My gram hid those things and then forgot where. If I find cash, we'll be gone before the old guy notices it's missing."

"He's family. Not that the universe likes us stealing from anyone."

"I didn't say, 'let's kill him,' although…if there's a will in here, and you're in it, he does have medical issues—"

"You did not just say that, Jax. And why would I be in his will? He has children and grandchildren."

"He likes you. At least hit him with my patron angle. Without money we push the camper back to Maine."

The universe and their followers could not want that. "I'll ask him for a small loan to fix the water hose and fill the gas tank. Just stop going through his stuff."

"Go to sleep, Maisie. The universe and I have got this."

* * * *

In the morning, she found him asleep in the desk chair. She tried to push her uncle's papers back into the drawers. She put her charged phone in her robe pocket. On the living room's balcony, she videoed the marina with commentary about their upcoming boat ride.

She posted it to @Maisie and Jaxson just as she heard her uncle's motorized chair.

"Good morning, my dear."

"It's paradise here, Uncle. You're living your best life."

"My best life is behind me," he said. "But the food's good. Join me for breakfast downstairs?"

After breakfast, the doctor left her in the dining room, saying he had to speak with the dockmaster. The woman from dinner who'd had the young man with her beckoned to Maisie from another table.

"Is Dr. Shandi coming back?" the woman asked. "Make sure you try the scones. Or have you?"

"No, I haven't."

"I understand you're famous," the woman went on. "My grandson Charlie has seen you on Instagram or something. He also recognized your vehicle."

Maisie's heart leaped. "He recognized me?"

"Yes. Try one of these blueberry ones. Charlie—my grandson—called you the 'It' girl. I hope Ben Shandi provided you with a visitor parking pass for that horror in the lot. If not, management will tow it."

"The 'It' girl?"

"And he called your boyfriend 'Wacky Jackie.'"

"Jaxson probably wouldn't mind that." Maisie's universe had given her the boost she needed.

She picked at a scone and resolved to ask her uncle for a loan and then negotiate with Jaxson's father. She and Jax could get jobs at a Walmart until they'd accumulated enough money to get back on the road. If a stranger in coastal Virginia recognized them and their Maine license plate from a video, it was a sign that her website would be built.

"Charlie—my grandson—wanted to ask you last night if life on the road is as delightful as you make it look. I wouldn't let him interrupt your dinner."

Fame had revived Maisie. "I'd love to answer his questions. Maybe we could do a video interview."

"The whole truth is…." The woman stirred her coffee. "None of us like Dr. Shandi. We avoid him. No offense if you're related."

"He's my mother's uncle."

The woman sniffed. "Your great uncle was only in this residence two days when he walked up to me and my gentleman friend and predicted my friend's death would be in two weeks."

"Oh, dear," Maisie said.

The woman shook her head. "Surgeons. No one here needs their brilliant insight on our impending deaths."

"Did your friend—"

"Eight days later." The woman took a sip of coffee. "I don't believe surgeons have consciences. They can't afford them, can they? It might cause them to hesitate."

Maisie thought about her conscience. She wanted to become an RV influencer so much that she'd almost offered to help Jaxson look through her uncle's desk the night before.

"Money isn't everything," the woman said. "Dr. Shandi's grown children never visit."

"I don't think any of them live near here."

"Still," the woman said as she picked over the scone crumbs left on her plate. "My grown children visit often enough to stay in my Will."

* * * *

An attendant from the residence helped the doctor down to the boat ramp, but Maisie's great-uncle wheeled himself onto the deck and took the helm.

"Life preservers are required," he said. After that, she and Jaxson obeyed a steady stream of commands regarding how to undo ropes and avoid buoys. The doctor deftly navigated the cabin cruiser into the outgoing ship lane that linked them to the bay.

Jaxson, in his orange life vest, claimed the most comfortable deck chair. "You really know how to live, Doc."

The doctor told them the history of the bay from oyster management to pirates, and about the Bridge-Tunnel that allowed container ships to pass through it.

Maisie videoed everything to upload later.

"You maneuver this craft so well," she said. "You make it look easy."

"Dexterity in the operating room applies everywhere," her uncle said. "My hands are unaffected by the weakening in my legs. Precision and focus—they're gifts. By the way, my left side is my best profile. After countless magazine and newspaper shoots, one learns these things."

Maisie, too, had learned those things since leaving Maine. Jaxson hadn't care to. She turned to video Jaxson, who waved at her with the beer can in his hand.

She joined him. "You agreed we wouldn't have alcohol in our videography. Where'd you get it?"

"I brought it from his apartment. Along with these." Jaxson produced three platinum credit cards.

"Oh no, you didn't. Give me those!"

Her uncle called out a warning. He needed to increase the cruiser's speed to minimize the impact from another boat's wake. With the credit cards in one hand and her phone in the other, Maisie lacked a hand to balance herself. The cards slipped from her hand to the wet deck and her phone fell on the wet railing.

"My videos!" Maisie didn't hesitate to reach out and grab the phone, but it caused her to slip again. She and the phone in her hand fell further and in a moment both went overboard.

"She's in the water!" Jaxson shouted.

Dr. Shandi idled the engine. "What?"

"She's floating in the water holding her phone up in the air. How do we get to her?"

Both men stared at the credit cards strewn on the deck between them for a moment.

The doctor looked at where Maisie bobbed in the water in her orange life vest with her arm high in the air protecting the phone. He carefully put the boat in reverse. "Drop that rope ladder over the side," he ordered Jaxson.

Maisie handed the phone up to Jaxson so she could climb the ladder using both hands. Once on deck, life vest dripping water everywhere, Maisie grinned.

"That was energizing," she said. The doctor asked to see the phone. She'd put a waterproof cover on it before they left.

Jaxson bent over and appeared to be mopping the deck where the cards had been.

"I'll go get you more towels from below," he said.

The credit cards on the deck had vanished.

"I want to take this dripping vest off and go below to dry off, Uncle."

"Be careful not to slip," her uncle said. "There's a dry vest in the galley."

Jaxson lay on a bunk below with his own vest unhooked. "I can't breathe in this stupid thing."

"The water's calm but if I hadn't had mine on, we'd have lost our camera." She pulled open a few drawers and found towels and a dry life vest. Why are you lying down?"

Jaxson slammed his hand against the wall. "Your universe stinks," he said. "The old man saw the credit cards."

"Give them to me," she said.

He grabbed her wrist when she reached for them. "Those cards aren't all I found in his desk. There's twenty thousand bucks in cash that's ours if we go back without him. I could do it."

"Do what? Let go of me."

"Push him in like you went in. No one knows who we are or who you are to him."

"I told a woman that I'm his niece. Her grandson recognized both us and the camper from the internet. You're scaring me, Jaxson." She pulled away from his grip with the cards in her hand. She found a baggie to put the cards in on the galley's kitchen counter. She removed two sandwiches from the cooler and took them up to the deck.

She sat in the co-pilot's chair and handed her uncle one of the sandwiches. Then she set the credit card baggie down where he could see it.

"I'm heading back," the doctor said. "To the marina."

Maisie took a deep breath. Saved by the universe again. "Oh, good. That is an excellent idea."

"The sandwich you made is delicious, but I can feel your heart racing from over here, Maisie. Did you not know till now that your boyfriend's a thief?"

She put down the half sandwich in her hand. "I think he just feels desperate…"

"Is the broken-down RV stolen, too?"

"It's his father's. He wants it back right away."

The doctor handed Maisie her phone. "Your determination to hold onto this thing impressed me. It's working."

"That phone's my world. I hate giving up."

"I see that." The doctor held up the bag of credit cards. "I've brought people back to life because I refused to give up. Who paid for your travel blogging adventure?"

Maisie played with the wax paper wrapping around her sandwich.

"I see," he said. "You did. He didn't mind taking your money."

"We're broke, Uncle. Could you lend me money to get us back to Maine?"

"We'll talk about it later. The boat's gas line needs to be flushed before we reach the channel. It clogs like an artery in dry dock. Call Jaxson up here."

"I think he should stay down there. Can't I help?"

"His arm is longer, and it's housed halfway down the side. Tell me if you're afraid to let Jaxson come up, Niece."

She touched her uncle's arm. "Do you believe the universe provides?"

"I believe in seizing opportunities when they present themselves. Please get Jaxson up here."

In the minutes after Maisie left to get Jaxson, Dr. Shandi idled the boat and wheeled his chair to the stern. He bent far enough over in his chair to reach the top of the rope ladder, and then threw it in the bay. He returned to the helm as Jaxson and Maisie arrived on deck. She stood between the two men.

"Put your life jacket back on, Jaxson. The gas line is in the stern on the outside. It's quite a reach, but once you lean over and open the cabinet it's stored in, I'll do the rest," the doctor said.

Once Jaxson had leaned far enough over the side, Dr. Shandi hit the throttle. The boat took off at a speed that caused Jaxson to lose his grasp on the boat and he fell overboard.

The doctor then steered the cabin cruiser in a wide circle to get close enough to Jaxson to throw the bag of credit cards at the bobbing man. "Precision and focus," the doctor said.

Maisie threw Jaxson a ring buoy. "Where's the rope ladder, Uncle?"

She watched as Jaxson grabbed the flotation device.

"Don't worry, Maisie," the doctor said. He held up his cell phone. "I'm contacting Coast Guard Rescue."

"Hey, you guys!" Jaxson shouted, "You guys!"

The doctor kept his phone by his ear and the boat beyond Jaxson's reach.

"I know one of their officers," Dr. Shandi said while he waited for the officer he'd requested to come to the phone. "I brought the man's mother back to life."

"But shouldn't we—"

"His mother had an aneurysm right in the middle of her bypass operation—Joe? It's Ben Shandi. We need a rescue by the channel as soon as possible. He's a young man in good health, wearing a life preserver and holding onto a flotation ring. I'm wheelchair-bound, and my niece can't find the ladder and doesn't know how to maneuver a boat. We're almost out of gas, so I'm heading back. His coordinates are on the screenshot I just sent. Is your team nearby? Five minutes? Thank you."

The doctor steered the boat away from Jaxson and into the channel.

Maisie watched as Jaxson got farther away. "You're sure they'll rescue him in time? He's been drinking."

Back at the doctor's apartment, Maisie showered and dressed while her uncle made more calls.

His contact at the Coast Guard reported that Jaxson was safely on shore—with three of the doctor's credit cards on him. Did the doctor want to take out charges?

"Yes. Can the police notify the magistrate without me?"

Another call and the Public Defender's office agreed to arrange for an attorney for Jaxson. The head of the office thanked the doctor again for her Dad's life-saving triple bypass twenty years earlier.

Maisie walked in as the doctor hung up from canceling his credit cards.

"He's fine, dear," the doctor assured her. "I used my influence."

* * * *

At Jaxson's bench trial, Maisie stood by her uncle in court rather than standing by Jaxson in his jail jumpsuit.

The judge and the Commonwealth Attorney agreed on Jaxson's release, provided the doctor drop the charges and that the defendant leave the area the same day. Getting the defendant back to Maine turned out to be the easiest part, since Jaxson's arrest had triggered a fugitive warrant for theft of property and local police delivered him door to door.

* * * *

"My grandson Charlie and I toured the inside of the doctor's RV," the woman from the dining room bragged to the other residents of Marina Village a few weeks later. "It's huge inside. Nothing like that monstrosity the management towed out of here."

Maisie's uncle sold his cabin cruiser after the trial. He spent $400,000 on a wheelchair-accessible RV fitted with an eight-hundred-dollar composting toilet, two bathrooms, two bedrooms, a spacious kitchen, and a media center.

"It's got hand brakes and gas pedals so the doctor can drive it himself," the woman said. "His eyesight's remarkable. The hydraulic lift puts his chair right behind the wheel. Charlie—my grandson—offered to design a website for the niece. He and Maisie spend hours together working on it. She's famous, you know."

On the day of their departure, Dr. Shandi turned in his apartment fob and mailbox keys. Charlie videoed them in the parking lot before they headed out.

"Jaxson had to end his journey," Maisie said into the camera. "The universe, however, supplied me with a new travel companion—renowned heart specialist and my uncle, Benjamin Shandi. It also brought me a brilliant webmaster."

Charlie followed her as she walked toward the doctor who sat outside the mammoth RV. "Uncle, say hello to our online friends."

She reminded Charlie which side her uncle looked best on.

"This young woman has managed to remind me what living is," Dr. Shandi said. "If a heart problem makes you hesitate to join us on the road, my expertise as a heart surgeon and my answers to your published comments may allay those fears. I'll be available to meet with you at campsites across the country. We'll also recommend products to make your life on the road a success."

The doctor had spent his last days in Marina Village contacting executives in the travel industry. One of them had a parent the doctor had operated on. Promotional agreements from RV manufacturers and brand advocates had already come in.

"I'll cook heart-healthy meals in our state-of-the-art kitchen," Maisie chimed in. "You'll still see me eating breakfast yogurt on beautiful mornings outdoors. All our videos will help you live your best life."

"And products that may extend your lives," the doctor added.

"Charlie," Maisie interrupted as she joined him. "Turn the camera and say hello to our followers. Meet Charlie, our amazing web designer. He'll leave links for subscribers."

* * * *

Charlie's grandmother added details to her story about Dr. Shandi's RV whenever there was a lull in conversation on the residents' porch. "It's amazingly comfortable," she'd say. "Did I tell you what it's worth? I suppose selling his apartment amortized the cost. They plan to drop in on his grown children and two of his ex-wives. Charlie says that content will be fascinating. None of the doctor's relatives are expecting him. Charlie—that's my grandson—thinks boomers with aging parents will flock to the website just to see how awkward those situations get."

She went on to suggest that Maisie and her uncle might quadruple their number of followers and brand agreements if it went as planned.

"But we know Ben Shandi," she always added. "How long can he put up with being Maisie's driver or helping seniors follow nutrition plans? Any day now he'll ask her to turn the camera on him so he can start bragging about himself. He'll either turn off their following or start guessing death dates of seniors he sees on Facebook."

Relieved that the doctor had moved out, many residents of Marina Village followed Maisie's social media platforms to chart Ben Shandi's rise or fall.

The universe approved of their venture, though, and the website took off. The doctor's adult children and ex-wives enjoyed finally getting their share of his notoriety, and Maisie kept those visits short. She and Charlie skyped weekly to discuss new promotional agreements or to strategize how much video time to allot to the doctor or to Maisie alone.

After a few months, Dr. Shandi began a secondary website of his own. Maisie started calling Charlie just to hear his voice. Charlie added animated heart-shaped gifs, which floated onscreen every time Maisie appeared in a video. Her legion of followers gave those a thumbs up.

CARAVAN AND CHALICE

MAX JASON PETERSON

OLIVIER LOVED his adoptive mother, Éléonore, with the strength of an entire family. Ollie and Ellie. A perfect pair, as far as it went. But with Ellie once again succumbing to her twilight years, Ollie reached an inescapable conclusion: to survive and pass the legacy of love on to the next generation, this family needed some fresh blood.

They toured the highways and byways of America on perpetual vacation in a battered RV caravan they'd named the White Witch (also affectionately known as Stevie), like John Steinbeck and Charley in the camper Rocinante. When they needed cash or hungered for the stage, Ollie and Ellie worked traveling carnivals. Together, they put on an amazing magic show. About half the tricks were skillful illusions; the other half were real. Under the banner "Ellie's Insight," Ellie reigned like the queen she was at the divination booth or fortune-telling tent. Ollie played the strong man, with dazzling demonstrations of martial skill.

The open air refreshed them, and when they moved on, the blur of passing greenery and towns felt like home to Ollie from his days of knight errantry and riding to war. Parked at campsites or docked at the occasional trailer park, they attracted little notice outside the carnival circuit. Arriving in Hampton Roads, Virginia, they enjoyed the beach life, even with late summer heading into fall. They especially loved all the campsites in forested parklands.

"I found one for you, Ollie," Ellie said, snapping the obituary section. (They supported print media when they could. Both of them loved the scent of newsprint with their coffee. And campfires. Newspapers made excellent kindling.)

He set down his toasting fork in its crook and came over to Ellie's velvet-draped chaise lounge. He reached out a long arm—"elegantly shaped," as Ellie approvingly called it when helping him gussy up for his latest conquest—and snagged the section, scanning it quickly for pertinent details. These notices seldom contained a picture—at least, not of the people he and Ellie were most interested in.

"Seven children," Ollie remarked with warmth in his tone.

"The widow's a schoolteacher."

"That may be a bit too Ichabod Crane even for me."

"You never know, Ollie. Ichabod Crane lived a happy life, while it lasted. Think of all that fresh apple pie."

"I'll take it under advisement," Ollie said cheerfully, circling the lucky widow's name. As well as the mysterious elements of her wealthy young husband's demise.

"There's more where she came from," Ellie observed, holding out a withered hand for the paper.

Ollie, however, had spotted something. He smoothed the paper on his knee. "She's beautiful," he murmured, folding the page on a different notice and holding it up for her to see. He didn't want to relinquish it just yet. "And she looks—brave? Sad?" He felt a deep spark of recognition he couldn't account for.

"Not bad," his mother acknowledged. "Only two kids, though."

"She's young enough to have more," he said thoughtfully.

Ellie cackled. "How can you tell from that photograph? It could be twenty years old!"

"Well, at least she picked a photo of the whole family," Ollie said. "She only needed to include one with him."

"True, true," Ellie agreed. "A good sign."

"The kids might be from a prior marriage. They'd only been married a month." This was one of the potential signs that they'd located their quarry.

Ellie snatched the paper with nimble fingers, displaying the grace and charm that went along with being one of the most prized itinerant stage magicians in the land. Even if, for too long a time, she'd had to masquerade as the assistant of one husband or another.

She handed back the obituary section. "Well, don't go falling in love with a picture," Ellie concluded. "You know what happened to Dorian Gray."

"At least this one's closer to my age," Ollie commented wistfully. It was all very well to say age didn't matter, but he liked a certain level of experience. Plus, since most people only got a limited span of years with their beloved, better if you both progressed along the timeline from what looked like the same starting point. Right now, he could pass for thirty-three.

"Don't kid yourself, old man," his mother cackled.

Ollie flushed: it was true. He was technically 376 years older than Ellie. And yet his heart went out to this rare flower, who had lost so much—exactly what, it was plain for all the world to see in the photograph she'd chosen. A loving family. She might be a woman after his own heart.

Or exactly the opposite. Either way, it was win-win. One had to take turns between the good and the bad, after all.

Ollie and Ellie played a few hands of hearts. Then, by the light of the moon and her flickering plasma globe, Ellie told his fortune, just to keep her hand in. Afterwards, Ollie laughed gamely at all her jokes and told a few of his own, new ones he'd made up when the winter nights grew long. He won several hundred dollars from her at rummy. Through it all, he never referred to the slip of newspaper he'd tucked into his breast pocket, though he patted it from time to time.

He slept on it. When he rolled over and the page crinkled in the breast pocket of his pajamas, the young widow wafted into his dreams on the perfume of newsprint. There was definitely something about her. Their off-the-grid lifestyle in the White Witch meant that most of their research happened in "guest mode" on library computers; but they'd gotten quite adept at ferreting out the facts: who'd died, how, and when. They had contacts tangentially connected with law enforcement across the country. They'd also learned to recognize certain "tells" for the quarry they hunted.

This young-looking woman might be a black widow of the highest order, a hardened actress of love and grief (like he and Ellie had, by necessity, become). Or she might have a soul wise and true.

He dreamed of her. Something about a battlefield, lifting his sword to follow her with absolute belief. When he woke the next morning, he was certain she was the one. He dressed up in the top hat and tails he preserved for days on stage with Ellie, descended the steps of their cozy caravan, and headed off to meet the destiny that would make his family complete again.

For a time.

* * * *

Reports of Ollie's prowess in bed had made the rounds, back in the day. He was, after all, *that* Olivier de Vienne, bosom friend of Roland—one of Charlemagne's paladins, counted among the original Twelve Peers of France. There was one especially risqué epic poem that had Olivier making good on his boast to bring off the emperor's daughter a hundred times in one night. Which may or may not have been true…

Ollie remembered that night. It had indeed been epic. But their salacious escapades had been as much the princess's doing as his, and after a certain point, he hadn't exactly been counting.

In truth, Ollie was a romantic. Even though the chivalric romances might be so much fiction. War was gruesome. Slaying enemy after enemy killed the heart; executions, even more so, no matter how just. He knew of just one way to revive the spirit. Aside from his harmonious companionship with Ellie, the thing he wanted most in life was love. A good man or woman.

The bad…were a necessary evil.

One he had, however reluctantly, accepted as his mission to weed out.

Ollie and Joanie went on their first date on October 1. It was the perfect time of year: most of the tourists had gone home; kids, teens, and twenty-somethings were back in school and college; and the locals had the vacation destinations all to themselves. Plus, fall in Tidewater, Virginia, was so mild, the weather was actually comfortable for outdoor excursions.

With Halloween approaching, Ollie took Joanie and her two children—a daughter and son, ages ten and eleven—to the hayride and miniature petting zoo at Haunted Hunt Club Farm in Virginia Beach. They loved the pumpkin-themed amusements of Cox Farms in Centreville, Virginia. And the Haunted Horse Rides on the restored Hampton Carousel got their blood pumping.

They turned the whole month of October into a delightful Hampton Roads Halloween vacation for four—sometimes five, since the children loved Ollie's mother like a grandma.

And Ellie was, of course, just that fun. Especially with so much magic at her command. She found silver dollars and gold doubloons behind their ears; hexed their Halloween balloons to follow them all day; and summoned toy black cats and owls from her sleeves. The owls gave a slow blink when exposed to light, and the cats engaged in a tiny tussle and leapt into the children's hands. Ollie's heart swelled with pride and love.

Of course, grief seemed to cast its black veil over Joanie from time to time, putting her in a somber, pensive mood as she looked at him with so much sorrow. But that often happened with Ollie's conquests, considering how he found them. He hoped it was a sign that she'd actually cared about her husband—even if the kids did not seem overly troubled by the death of their dad.

One day at Busch Gardens, the kids played at haunted Sesame Place with Ellie so Ollie and Joanie could enjoy some of the scarier attractions. Waiting in line for a maze rife with living skeletons and undead vampires, they finally got down to discussing matters of life and death.

Ollie said, "If I got mystically revived, I'd rather wake up in a crypt or mausoleum than buried six feet under."

She laughed. "One of those tombs like a sarcophagus, where they have a statue of you on the lid. Like a knight of the old guard."

"The very old guard," he agreed, bouncing on his toes. Oh, how he wanted to tell her about his time with Charlemagne. It had been too long since he'd had an understanding soul he could trust that much. For a moment, his heart pinched as he thought of his last true love, Maurice. Husband of forty-nine years. How much more time he'd wanted with that lovely man.

"Good thing I had Clement cremated," Joanie continued, linking her arm through his and resting her head on his shoulder. "That way we don't have to worry about him coming back."

"Whatever happened to dear Clement?" His heart picked up the pace as the line moved. This was part of it: collecting evidence. The murderers he and Ellie sought were too clever to leave cut-and-dried clues strong enough to convince a court, even when people *knew* what had really happened. They would never be caught by conventional means. Magic often helped, but with something like this, Ollie and Ellie wanted to be sure. The best proof was handed to them by the culprit—one way or another.

"Why do you want to know?" She clung tight to his arm as the line moved closer to the entrance. In this eerie, dark alley, skeletal "statues" suddenly moved, startling shrieks from the guests.

"Just wondering what fate has in store for me," he said softly.

She leaned close, soft lips brushing his ear. "I think it's my fault. He had a weak heart. We'd been arguing so much about everything—where to go on vacation, where the kids should go to school. He wanted to ship them off to boarding school, can you believe it? They're just little kids. They don't want to leave home, and I want them near me. I want us to enjoy their happy childhoods together. That's time you never get back. He'd never have suggested that if they were his own kids."

"They weren't?"

"Oh, no. And I love them like my own, but they're my stepchildren, technically. My previous husband—he died early, too." Her eyes gleamed in the eerie blue lights. Tears? Or triumph?

He kissed her forehead. "Children should be cherished, no matter where they come from. A family is the greatest thing on earth. I'm so lucky to have found you."

"That makes me the lucky one," she said, squeezing his waist tight.

In the maze, skeletons stalked them. Joanie shrieked and cowered against Ollie. Then, when the skeletons leaned close with menace, she leapt at *them*, claws outstretched, snarling "Begone, fiends!" and "Back to hell, revenants!"

Ollie put a hand over his heart, captivated.

It was time. Guilty or innocent.

In the next haunted house, he proposed.

He waited till they reached the parlor with a witch reading tarot cards. On a nearby shelf, a cat's skeleton oversaw this spooky work.

As Ollie dropped to one knee, the witch turned over the cards for Death, The Lovers (reversed), The Devil.

Joanie chuckled, beaming at him. "Yes, you fool." He kissed her hand.

The fortune teller met his gaze with a humorless, thin-lipped smile.

"A Halloween wedding!" Joanie's teeth glowed in the black light. "As a widow, that feels oddly appropriate."

As they left the tarot room, the witch's laugh echoed. He heard the slap as she turned over more rectangles of stiff cardboard. "Judgement," she announced. "The Fool."

Ollie's back prickled. He placed a hand between Joanie's shoulder blades and guided her quickly on.

They celebrated their marriage swiftly, all of them dressed in sober black, by Joanie's request. Respect for the dead? Halloween tradition? Ollie found he was too happy to care. It was often like this—so good at the start, before he knew for certain. If she were innocent, hopefully they'd have years to explore their deepest truths. Today, her kisses tasted like champagne. That was good enough for now.

In camp that night, Ollie and Joanie set up their own tent. "It's all terribly romantic," Joanie said, her eyes flashing with tiny reflected candle flames as she stripped to reveal black lace. "But aren't you worried about security?"

Ollie folded her in his arms. "I'll protect you from the night," he promised. He kissed her for all his life was worth. She kissed him back as if her life depended on it. Soon Ollie found himself entering that lightheaded state where he wanted to share his soul. "Of course, in the old days, my horse would have waited outside the pavilion. With his superior senses, he'd have given me plenty of warning if anything was wrong. Long before a snake had time to strike."

"You don't like snakes?" Joanie…was a top. She commanded with force and finesse, with the assurance and fervor of the battlefield.

And Ollie…sometimes liked that, rather a lot. So he found himself answering without hesitation. "I woke up one morning and found my charger, Emeris, standing sentry with a snake's skull crushed under his front shoe." Emeris would have done anything to protect him. That beloved horse, who nuzzled his mussed hair affectionately when he arose from sleep each morning, had died on the battlefield, wheeling to save Olivier from a spear in the back.

Which reminded him: no matter how charming Joanie was, Ollie needed to stay on guard, in case she decided to pour poison in his ear once he fell asleep, like Claudius with his brother Hamlet Sr.

So at an apropos moment, Ollie took the reins. He knew a million ways to distract a partner to the point of gibberish. Pillow talk was the best for ferreting out elusive secrets. "Speaking of antique things, I don't know much about your past. How did your previous husband die?"

"Which one?" she gasped.

"So many times a widow. And still so young," he lamented.

"We all have our crosses to bear. You're a widower yourself, aren't you?"

"Many times over, I'm afraid."

"How many times?"

"Answer my question first," he growled.

"Dear Randy shouldn't have ridden the Ferris Wheel with that heart condition. I told him he didn't need to come with me."

Randolph had been husband number four, according to their research. At least, as far back as they could take it. "Really? I thought his death was a bit more unusual than a heart attack," he prompted, pressing his point.

"When the pain struck, I guess he thought it was the seat belt. He panicked and ripped it off. Fell to his death, poor fool. It's a lucky thing I work out so much. When the car tipped over all the way up there, I managed to hang on."

"Very lucky. And the husband before that?"

"Paul was a deep-sea diver. We were studying coral reefs together when his oxygen line sprang a leak. That far down, he just didn't have a chance to reach help. And I was no use. I'd caught my ankle in the reef."

"So unlucky," Ollie murmured.

"And what about you? Your last wife? Susannah, was it?"

"She was a lovely person. Such a passion for life. She cultivated some amazing gardens. Everything you might want to find—which, apparently, her previous husband found a lot of hellebore? Mostly in his salad? Anyway, you should have seen it. Acres of flowers. Birds and bees everywhere. I guess she never knew she was allergic to stings."

Was that a wicked gleam in Joanie's eyes? "And the one before her?"

"Marianne was our stage magic assistant. On the side, she also tamed lions with her husband. Until he got mauled. Apparently, there was a bit of a mix-up, and some of our rabbits ended up in the ring with his big cats. But that cat act was plagued with problems. One day someone forgot their feeding, and Marianne happened to enter their pen when they were hangry. I guess it didn't help that Ellie and I were working on a scary stage show that involved spraying our assistant with blood. Unfortunately, she didn't know the blood was real…"

Joanie drew back a little, rising up on her elbow. "Who was in charge of feeding the lions?"

"Well, as her new husband…that would be me."

She challenged Ollie with her frank gaze, like an unsheathed sword. At last, Joanie smiled.

Challenge accepted, Ollie thought giddily.

It was a most memorable wedding night.

Life got interesting again. Ollie now played chess with family members, enjoying moments spent here or there with the kids, trying to find time with his mother without leaving Joanie alone for too long.

One evening while Joanie took the tots to the movies, Ollie and Ellie propped up the awning on the side of the White Witch. The bright harvest moon guided Ellie's crocheting (though by now, her talented fingers could have created an entire afghan in the dark). The firelight glinted on the sharp edges of Hauteclere, the sword Ollie polished across his knee.

"I hate it when it's my turn," Ollie said. "It feels like such a lie."

"You're doing good work, Son. Never doubt it."

"Isn't it overcompensating? Two wrongs, and all that."

"We're still here, aren't we? The Chalice would reject your offerings if you weren't still a peerless defender of right."

"I don't know about peerless." He pressed his shoulder to hers in a friendly jostle. "We make a pretty good team."

Ellie passed him the cocoa. He sipped, peering into the darkness, listening to the wood snapping in the fire, to the lonely owl challenging the night.

"The children are settling in well." Ellie sprinkled tiny marshmallows into his mug, where they floated like little stars.

"They're good kids. They might even grow up to be heroes."

"With the right training."

"And love. Don't forget love."

"The secret ingredient." Ellie smiled, stirring her own cocoa. "Oh, the times we've had together. Raising children, grandchildren, great-grandchildren. So many of them became heroes, one way or another. Firefighters, nurses, novelists, musicians whose work saved a life. They're all so talented. You know, Ollie…" she hesitated. "I still miss the children of my first lifetime. Especially Henry, Richard, and Joan." She smiled. "And Marie, Alix, William, Matilda, Geoffrey, Eleanor, and John, of course."

"You'll see them all again one day," Ollie said softly.

Ellie shrugged, looking away. "Perhaps. If we ever get tired of this life. If people wise up, treat each other kindly, and stop needing us in this modern age." She looked up at him, reached out for his hand. "But honey, I couldn't do better for my lifelong son than you. One of Charlemagne's best."

"And you, Mother," he said, struggling to speak evenly through his emotion. "One of the wisest queens France ever produced. Staunch mother of lionhearted heroes and supporter of poets. And—my best friend." His voice choked off. For a moment, he allowed himself to face the enormity of it: she'd been Éléonore d'Aquitaine, a double queen, first of France, then of

England. She'd become his confidante and dearest friend. And his partner in crime. Through the good and the bad. His mother, as supportive of him as she'd been of her own brood.

"We've been so happy," she murmured, smoothing his hand. "Haven't we, Ollie? We've had a good run."

"We're happy now. Aren't we?"

"Yes," she said, with a slow sigh, easing back in her chair, drawing her crocheting up over her lap like a shawl. "Even now."

"Tolstoy said, 'Happy families are all alike.'"

Ellie snorted. "Hogwash. Never you believe it. Happy families are all happy. In as many different and interesting ways as there are days on this planet."

"But I wonder. If I hadn't thwarted Ganelon from killing Roland. If I hadn't stopped him from taking Charlemagne's army by treachery. If Roland hadn't offered me that Chalice, which was his by right. And then Ganelon's curse, before they executed him—"

"Your nemesis Ganelon may call this a curse. I call it a blessing." She raised her mug to him. "Here's to more good days than bad."

"Amen." He clinked his mug to hers. They reminisced for a bit. It was nice to share memories of the old days. Like when Ollie had befriended her, a great queen in what some felt sure were her final days. Thank Heaven the Chalice liked her, too. They publicized news of her death and hit the road together, traveling the world. Perfect freedom—except for their service to the Chalice.

Just like the canker in Ganelon's soul, there was an element of treachery required to keep the lifeblood of the Chalice flowing, and thereby their own lives and good deeds. Ollie didn't like to think about it. It was bad enough he had to do what needed to be done. Even now, he slept with Hauteclere near to hand, a special pillow cradling the burnished steel that glinted by the faint amber glow of the crystal in its hilt.

Ollie hated that this cherished blade sometimes functioned as executioner's sword. In his days as a paladin, amid life and death on the battlefield, Hauteclere had defended his homeland. As a knight errant, roaming the countryside and helping the helpless, he'd used the blade to save innocents. But truth be told, he'd also enacted the king's justice, even then.

The real crux of the matter was, he liked Joanie. He might even love her. But he hadn't been able to clear her. Or satisfy himself of her guilt, either, though research showed she'd survived at least twenty-five husbands, whom she'd married under a multitude of names. Maybe more. That was as far back as they could easily trace. Nor could Ellie's divination magic establish her guilt or innocence—the answers came up both ways. It was... perplexing.

The deaths of the wicked fed the Chalice and reversed the aging of Ollie and Ellie, giving them life and strength to continue to stop murderers. But the conditions were very specific. Perhaps fittingly for Ollie and Ellie's origins in the eras of chivalry and courtly love (which Éléonore had done a lot to promote, elevating the status of women as best she could for her times), they punished only those crimes which occurred within the context of marriage. And they had to be married to the evildoers themselves in order for the Chalice, with its medieval ideas of justice, to consider that they had the authority to punish those crimes.

Fortunately, the Chalice understood that marriage could exist even without being sanctified by officialdom, through sacred oaths alone, or Ollie would have been denied several true loves of his life, including dear Maurice. Though in Maurice's case, they were fortunate that the laws of the land changed in time for them to be legally recognized as husbands for the last five years of his life. Ollie's heart still melted at the memory of the smile on Maurice's beautiful, seventy-eight-year-old face.

But normally, they had no such luck; it was just one execution after another. Such grim doings sickened the soul. Sometimes, champions of justice or no, it felt far more curse than blessing. So Ollie and Ellie made a pact: they'd take turns nabbing the bad ones; and every fifteenth or twenty-fifth marriage, they could choose love.

Given what else they put themselves through, they really made it count.

These intervals of happiness—sometimes only a few years; a rare few lasting fifty—strengthened their hearts enough to endure the centuries. At the same time, especially if neither of them was actively hunting evildoers, it meant they were aging naturally, along with everyone else. Which was probably a good thing, especially for the ones they loved.

But sometimes…they did rather cut things close. Ollie, Ellie, or both had gotten so old they almost died of natural causes. And honestly, they were at peace with that. Especially since that meant they were so happy with their mates, they had no interest in doing anything that would take them from their lovers' arms, even to feed the Chalice. And after all they'd been through? To go out for the sake of someone they truly loved? Would not have been all that bad.

But unfortunately—perhaps due to their longstanding connection to the Chalice—they always lived to bury their spouses another day.

Meanwhile, there were so many wicked—murderers and rapists, abusers and torturers who'd never be caught. If Ollie and Ellie kept at their mission nonstop, it would crumble their hearts and poison them to the goodness of life. Especially since the Chalice demanded as part of the process that they take these monsters to the marriage bed. So, they didn't choose heart's love now and again just for pleasure. It was an essential chance to reconnect with all that was good in life. Love—was the very stuff of survival.

The only problem was—due to the uncertainty inherent in uncovering the truth—Ollie didn't always know if the person he'd wed would be facing justice.

Before he found out, sometimes he'd already given his heart.

Of course, there was one way to test the theory. By leaving himself open to apparent risk.

At some point, a black widow might try to poison his drink or murder Ollie in his sleep. Fortunately, as a roving knight, he'd long ago learned to sleep like a cat. And recognize the taste of most common poisons, to which he'd acclimatized himself by ingesting slowly increasing amounts, like the Count of Monte Cristo.

So, when Joanie asked solicitously at breakfast, "Would you like more orange juice, dear?" he took the glass willingly and sipped, savoring the taste while giving his tongue time to warn him.

Nothing happened. That didn't mean it wouldn't. Maybe Joanie was truly innocent. Or maybe she was waiting him out, selecting her time. Meanwhile, when Joanie worked as a paramedic and the children went to school, Ollie and Ellie continued their research and investigation. Ollie hit up contacts tangential to law enforcement. Ellie cast divination spells and read her cards. But even the cards' explicit clues did not turn up actual evidence.

Meanwhile, Ellie bonded with the children. They played rummy or chess on rainy afternoons. Ollie took them to the library. Joanie sometimes had to work different hours and asked him to pick them up after school. He welcomed the chance to talk with them. Mostly he kept the conversation light. But from time to time he told selective stories from his long life and asked them about their lives before.

Brian was serious, guarded, but said their most recent stepfather had been mean to him and little Sophie. He wouldn't repeat the details, but vehemently asserted that he was glad of the man's death, that he'd been dangerous. Sophie said gravely that Clement hadn't hurt them—their mother protected them—but he had hurt his previous family. Ollie found he trusted the kids.

For her part, Ellie loved playing with the children, teaching them how to tell fortunes and do close-up magic. She told Ollie they had the gift—even for the parts that were not illusory. Maybe, at some point, the whole family could take the stage.

Every night before bed, Ollie set up voice-activated recorders, in case Joanie talked in her sleep due to a guilty conscience. But not much got past her. One morning, she greeted him with a slim recorder on her palm, her expression carefully set to Polite Questioning. Fortunately, he'd just discovered a motion-activated camera she'd hidden and offered it to her in exchange.

With blushes that radiated sincerity, she explained it was just a way to immortalize a beautiful experience while they were young and pretty. Ollie had no intention of telling her how young he wasn't, but he couldn't help admiring her spirit.

The frustrating thing was, so much other evidence hinted at—but did not *absolutely* prove—her guilt. Police reports, news articles, evidence from neighbors who had no idea what they'd truly seen. If this were a detective show, the audience would be clamoring for her to be caught. But there was still a margin for error, and to do away with Joanie, Ollie must be utterly convinced.

Meanwhile, as the time passed, they treated each other to romantic gestures small and large. Perhaps Ollie had let certain things slip, from time to time, regarding his interest in knights. One day on a family outing, she surprised him with a side trip to a costume museum full of medieval fashions. Another time, Ollie and Ellie returned from a Saturday filled with performing magic at three different birthday parties, to find Joanie had baked Ollie's favorite brioche and cinnamon rolls from scratch. So, he made her a magically ever-blooming rose bush and wrangled box seats to her favorite operas.

As much as he loved her brash and confident exterior, Joanie had a vulnerable side too, a wariness he wanted to soothe, a glisten to her eyes as if she hoped he wouldn't break her heart.

"You know, Joanie, we might really have something here."

"The start of a beautiful friendship?" she teased.

"Or a lifetime love," he growled.

And maybe he'd struck lucky this time. He hoped so…

"I'm in over my head," he confessed to Ellie a few days later.

"There, there," she consoled him, with a motherly pat on the back. "I was afraid you might be."

"Really? How did you know? Was it the cards? No, I've got it. Motherly intuition."

She tapped the side of her nose with a wink. "It was the lack of attempts to give her a good opportunity to murder you over the last few days."

"Got me," he said ruefully.

"Her too, apparently," Ellie said with a chuckle.

Ollie realized he'd gotten so caught up in their burgeoning romance he'd failed in his mission. Maybe she was just lulling him with a false sense of security, working up to something big. But what if…this was real?

As per their wont, in the course of a year, Ollie and Ellie moved the caravan here and there. Sometimes they took the family on extended trips to a secluded beach. But they always returned to Hampton Roads in time for the kids to keep up with school. They settled at the edge of a trailer park near the woods they loved, and Ellie and Ollie worked their magic to fit up the White Witch as a cozy doublewide, with enough space for everyone who wanted separate rooms. The breakfast nook allowed Ollie to demonstrate his flair for making pancakes and pizza, or for the whole family to join in on board games and puzzles.

When Ollie and Joanie wanted a date night, Ellie cared for the kids. They all loved every minute together. When Ellie had magical clients or colleagues she needed to see at the homestead, whether afternoon or evening, Ollie took his new brood to the movies or the arcade. It would have been a beautiful, even idyllic existence, were it not for the nagging question of all of Joanie's dead spouses.

Even thinking about that made Ollie feel a bit guilty, though. What about all *his* dead husbands and wives?

"Sweetheart, would you tell me something?" Olivier asked, after a long, loving night together, the two of them bundled up in a quilt Ellie had made for the most recent husband she'd adored, whom she'd only gotten to love for five years before he passed in his sleep. From various quilt panels, round-cheeked cartoon moons smiled up at them, dappled with moonlight from the narrow window. "What did you love best, and what annoyed you the most, about each of your husbands?"

He hoped for a clue in the tone of her voice, in the details she chose.

But everything she told him was as mundane as a meme.

Ellie tried to help, reading Joanie's palm, her cards, her tea leaves. They sprung facts on her, from her prior marriages—things they shouldn't have known. They never managed to trip her up. She had so many reasonable explanations, and spoke in such calm tones, it was hard not to believe her. Ollie could find no flaw. And damn it, he was falling harder for Joanie with every passing day.

Maybe Joanie was doing the same. She sure did want to know a lot of details about his life, down to the level of excruciating minutiae. Sometimes, she skirted a little too close to the edges of his alibis and identities.

"Honey, what was your major in college? What was your GPA in high school? When is your grandfather's birthday? Where did you go on honeymoon with each of your spouses?"

He laughed and told her about the honeymoons, because why not? Those were good times. At least, until pillow talk and trace evidence finally revealed what his partners had done, and he'd been forced to execute their sentence, as the rules of the Chalice dictated.

He always waited to deliver the coup de grace till he'd proven their guilt beyond his reasonable doubt. To be perfectly certain, he relied most on one tried and true method: catching them in the act.

When Ellie or Ollie were married to a suspect, they set warning spells on each other, so they might help if a murderer decided to strike. They kept the means to defend themselves on hand, like personal magical alerts to wake them, or Hauteclere on its silken cushion by Ollie's head. In addition, each had many years of wiliness and working out in their favor.

But morning after morning, Ollie woke to find Joanie slumbering, curled into his side, her normally watchful face beautifully relaxed.

If Joanie was a murderer, why wouldn't she cooperate by trying to do away with him?

Meanwhile, he kept having to save her from all sorts of dangerous situations. Did his sweetheart have a death wish? He grabbed her just in time when she leaned too far over the balcony at the Virginia Symphony. When the family swam at Virginia Beach and a sudden storm swamped her, he battled the waves to save her. She struggled in his arms, possibly out of fear; he really had to fight to get her out. He thanked his continued knightly fitness regime for that one.

Might it actually be safe to love her?

One night, he ostentatiously downed a large mug of Ellie's home-brewed eggnog, liberally spiked with rum. "Well, I'm turning in," he said loudly. "I'll probably sleep like a log."

"Goodnight, dear. I'll come to bed after I tuck in the children."

Having long since developed a head for his mother's eggnog, Ollie lay still with his eyes closed, pretending to snore while Joanie crept into bed. As she snuggled in beside him, Ollie counted kills as a means of staying awake, timing them to the growl of each fake log he sawed. So many dead. But he mustn't lose count, mustn't forget. There'd been his wife Hermione, who'd poisoned her previous husband's wine when he found out about her affair with a chocolatier. His husband Edison, whose bitter fight for sole creative control of the film company he owned with his last husband ended in "accidental" drowning in their backyard pool. Dear Geraldine, whose young sister had ostensibly overdosed in the arms of a man who'd led her into a life of drugs. Deeming him a predatory Bluebeard, Geraldine disguised herself, seduced her way into his arms, and helped him to an overdose of his own medicine.

That one still smote his heart. If it was wrong for Geraldine to coldly avenge her sister, how different was Ollie's work? But the Chalice demanded it, in no uncertain terms. Maybe he and Ellie really were bound for hell.

As, indeed, Josefina had proudly declared, when Olivier sentenced her—after she'd drugged and tried to hang him, like she'd done to her rich husband, a supposed suicide. Of course, she waited to do it till she had ample proof of the haul Ollie amassed over the centuries. He'd let that information slip on purpose, but she waited so long her attack took him by surprise. Ellie saved him. His guardian angel.

Upon which comforting thought, he must have fallen asleep…

Vaguely, he became aware of movement at his side. In the moonlight, a shadow lifted Hauteclere from its pillow.

Woozily, he fought the banging in his head. She must have drugged him after all. She'd passed him the eggnog. What had she given him?

Why was he still alive?

Swaying, he checked the trailer. Everyone slept. Except the missing Joanie. He made his way outside but stopped at the sight that greeted him at the edge of the forest.

Joanie stood in front of the high, portable bistro table that Ollie and Ellie used as an altar when they did rituals with the Chalice to enact justice and renew their lives. Joanie cut quite the figure, looking like she was wearing black-enameled armor in her form-fitting black leather jeans and jacket, which caught ripples of moonlight like water.

Atop the table rested the silken cushion. On it lay Hauteclere, bosom companion of the battlefield, the gem in its golden hilt winking up at the stars.

Joanie held another sword high above it. A series of unearthly shimmers stretched between the two blades like strings of party lights. By this effervescent glow, Ollie made out five crosses etched into Joanie's blade near the hilt.

Had he seen that sword before? Something about it nudged the back of his mind, from long-ago days riding to battle on behalf of France. A sword raised in the hand of a young maid, with five crosses near the hilt—a relic she'd found in the Church of Saint Catherine of Fierbois.

Silently, he watched as she murmured something and more sparks flew through the air between the two swords. These small bits of fiery splendor winked out, to be replaced by new fireflies, drawing ever-shifting constellations, a beautiful, intricate pattern whose lines buzzed like a harmonious hive hard at work.

In the midst of the pattern, images arose. Ollie watched, neck prickling with danger. Out of all context, the executions began to appear. Evildoers he'd slain, whose continuing swath of destruction he'd ended—murderers too careful to ever have been caught by conventional means.

In his hand, Hauteclere had always been swift, certain. One stroke in battle could sever a head, split a skull. Beheading the ones who needed it had seemed a mercy.

But the two swords that hummed to each other now, crafting a mystical web to reveal secrets, were only showing the executions, not the murders that had led to them.

His sword loved him. He knew that. It had preserved his life against all odds, all dangers, acting almost as an independent ally. "Hauteclere," he called in a raw voice. "If you're going to show that much—exert yourself. Show the whole truth."

And then—it did.

Or, rather, *they* did. Two swords, singing together, the sound solemn, ethereal. The lights brightened and spread, and Ollie recognized that amber glow as Hauteclere's.

In the intricate web, faces and deeds shone stark and clear.

The evil that had been done. The way Ollie and Ellie had stopped it.

And—Joanie too.

Ollie shivered and ran toward her as he recognized this story. Somehow—it all made sense.

Joanie had a Chalice of her own. And those hadn't been murders, but her own hard-won justice. No wonder the evidence and Ellie's divinations had been so oddly ambivalent.

As the spell ended, he caught her in his arms.

"Joanie. *Mon Dieu!*"

Her smile lit up her eyes in the moonlight, by the fading glow of their swords. "I recognize you now. You fought by my side at the Siege of Orléans."

"Your blade—"

"It's the sword of Charles Martel. I found it at the Church of Saint Catherine of Fierbois," she confirmed. "My patron saint."

"That sword belonged to Charlemagne's grandfather," Ollie said.

She held it out, and he touched the hilt reverently. This wasn't fear, running like lightning over his scalp. This was—recognition—standing in the presence of something connected to his old life, something older in fact than he was. Something holy.

"And you—you wielded *this*."

"Well, you know—" Joanie sighed. She spoke in a low voice, and he leaned close to hear. "Once upon a time, I rode at the head of an army, wearing men's clothes, which even the Church deemed attire suitable for my work. But the English burned me for it. Or tried, anyway."

Shivers ran up and down his spine. He whispered, "Jehanne d'Arc?"

"Yes, darling?"

"I'm Olivier de Vienne."

"One of Charlemagne's true knights." Her voice brimmed with joy.

And here it was—the age gap. "I'm 664 years older than you are, darling."

She laughed, kissing him. "I don't think the age gap matters much, after the first few hundred years."

"And you—you wanted to find out if *I was a murderer*," he said with awe.

"I know better now. I couldn't figure it out, at first. You mowed down spouses like mortal enemies, but my Chalice insists you were blameless. I kept giving you chances to kill me, but you proved yourself a perfect knight." She laughed.

"Say rather executioner, and you hit nearer the mark." He sighed heavily.

She kissed him, hard. Then said, in a ringing voice, "I speak for those who cannot. I wreak vengeance for those who cannot avenge themselves. I wield the sword of justice."

He shivered, then gripped her shoulders hard. She'd spoken to him in medieval French. And her words—

"You're like me, Olivier," she said, holding him close, looking up at him with that absolute sincerity that commanded belief. "You're not a murderer. You save people. It's not easy, I know. It's the hardest work, in fact. But—ask Brian. Ask Sophie. It's worth it. They were—when I entered their lives, their own father—let us just say their mother died standing between him and them." She stopped, swallowed. Her jaw clenched. "And there are so many more. Children who need saving, spouses who might otherwise be murdered…"

"We can't save everyone."

"But we've devoted our lives to saving those we can. That's worth doing."

"I'm not sure that makes up for the selfishness of what I'm about to say. Joanie—do you realize—we could have everything? For a little while at least. If we just—stick together—till the end." Who knew what would happen when two Knights of the Chalice stayed married to each other? "We could stop here."

"We'd all age then," she cautioned.

"Would that be so bad?"

From the shadows near the caravan, a throat cleared. Ollie looked toward the White Witch to see Ellie leaning on the railing of the little deck they'd installed. The picnic table held five burning candles, a globe as big as a bowling ball, and three carved wooden boxes that held her favorite decks of cards. "Sorry, it's a good moon night," Ellie said. "But just to throw in my three cents, I'm unattached. If you two lovebirds want to stay together, I'm free to take the reins for a while."

"Mother, that's really heavy. I don't want to leave you with all the work."

"You're not. I'm volunteering. We don't get nearly enough time for happiness in all these centuries. Let alone a love as well-matched as this."

Could such happiness be in his grasp? He took Joanie's hand—each of them holding a sword by their sides—and approached the queen. "But— the children?"

"They won't notice for a while, at least. They won't want their parents to age. It'll be no different than we'd planned. And I can cohabit with my new spouses if we need to keep them away from the kids. When they're old enough, we'll tell them the truth."

"But Mother—you can't do this forever," he pleaded, hoping she'd actually have an answer. He slipped his arm around Joanie's shoulders, holding her close while she wove her free arm around his waist.

"Maybe not. But I can spell you for a while. We've done it before."

"I know," he murmured. "But it takes so much out of the one who's carrying the burden alone."

With a worried look at him, Joanie spoke up. "I have my mission as well. Do you know how many murderers never get caught? Including the ones who stalk and kill the abused wives who escaped?" Looking from Ollie to Ellie, her eyes pleaded for understanding, their liquid darkness reflecting the glow of Ellie's candles as she told them grim tales that horrified Ollie, despite all he'd seen. He read the same deep grief on his mother's face.

"That's an important mission," Ellie said slowly, her voice heavy with a queen's gravity.

"But you're in so much danger," Ollie said, distraught.

"So are you," Joanie said gently. "Don't think I didn't notice how many risks you took to be sure of me. You're so careful to find the truth, I'm amazed you've survived. I've seen what evidence you've gathered on me, and it really is clear enough that I brought about Clement's heart attack with digitalis, even if you probably couldn't prove it in court. You've got to harden your heart a bit more, Ollie. If we weren't on the same mission—I could have killed you, dearest. And if I weren't a Chalice-bound and honorable knight—you *should* have executed me."

"Oh, Ollie can do the job," Ellie put in staunchly. "He's more than brave enough. If anything, he's so strong he has the *luxury* of mercy. He can hold on as long as he needs to give the suspect every last chance to exonerate themselves."

Joanie cocked her head fondly. "Spoken like a doting mother."

"That doesn't mean it's not true."

Ollie spoke up. "Have you ever thought—maybe *not* hardening our hearts—is the only way to survive this? The only way we can be sure? The moment we lose the ability to empathize—the moment we see only the facts—we'll be setting aside the insight we need to get it right. Lives are at stake, yes—but not only those of future victims. *The lives of the innocent.* Joanie—I could have killed you just as easily as you could me."

He saw it, then—her lips forming that *O*—the quick skate of fear across her cheeks, chased by compassion. She reached around, grabbed the back of his head, and kissed him, kissed him till he hadn't any air, till he didn't want any, till he felt the sizzle of the sparks up his arm as the two swords they'd almost forgotten swung together at the ends of their arms, meeting with a gentle clang like a sonorous bell.

When they parted, Joanie said, "You know I love you. Right?"

"Right," he said, breathless. "And you have my undying love. Literally."

"But we can't forsake the mission forever. At least—not as long as we plan to continue it."

"But the mission—requires marriage. Of whatever sort. How does the Chalice feel about bigamy? I can't give you up, Joanie. Now that I've found you—God, I don't want to give you up."

For the first time, her commanding features looked uncertain.

"Really, Ollie?" his mother chastised. "Since when do we need marriage to commit our hearts to a lover? Just get an annulment. Hell, I annulled my marriage to the *King of France*. When one of you is on the job, marry the suspect as usual. In between jobs…you have each other."

God, could it be this easy? Facing each other, they twined their free hands, swinging them a little. "Soul's respite," he murmured. *"Forever."*

She smiled. "Our vacation from death. From loneliness."

"Nothing is ever perfect in this life," Ollie said as he sank into the kiss greedily. "But that sounds damned close."

Then he had no more space for words.

They'd been kissing for a while when Ollie felt a tug at his sword. He recognized the touch and let Ellie pull the blade from his hand. A moment later, he felt both of Joanie's hands on his shoulders.

With a tiny part of his mind, he heard the deck stairs creak, the rustle and clank as Ellie gathered her things, the swoosh of the metal track as she slid the French door closed.

But mostly, there was only Joanie. Twining her hands in his hair. Kissing him like there really was a tomorrow.

Love of his life.

No matter how long that might be.

SILVER FOXES FIGHT BACK

SHERYL JORDAN

THE SUN SHINED brightly as a gentle breeze softly swept her hair from her face. *What a beautiful day.* Saundra enjoyed her walk to the Silver Fox Tactical Training Complex, the business she and her husband owns with their closest friends, Robert and Vangie Whitford. Located on the Virginia Beach Boardwalk, the grand opening of the business was less than a week away.

As Saundra entered the building, she smiled at the beautiful space she designed with Vangie. She headed to the office at the far right of the door and logged onto the computer to check on the classes scheduled for the grand opening week. Pleased to see that all the classes are full, her smile broadened. Saundra checked the refrigerator to ensure it's stocked with water, protein drinks, and fruit juices. She heard the door open.

"Hey Saundra, where are you?" Vangie called out.

"Good morning. I'm in the refreshment area," Saundra walked around the counter to greet Vangie.

"Are we all set for next week?" Vangie asked.

"Yep, and all classes are full for the week."

"That's fantastic." Vangie clasped her hands. "We're going to be busy."

"The guys should be here soon to do their final walk through before we head over to the hotel for the family reunion. I'm going to get the towels set up and take the trash out. Can you make sure the cash register is locked and put the sign-in sheets out on the receptionist desk?" Saundra asked unwrapping the freshly laundered towels.

Bang!

"What was that?" Vangie asked.

"It's probably someone throwing trash into the dumpster out back," Saundra said.

"Oh okay. I still get a bit jumpy after all the break-ins around my neighborhood and that rogue CIA agent threatening to kill us last year. I'm always on high alert."

Last year Vangie, Saundra, and their families thought Vangie's husband Robert suffered a heart attack and that Blake had died. It appeared Saundra was being stalked by someone from her past. It turned out Blake, a former FBI agent, had faked his death to help his closest friend and the CIA catch a rogue agent who was threatening to kill their families.

"Better to be safe than sorry. Especially now that it is tourist season and there is so much happening down here. Jackson said the number of crimes tend to increase during the summer months around here," Saundra smiled, proud of her son Jackson, a detective with the Norfolk Police Department.

"I'm glad we're opening tactical training centers to teach old folks like us how to defend themselves," Vangie said.

"Yeah, everyone needs skills to protect themselves. I'm going to take this trash out," Saundra said opening the back door.

This is going to be a great day, Saundra thought walking to the dumpster.

Thud. Thud.

Saundra squints from the bright sun. A scream escapes her mouth as a man comes from behind the dumpster running full speed towards her.

Thud! Swoosh.

Saundra punched him in the stomach. Then swung the bag of trash at his face.

"Hey, what's your hurry!" Saundra screamed falling to the ground after swinging the trash bag again. The man high-tailed it to a car which sped off before he shut the door.

Saundra saw Blake and Robert burst out of the back door to the alley as a car barreled out of the alley, missing them by inches.

* * * *

"What the hell is going on?" Blake asked while running past Robert. He reached Saundra as she got up. "Are you okay? He pulled his wife to him looking her over for injuries.

"I'm fine. I was taking the trash out and heard a couple of thuds. When I looked up, this guy came running at me from behind the dumpster. He pushed me and I hit him with the trash bag," Saundra laughed.

"Oh, my goodness," Vangie joined them by the back door. "I knew I should have come out here with you after we heard the loud noise."

"What loud noise?" Blake raised his eyebrows.

"We heard a noise like the dumpster lid slamming shut a few minutes before Saundra took the trash out," Vangie said.

Blake and Robert walked closer to the dumpster looking for anything out of the ordinary. Not seeing anything they walked back into the training center.

"Should we call the police?" Vangie nervously looked at the others.

"No, it was probably just some youngsters fooling around," Blake gestured his hand dismissively.

"You're probably right." Vangie said.

"Since that's settled, let's discuss next week," Saundra said. "With the class schedules full, Blake and I will teach the Hand-to-Hand Combat class while Robert and Vangie teach the Utilizing Ordinary Items as Weapons Class. Both are from nine to eleven o'clock. We break for an hour, then have the next sessions from twelve to two. And Blake and Robert will cover the Firearm Basics session from three to five. Is everyone good with the schedule?"

The group nodded in agreement.

"Good morning. How's everyone on this beautiful day?" Reanne, the Whitfords' niece and their receptionist, walked to the desk setting her belongings down.

"Hey Reanne. We're doing well. We had a little commotion in the alley earlier, but it wasn't anything,"

"What happened?" Reanne said.

As Blake explained the situation, the door opened.

"Sir, we are not open for business yet. Our grand opening is next week if you can come back on Monday." Reanne smiled at the handsome older gentleman.

"Hi, I'm interested in your self-defense training. I'm here on vacation for four weeks and want to get some training in while here."

"We have a variety of classes." Reanne handed him a brochure of the classes offered. Do any of these interest you?"

"All of them do but I will try the Hand-to-Hand Combat session first to see how it goes," the man said.

"The sessions are $75 each which includes protein drinks, water, fruit juices, and protein bars after each session. We're fully booked next week, but you can register for the following Monday. Will that work for you?"

"I would like to start next week. Can you fit me in? I fear my life is in danger."

"Whoa, what's happened to make you think that?" Blake asked.

"I've received several death threats. I think they are from a business partner back home."

"Let's talk in private." Blake waved his hand toward Robert and the man to follow him to the office.

"Start by telling us your name and where you're from," Blake said.

"I'm Jonathan Chadwick from New York City."

"The Jonathan Chadwick, CEO of Chadwick and Moore Industries, the multi-billion-dollar government contractor?" Robert looked at him in disbelief.

"Yes. My partner Michael Moore has been embezzling money from the company. I told him if he didn't repay all the funds, I would report him to the authorities. Over the past few weeks, my home was broken into and vandalized, I was almost run over by a truck, and most recently, he threatened to kill my family."

"Have you gone to the police in New York?" Blake empathized with Jonathan, recalling the feelings of anguish and fear he felt less than a year ago when a madman threatened to kill his family.

"No, I was going to but when he threatened my family, I sent my wife and kids to stay with friends from her college days and I came here." Jonathan said. Also, Michaels's cousin is with the New York City Police Department, so I didn't feel it would be safe going to them."

"We can train you in tactical self-defense, but if Mr. Moore has hired professional assassins to take you out, it isn't going to help you," Robert said. "You need to seek help from the authorities. Does anyone know you're here?"

"No, I told everyone I was taking the family to Dubai for a few weeks."

"I think you'll be safe for now but let us make a few phone calls and see what we can do from here. Where are you staying?"

"I'm at an Airbnb a few blocks from here. My wife's stepfather, William Mason rented it for me."

"So at least one other person does know where you are," Robert said.

"No, I told him an employee is having some personal problems and needed to get away for a while but didn't want his family or friends to know where he was going. He thinks I'm in Dubai with my wife and kids."

"Okay, so when you come back on Monday, we'll go through some training sessions and keep watch over you. We have an event at the Hilton Hotel this weekend but will be close by. Here are our cell phone numbers to contact us, if needed." Blake handed Jonathan their business cards.

"Turn your cell phone off and buy a prepaid cell phone. Do not use your credit cards. Pay for everything in cash," Robert said.

"I have a prepaid phone and enough cash to last for several months. I haven't used any credit or debit cards after I left home," Jonathan said writing the Airbnb address and the burner phone number on a piece of paper.

"Everything will be okay, Mr. Chadwick. We'll do all we can to help you out of this situation." Blake shook hands with Jonathan.

"Thank you both so much Mr. Anderson and Mr. Whitford," Jonathan said.

"Sure thing, but one more question. How did you just happen to come here of all places for help with your situation?" Robert raised an eyebrow staring at Jonathan.

"The Airbnb had a brochure about your tactical training center with your bios, so I googled you both and saw how you teamed up with the CIA to catch that rogue agent. "It felt like God led me to you," Jonathan said.

"Well, I can't argue with you on that. God has a way of putting people where they can help others. And please call us Blake and Robert," Blake smiled.

"We'll be in touch real soon." Robert patted Jonathan's back as they exited the office.

"Goodbye everyone, see you on Monday," Jonathan left the center.

"What was that all about?" Vangie and Saundra asked.

"We need to make a few phone calls and get to the family reunion. We'll tell you all about it after the reunion kick off tonight," Blake said.

"You ladies go over to the hotel, and we'll be there shortly," Blake dialed his son's cell phone while Robert called his friends from the agency.

"Hey Jackson, call me back as soon as you can. It's urgent," Blake said to his son's voicemail.

"Connor at the CIA is looking into Chadwick and Moore. He'll call me back when he's done," Robert said. "Let's lock up and get to the reunion for some fun."

* * * *

The reunion was in full swing as people showed up from both sides of the Anderson and Whitford families. The adults reminisced about the fun times they shared in the past, while the children played games and sang karaoke. Some were meeting for the first time while others were reuniting. Blake and Robert planned the two-family reunion because their families have known each other for generations.

"Hey dad, I just listened to your message. What's going on? Did something happen to mom or Bianca?" Jackson's voice quivered at the thought of his mom or younger sister, a Virginia Beach Assistant Coroner being in danger.

"No son, they're both fine. Let's find somewhere private to talk," Blake nodded at Robert to come along.

Jackson and Robert followed Blake to the patio off the reception room.

"Jonathan Chadwick visited the training complex today. He wants training to protect himself," Blake said.

"Jonathan Chadwick as in multi-billionaire Jonathan Chadwick?" Jackson said.

"Yes, that Jonathan Chadwick. Robert told Jackson everything that transpired earlier.

"Unbelievable! What do you need from me? I want to help save this guy and see his partner behind bars if it's true," Jackson said.

"For now, we just need to keep him under surveillance. Connor at the CIA is looking into both Chadwick and Moore. If Chadwick's story checks out, we must keep the man safe until Moore is locked up."

"It sounds like you're on top of it. I will contact my buddy, Virginia Beach Police Chief Edwards to give him a heads up and see if he can have units patrol the Airbnb more frequently. If not, I'm off work next week so I can do it, if no Norfolk homicide cases come up," Jackson said.

"Perfect, we'll let you know what Connor comes back with," Robert said.

"Let's get back to the reunion before we're missed." Blake opened the patio door.

The meet-and-greet went on until eleven thirty. Everyone said their good nights and retreated to their rooms for the night. Blake and Robert gathered with their wives, Reanne, Jackson, and Bianca, to discuss what was happening to Jonathan.

"I feel for him after what happened last year," Blake said.

"I think we all want to keep him and his family alive," Saundra said.

"Let's get some sleep. The main event of the reunion is tomorrow so we have a lot to do. I want to visit the Airbnb to check on Jonathan in the morning and wait for Connor to get back to me," Robert said.

"Dad and I will go with you," Jackson said.

* * * *

Robert met Blake and Jackson in the lobby early that morning. "Are y'all ready to go?" Robert asked, grabbing a cup of coffee from the complimentary beverage counter.

"I'll drive," Blake walked outside to the valet.

"Do you think this guy is legitimately in danger?" Jackson asked.

"Yes, he seemed distressed when he came to talk to us. He was truly relieved after he told us about his dilemma," Robert said.

"If not, he's a damn good actor," Blake said. The valet pulled Blake's black Mercedes SUV up to the entrance.

Chatter filled the air as people were out walking and shopping along Atlantic Avenue. Dog walkers, teenagers, and families enjoying the perfect day with low humidity, and a light breeze. Blake entered the address in the navigation system, and they were on their way. They pulled up to the house a few blocks off the boardwalk and sat for a few minutes to survey the area.

"That looks like the same car that came barreling out of the alley at us." Robert was looking at a dark blue mustang with tinted windows and New Jersey plates.

"It could be the same car," Blake said. "There's someone in it, Jackson go have a chat with them."

"Already on it." Jackson exited the vehicle and walked past a couple of houses, then turned back and walked to the mustang.

"Hey, I think I'm lost. Do you know where 125 21st Street is?" Jackon gazed around confused then looked in the car at college age males smiling at him. The skunk smell of weed stung his nostrils.

"Naw, I ain't from around here. We're just here on vacation," the driver slurred.

"Yeah man, we from Jersey," the passenger snickered.

"Toss your keys out the window and put your hands on the dashboard," Jackson flashed his police shield.

"Ah hell," the passenger mumbled.

"What'd we do, officer?" the driver asked, coming down a notch from his high.

"We're about to find out," Jackson said.

Tap.

"Holy crap!" the passenger screamed and ducked in his seat as Blake knocked on the passenger side window.

"What were you doing yesterday in the alley behind The Silver Fox?" Blake asked.

"What's a Silver Fox? We stopped at the first alley we came too because Antonio had to pee," the driver said.

"Shut up, stupid," Antonio said catching his breath.

"Do you always push women down and then speed off almost hitting pedestrians?" Blake asked.

"No sir. I got scared when the lady came towards the dumpster where I was peeing. I just ran to the car and told Dominque to get out of there. I didn't mean to knock her down. She punched me on my back and hit me in the face with a trash bag," Antonio said, looking at Blake.

"Well, that woman was my wife. You could have hurt her. And you almost hit me and my friend speeding away like that," Blake said. "You just don't know; she would've kicked your butt if you weren't running."

"We're sorry sir." Dominique said.

"Smoking weed and driving is illegal. I suggest you get out the car and walk to wherever you're going," Jackson shook his head. "That woman was my mother, and this is my dad. If you would have hurt them, I would've made the rest of your lives miserable."

"So, we are not being arrested?" Antonio asked.

"No, get out of here and enjoy your vacation. Stop peeing in alleys," Jackson said.

Blake and Jackson returned to the SUV while Robert was on the phone with Jonathan.

"Hey Jonathan, this is Robert. How are you doing?"

"I'm doing well, I just spoke with my wife. She and the kids are safe and sound," Jonathan said.

"Great to hear. We're outside in a black SUV. Go to the front left window and wave if you are safe." Robert looked at the windows on the house. Jonathan waved from the left window.

"I'm safe," Jonathan said.

"Good, we're going back to the hotel, but call or come to the hotel if you need us for anything at all."

"I will," Jonathan hung up his phone.

* * * *

"How's Jonathan doing?" Saundra asked as the waiter left their table after taking their order for breakfast.

"He's safe. We didn't see anything suspicious while we were there, except the guy who ran into you," Robert said.

"He was getting high in a car parked down the street from Jonathan's hideout when we surprised them. They're harmless, just a couple of weed smoking, carefree, kids from New Jersey on vacation," Jackson said.

"I'm glad you talked with them. I wanted to whoop his behind," Saundra said.

"I let him know you could have," Blake said.

"What do you all want to do before the main event starts this evening?" Vangie asked.

"Let's go to the beach and hang out with the families. I know some folks want to walk the boardwalk to sight see for a while," Saundra said.

"I'll suggest it in the group chat so everyone can meet up if they want to," Bianca said.

An hour later the families were sitting on the beach tossing frisbees, swimming in the ocean, and enjoying each other's company. Some hadn't seen each other in years. It was a time of nostalgia and new memories.

Buzz. Buzz.

"Hey Connor, what's up man? Robert asked.

"Michael Moore is a bad dude. He's being investigated for embezzlement and a list of other charges from an organization whose Board of Directors he sat on as treasurer. He argued with the president of the organization about it on several occasions. The president has been missing for eight weeks."

"Anything on Jonathan Chadwick?" Robert asked.

"No, he's clean. A wife of twelve years, three children, gives to numerous charities, active in his church. He's a solid guy."

"Do you know the whereabouts of Moore and if he is associated with any shady characters?"

"He was at their office on Friday, but no one we've talked to has seen him since. He told his people at the office he was going out on his cabin cruiser all weekend. We're trying to locate his boat now," Connor said.

"Thanks, keep me posted," Robert ended the call.

* * * *

"Thank you all for making it here for the first reunion of the Anderson and Whitford families. We felt it fitting to get the families together after last year when you all were told I had died and Robert had a heart attack," Blake said into the microphone. "We did it all to protect our immediate families and to put a rogue CIA agent away for a long time. We hope you understand we hated putting you through all of that."

"We're glad it wasn't true!" Someone yelled from the tables.

"We are too. It's a blessing to be here with all of you. I'll turn it over to Deacon Frank Whitford to bless this gathering and the southern style cuisine prepared by the hotel chef."

Chatter and laughter filled the ballroom as they ate. After dinner, the DJ played music and people danced and played games. Several family members and friends took an evening stroll down the boardwalk.

"Can we see your training center?" One of the guests asked.

"Sure, it's a few blocks away," Saundra said grabbing her purse. "We'll take them, and you and Blake can stay here with the other guests.

Saundra and Vangie led the small group out of the hotel and down the boardwalk. Lights shining bright from the many stores along the strip illuminated the crowd of folks enjoying the warm summer evening. The group took in the sights as they walked towards the training center. Suddenly police, ambulances, and fire trucks blared their sirens as they drove towards the training center.

"What the—"

"They're at the training center," Vangie said as the group ran the rest of the way.

Emergency vehicles blocked the front of the businesses surrounding the training center. Vangie and Saundra ran up to an officer.

"What's going on," Saundra asked the officer.

"Stand back, ma'am," the officer said.

"We own The Silver Fox," Vangie said.

"Come with me." The officer led them to the detective in charge.

"I'm Detective Collins, I need to ask you a few questions." The detective took their names, addresses, and phone numbers as the coroner's van pulled into the alley.

"Is there a body back there?" Saundra asked.

"I can't tell you anything right now. When was the last time you were here?" the detective asked.

"Friday afternoon around two o'clock," Vangie said while Saundra called Blake to tell him and Robert to get to the training center.

"Did you happen to come into the alley while you were here?" Detective Collins asked.

"Yes, I was taking some trash out and a kid came running at me, but I punched him in his stomach and hit him with a bag of trash," Saundra said. "He got into a car, and they pulled out of the alley almost running over our husbands."

Vangie explained the rest of what happened to the detective. The detective told them not to leave. He walked over to the coroner as they were removing a body.

* * * *

Blake, Robert, and Jackson walked up to the business as the women walked back to the group they had brought with them.

"There's a body back there but they won't tell us anything," Saundra said.

"They can't yet," Jackson said. "I'll see if I can find anything out."

"I sure hope it's not that fellow who came here on Friday," Vangie said.

Robert pulled out his cell phone and called Jonathan. He didn't answer. Robert let Blake know, and they turned to go to Jonathan's rental. A large crowd had gathered on the block trying to see what was going on. Weaving between people, Blake thought he saw Jonathan, staggering toward them.

"I think that's him," Blake told Robert, pointing, as the crowd began parting around a man who had blood on his shirt.

"Oh, dear Lord!" A woman near the man screamed.

Blake and Robert ran to the man grabbing hold of his arms just before he fell to the ground.

"It's him," Blake said as they laid Jonathan gently to the ground on his back.

He raised Jonathan's shirt to see where he was bleeding. He saw a hole in his side where dark, thick, blood was gushing. The strong smell of blood filled his nostrils.

"Stay with me Jonathan," Blake said. A bystander handed him a towel which he pressed on the wound.

Officers on boardwalk patrol called for an ambulance and took over working on Jonathan. Blake stayed by his side, trying to ask him what happened. Jonathan was in and out of consciousness. Blake stood as EMT's arrived and began working on Jonathan.

The officers questioned Blake and Robert about what happened. They told the officers everything they knew.

"Did you see what happened to him?" one officer asked.

"No, we were at our self-defense training center because apparently there is a body in the alley behind it. We were going to walk to Jonathan's Airbnb to check on him, when we saw him coming down the street towards our place," Robert said.

"You need to come down to the station, our chief will want to talk with you two," the officer said.

"Yes, of course," Blake said. We need to go check on what's happening at our business first."

Robert and Blake returned to The Silver Fox. The crowd had thinned, and they were allowed to enter the building. Detective Collins was talking to Jackson away from everyone.

"Unofficially, the body has been identified as Michael Moore," Detective Collins said. His wallet was still on the body, and his driver's license matched his face. The coroner's office will have to make an official ID after they process the body."

"This doesn't make sense. Moore was the man who was supposed to be after Jonathan Chadwick," Jackson said.

"Is that right?" the detective asked.

"You need to talk to Chadwick and see what's really going on," Jackson said.

* * * *

Two detectives entered Jonathan's hospital room. "Mr. Chadwick, we found the body of Michael Moore in the alley behind The Silver Fox."

"What can you tell us about this?" Detective Collins asked.

"I didn't think he would find me. I was walking on the boardwalk after dinner when he and his goon pulled up to me. I tried to run, but I tripped, and they forced me into the alley at gun point. He was rambling on about how stupid I was to think I could hide from him. The goon was about to shoot me when I heard shots and saw Michael get shot in the head. I ran as fast as I could and hid about a block away behind some houses where I passed out. When I came too, I realized I had been shot and I couldn't find my phone. I was trying to make it to Robert Whitmore and Blake Anderson," Jonathan said.

"So, you were walking to the Silver Fox?" Detective Collins asked.

"I was just walking and didn't realize I was there, "Jonathan said.

"We're holding you until we can verify your story."

"Cuff him to the bed and I want an officer here at all times," the detective said to the officer.

"Please contact Blake and Robert," Jonathan said.

"We already have."

* * * *

Officials cleared the businesses to re-open the following week. The Silver Fox had their grand opening, and people were signing up for their classes even more because of the body being found in the alley. The police verified Mr. Chadwick's story, and he tested negative for gunshot powder on his hands and clothing, clearing him of the murder. He was released from custody but remained in the hospital for the rest of the week. His phone was found in the alley and returned to him. The Andersons and Whitfords visited him in the hospital several times during the week.

"Hi Jonathan," Saundra greeted him one morning before going to the training center.

"Hello Saundra, it's so nice of you to visit me. I appreciate all of you," Jonathan said.

"We don't mind. "We want to make sure you're recovering well and having people who care helps the healing process," Saundra said.

"Thank you. Can you go by my rental and grab me some clean clothes and a few things? Blake bought me a phone charger already, so I called my wife."

"Sure. How is she doing? Saundra asked.

"She was shaken up when I told her what happened. She and the kids are still safe though," Jonathan said.

"That's great to hear. Have the police found out who shot you and Mr. Moore?" Saundra asked.

"No, but whoever it was probably saved my life," Jonathan said.

"You're right about that. I keep wondering who it was though, Saundra said.

"Me too. I just don't understand how Michael found me,"

"Yeah, that is a mystery. I'm sure the police are still working on finding the perp. Give me the key to your place and Vangie and I will go by this evening to grab you a few things."

"Thank you." Jonathan handed her the keys from his personal items next to the bed.

"You're welcome, see you later this evening," Saundra said leaving the room.

Later that evening, Saundra and Vangie went to Jonathan's place as promised. Saundra unlocked the door and reached for the light switch.

"Ouch," Vangie shrieked as something hit her from behind.

"What's wrong with—"

"Help!" Vangie yelled, elbowing a person in the face as he tried to grab her from behind.

"Ugh," a man grumbled as he covered his nose with his hand.

Saundra turned around and saw what was going on. She punched the man on the back several times. When he tried to grab her leg, she turned around and kneed him in the groin. While he was down, Vangie grabbed a vase from a table by the door and hit him over the head. Saundra called 9-1-1. The police arrived just as the man regained consciousness.

"Good riddance," Vangie said, punching the man in the stomach before the police put him in handcuffs.

* * * *

Saundra called Blake. He and Robert arrived at the house and hugged their wives.

"What were you two thinking coming over here alone, when the suspects in Moore's murder and Chadwick's shooting are still out here somewhere?" Robert asked.

"We wanted to bring Jonathan some things to make sure he was comfortable at the hospital," Saundra said.

"You could have been killed." Blake's voice raised with anger. "Coming here of all places."

"You're right, we just thought whoever did those things would be long gone," Vangie said, looking away from her husband.

"Let's get over to the hospital to talk to Jonathan," Robert said.

When they arrived at Jonathan's room, police officers were talking to him. He was terribly upset about the conversation.

"How could he do this to me? Risk my life for money?" Jonathan asked, shaking his head.

"We have arrested him. We got a confession out of him, and he probably won't get a bond," Detective Collins said.

"Who are we talking about," Blake asked.

"Detective Collins just told me about what happened to Saundra and Vangie at my place. I am beside myself with guilt, asking you to go over there. I wasn't thinking," Jonathan said.

"But who was arrested?" Robert asked.

"My father-in-law, William Mason."

"You told us you didn't tell him you were coming here," Blake reminded Jonathon.

"He must have figured it out when he talked to my wife. Michael bribed William into telling him where I really went. Michael hacked my computer and was monitoring everything I did. He had bugged my house when we hosted our annual holiday party last year," Jonathan said.

"Michael knew you were here the whole time," Saundra said.

"Yes, Michael hired someone to find out where my father-in-law lived and offered him $500,000.00 to tell him where I was staying. After my father-in-law took the money, he had a change of heart. William tried to return the money and begged Michael not to kill me, but Michael wouldn't budge. He came here to try to stop Michael from killing me," Jonathan said,

"Mr. Mason did just that. He confessed to following you and saw Michael and his goon tailing you that night. Mr. Mason had his gun and silencer and started shooting at Michael and his man. You got shot accidentally," Detective Collins said.

"William betrayed me, then saved me," Jonathan said. What happened to Michael's man?"

"He took off right after the shooting to go back to New York. He had lost a lot of blood and passed out on the side of the highway. Virginia State Police arrested the man on several other warrants when they checked the car and ran his driver's license," Detective Collins said.

"It sounds like this is over now," Blake said. "When are you going back home, Jonathan?"

"As soon as I am released from the hospital and the doctors say I can travel. I'm going to spend a few days with my wife and kids and then we are going home."

"Stay in touch, and if you ever come back to Virginia Beach, we must get together," Vangie said.

"I will. My family would love to vacation here. Now I must call my wife and break the news about her stepfather. Thanks again for your help," Jonathan said.

They left the hospital and drove back to the training center. They sat in the beverage and snack area talking about everything that occurred over the past few weeks.

"The Silver Foxes sure kick butts when we need too." Saundra high-fived Vangie.

THE EXPERT IN THE ROOM
JUDITH FOWLER

BEFORE THE KICKOFF SPEECHES at this year's regional Conference on Law and Crime, all city staff in attendance grouped around the governor. We posed on either side of her with our backs to the hotel, the ocean, and a naval aviation monument.

Some stayed to take selfies with a famous person. I hurried inside the hotel to see if I could locate the biggest fish at the conference, at least to me—Professor Garrett Sanchez, Ph.D., our keynote speaker.

It was during lunch that I saw him in the ballroom. The cloth-covered tables were set up for lunch, and waiters wandered through before most diners had taken seats.

Dr. Sanchez sat alone.

I took the chair beside him. "Do you mind? Maybe you want to be left alone before giving your keynote speech?"

"Not at all."

A waiter placed a bowl of chef salad in front of him. I introduced myself.

"Rebecca Sicario. I look like a mad fan interrupting your meal like this to a man who wrote a book on stalking. You probably don't remember me, Professor. I took your course on criminal deviance in grad school. It changed my life."

He glanced at my nametag. "'Rebecca Sicario.' I'm sorry I don't remember, but students from auditorium-style classes remain a blur all semester."

"Our class was standing room only. I got there early and sat up front so I could hear every word you said."

"I hope you got your money's worth of knowledge." He picked up his fork.

"The information fascinated me. I still go through my notes sometimes."

"Well, that's great." He dug into his salad.

"I've read every book you published since then."

He tilted his head. "You teach on the subject, then?"

"No." It was a sore spot that I hadn't worked hard enough to become an academic like he had. "I work for the city's jail services. I'm a medium-sized fish in a small pond. Not an expert like you."

"Everyone at this conference contributes to law and safety, Rebecca. Tell me about your work."

I wanted to discuss his last book. The ballroom had filled up and noise threatened to interrupt our conversation. "I help inmates with mental challenges learn their rights in court."

"That sounds worthwhile." He used the linen napkin in his lap to wipe a spot of dressing off his mustache.

My face felt hot. "It's nothing like being a renowned author and investigator. A leading voice in criminal psychology for over twenty years."

"Are these seats taken?"

Two women sat with us. I glared at them, hoping they wouldn't try to chat with us. I had so much I wanted to tell him. "I pre-ordered your new book, Dr. Sanchez—Crimes of Passion, Volume 2? I can't wait to read it."

"Call me Garrett, Rebecca. You're not in school anymore."

"Alright, Garrett."

"Most of my research ends up in other people's textbooks," he said. "It's nice to have a fan of my own books."

Reverb from a microphone squeaked from the front of the room. Chief Stanton stood at the podium.

"On behalf of your police force and our city manager, welcome. You folks make this city thrive. It's my pleasure to introduce our Commonwealth's first female governor, who will introduce our keynote speaker."

The governor posed with him for a photo while we applauded her. "Thank you, thank you. I'm proud of every city employee here today. This year must have tested each of you in the wake of the double homicide right here at the beach five months ago. Unsolved murders make it hard to assuage fears in our local citizenry. It also hits a city's tourism industry hard, as it has here."

Garrett would get up to speak in another minute. I wished I'd had more time with him.

"Today's keynote speaker is an expert on murder statistics and criminal behavior who understands that murders at the beach are practically a contradiction in terms. I've asked him to provide us with big-picture information, so we all get a feel for national trends. Dr. Garrett Sanchez is the author of many books."

"That's my cue, Rebecca," Garrett said. He got up and walked to the podium.

I took out my phone and turned around so it looked like he and I were together when I snapped the photo. I wondered if the women at the table would notice if I grabbed the napkin he'd left by his plate.

"Before I give you statistical data on unsolved crime statistics, let's address the elephant in the living room," Garrett said.

A tense tittering of laughter came from the audience.

"I'm sure you'd all like to forget that we are meeting today in the very hotel where the two brutal murders took place five months ago. I'm told this venue was paid for months before the murders, and couldn't be refunded. So here we are. The beach resort around us is one of the most popular vacation spots on the southeastern coast. You've got a lot of pressure on you to bring it back."

The audience clapped in agreement. The women continued to eat. I glared at them, because Garrett deserved their full attention. Court TV asked his opinion on cases all the time. He's done twenty or more YouTube interviews.

When the ladies finally turned their chairs so they could see him, I pretended to cough and reached over to scoop up his napkin. A silver pen lay under it. The staff might have grabbed Garrett's pen with the linens, so I left the napkin and pocketed the pen.

Ten minutes later the professor ended his talk on an upbeat note, but his mustache drooped in disappointment when he returned to find his plate gone. "They took my salad before I finished eating it."

I sympathized and told him how quickly the waiters had swooped in before I could stop them. A state administrator came over to ask if Garrett would consent to a brief lobby interview with a *Marina Press* reporter.

I'd had no time to give him back his pen. A panel discussion I'd agreed to participate in was about to start in one of the conference rooms.

Luncheon speakers sometimes leave after their talks. If he did, I'd have to send the pen to him.

At one point in the panel discussion, I saw him standing in the doorway. A uniformed hotel employee approached him and whispered something, and then both left. Maybe an Uber had arrived to take him to Norfolk International or the train at Newport News.

I ducked into each conference room, looking for him when my session ended, just in case he hadn't left the hotel. I even asked for him at the front desk.

"Has Professor Sanchez checked out? I have something of his. I could call his room or if you give me his room number—"

"We don't share guest information, ma'am. Especially since the incident."

I showed the clerk my city ID and conference badge. "He knows me," I said. "I have something of his."

The clerk looked in the computer and wrote something on a pad before some commotion from behind the desk area caused him to excuse himself.

While he and another clerk conferred in the back, I looked over the top of the counter and saw "Sanchez, Rm. 840" written on the pad.

My heart raced. I got into the elevator.

When I'm excited, I talk to myself. I was the only passenger all the way up. "Love Has No Pride" played on the intercom. I talked out loud about how he'd said he talked with the police chief, and how he's more curious than local police and that's why he's probably consulting on the murder case here. They hadn't found a suspect in five months. I wished I could tell him what I knew about that night.

On the eighth floor, the elevator doors opened. I walked along the corridor toward room 840. The empty hallway, with its pineapple-themed wallpaper, was cooled by air-conditioning. I continued to talk to myself as I turned a corner.

On the carpeting outside Room 840 sat a tray with congealed egg and leftover toast from breakfast.

I knocked on the door.

"You're still here," I said when Garrett opened it.

"Come in, Rebecca."

I felt for the pen in my pocket as he put his hand on my shoulder to usher me into the suite. In the living room, a huge window with a spectacular view of the Atlantic Ocean beyond the boardwalk greeted us. A lovely yellow sofa in front of the window caught my eye.

But Garrett and I weren't alone.

Chief Stanton and two of his officers stood off to the side of the room with a middle-aged man I knew. It was Jim—a cubicle mate of mine from the office. His presence threw me.

"What luck, Rebecca, that you came to my table at lunch and initiated a conversation with me," Garrett said.

I stared at Jim, and he stepped back behind one of the officers. "Why is he here?"

"Don't let her near me," Jim said.

I looked at Garrett. "I barely know him. He sits on the other side of a partition from me at work."

"Take a seat, Rebecca," Garrett said. "Please."

"I told them what you said. What I heard." Jim looked cockier, surrounded by police officers, than he ever had in our office.

I sat on the yellow sofa. "What did you hear?"

"What you said. I overhear you all the time."

Garrett sat in the armchair across from me. He twisted his graying mustache. "Jim claims you talk to yourself when he's working at his desk. He thinks you may not realize he's there at those times."

"Listening to you jabber to yourself always creeped me out, but what I heard two weeks ago? It made me sick," Jim said.

"Let me do this my way, Jim," Garrett said. "You can wait in the hall."

The chief motioned to one of his officers who escorted Jim out of the room.

The yellow sofa brought back memories of the man I'd once snuggled with, right there. A man I adored whom I thought adored me, too. We sipped champagne on that sofa on Valentine's Day weekends two years in a row.

I squinted—the sun's rays glared through the big window—to see if any dolphins swam near the shoreline.

"Did you find something of mine at lunch, Rebecca?"

"Yes, Garrett. I'm returning it to you."

I reached into my pocket and handed him the pen. "The cleanup crew could have thrown your pen out by mistake."

"Thanks." A smile filled the area under his mustache. "Actually, it's a recording device."

"It looks like a pen—"

"Chief Stanton and I want your help, Rebecca," Garrett said.

"My help? I'm flattered. The leading expert on crimes and predatory behavior needs my help?"

"Jim told us—"

I stood. "Jim's an idiot. Look, I only came up here to return that. I'm missing the afternoon workshops."

Chief Stanton put out his hand as if to make me stay. I sat again.

"Rebecca," Garrett said. "Jim has given the police a formal statement. He swore that he overheard you talking about the murders that happened five months ago in this room."

"We found the knife from the Valentine's Day sushi bar in the lobby," Chief Stanton said. "Now we have your confession."

Garrett connected the pen/tape recorder to a black box on the table. "Everything you said since picking this up got recorded." He showed me an earpiece. "I've listened to most of it."

"A lot of panel discussion," I said.

He leaned toward me. "Luckily, I always carry this thing to tape my talks. You had an active bug in your pocket at the front desk, in the elevator, and all the way to this room."

He connected the earpiece to the box. "When you sat at my table, I realized you were the Rebecca that Jim had told us about. He was going to introduce you to me after the luncheon. Let me cue this up." A female voice came from a speaker in the black box.

"The same floor. The same room."

The music in the elevator nearly covered my voice. "Classic, Garrett. Return to the scene of the crime. Think like the killer. Go to the room where my sweetheart always celebrated Valentine's Day."

My voice sounded angry. "That woman with my boyfriend laughed when she saw me at the door. They thought it was funny and asked if I wanted to share their champagne. He treated me like a nobody. Just last year's companion. As if we'd never been…us. I knew I hadn't been the first woman he'd taken to this hotel, but I'd told him how humiliating it would be if our relationship didn't mean more to him than the others. And what did my darling do? He put his arm on her shoulder when I showed him the knife, and said, 'It's the beach, Becca. Lighten up.' I only realized what he was when I watched them enter the hotel together."

"I needed them to understand," I said.

Garrett stopped the recording. "Officer, would you get the lady a glass of water?"

"Is it admissible?" I asked. Maybe I was still talking to myself. I watched Garrett unhook the equipment and hand it to the police chief.

"We had the knife," the chief said. "The city had your fingerprints on file, but we needed a confession."

"Will it hold up in court?" I asked Garrett.

He rubbed his mustache and smirked at me. "Maybe you can get your lawyer to evaluate your mental status," he said.

"Good luck with that," Chief Stanton said. "She's sane, and no judge or juror from around here will acquit her."

"I had no idea you'd been a student of mine," Garrett said. "But it's just so great when chance meets opportunity. When I put the device on the table, I had no idea you'd take it." His chuckle was deep and throaty. "Jim almost didn't go to the police—you terrify him."

That's when we both chuckled.

"What's so funny?" the chief asked.

"Jim hasn't read the research on love-crazed girlfriends," I said. "We aren't serial killers."

"Rebecca loves criminal psychology the way I do, Chief." Garrett handed over the audio equipment from the table. "It's a society of isolation for so many of us these days. People compulsively talk to themselves—I've caught myself doing it."

He grabbed the handle of a rolling suitcase. "Got to catch a plane, Chief. I enjoyed this. For the last five years, my own research has focused on predators who pursue their lovers to death. Rebecca pre-ordered my next book."

"Crimes of Passion, Volume 2," I said. "Will there be a Volume 3?"

The officer who'd brought me water handcuffed me. It hurt—like love. "The thing about a beautiful surround-style glass window like this, Garrett? It doesn't open. I couldn't hurl myself out afterward."

It struck me that I'd never see that view again—or any view. "I probably won't see you again, Garrett, unless prison television picks up Court TV."

He looked at his watch. "I'll have to read the trial transcript to find out how you managed to avoid detection by the police for so long—not just hotel cameras but everything, like your decision to grab the knife from the bucket behind the sushi bar."

The red sun would begin to dip into the horizon in an hour or two more. I looked at our yellow sofa and recalled the red rose petals my sweetheart had scattered on the floor beside it. I remembered the red blood on the knife I wiped on my dress before tossing it into a bucket of knives behind the sushi bar on my way out of the hotel. I hadn't taken a weapon with me that night. Of course, I knew about the sushi bar they set up there every year.

"It was a crime of passion, Garrett," I said. "What I did in this room was really your fault. You put the case of the wife with the knife in Volume 1."

His face went pale, and he covered his mouth. It hid his mustache.

"I thought I'd leave the conference with nothing more than your luncheon napkin, Professor. We can collaborate now. Put me in your next book. I'll tell you everything. Would you like that?"

RIDESHARE MURDER IN OBX
SHERYL JORDAN

"WHERE SHOULD WE GO for our birthday celebrations?" Katrina Collins sipped on Chardonnay while planning their annual birthday trip with her two closest friends, Morgan Baxter, and Hannah Allyn. Their birthdays fell within the same week.

"How about the Outer Banks? We can go shopping in towns and do some sightseeing," Morgan said searching for fun vacation spots near Virginia on her laptop.

"Sounds fun. I've never been to OBX but heard about some of the touristy stuff. Seeing wild horses run on the beach will be awesome," Hannah said.

"It's settled then, we're going to the OBX." Katrina grabbed her phone and made a call to her aunt Lydia.

"Hi Auntie. I hope you're doing well."

"Hello dear, I'm fine. How are you?" Lydia asked.

"Good to hear. I'm doing well. My girlfriends and I are planning to go down to the OBX to celebrate our birthdays. Are any of your properties available anytime in the next three weeks?" Katrina crossed her fingers.

"A guest opening for the week after next at the Kill Devil Hills beach house and the property in Corolla is available. Should I book one of them for you?"

"The week after next?" Katrina looked at her friends for approval, both nodded in agreement.

"That's perfect. I'll call you later this week to confirm the exact dates we will be there. Thank you, Auntie."

"You're welcome. I love you," Lydia said.

"I love you too."

* * * *

Two weeks later, the friends drove from Virginia Beach to the house in Kill Devil Hills. They arrived at Lydia's large two-story beach house and Katrina parked in the driveway next to her aunt's car. The aqua blue siding and tan trim on the house stood out against the beach background. A wrap-around porch spanned across both sides and the entire back of the house. The back faced the beach displaying the breathtaking view of the ocean. Lydia was at the house to show them around and to spend a little time with her niece and friends.

"Your house is beautiful, Miss Lydia," Hannah said. "I love how you coordinated the inside décor to match the colors outside."

"Thank you. It was my interior designer's idea." Lydia led them through the foyer into the kitchen.

"Being an interior designer, I can honestly say it's very classy and tastefully done," Hannah said.

While the ladies put away their belongings in the bedrooms upstairs, Lydia opened a bottle of Chardonnay and set pastries on the counter when they came downstairs.

"I thought you may want some refreshments after the drive in." Lydia poured the wine.

"You are so thoughtful Aunt Lydia," Katrina said. "Are you able to join us before you leave?"

"Yep, I thought it would be nice to chat for a bit before I head home." The women sat at the table in the kitchen eating area.

"Good. What have you been up to since you retired?"

"Traveling a bit. Ron and I went to Aruba for a week last month. A few months ago, we drove down to Florida to visit his family," Lydia said.

"Aruba sounds nice. We should plan to go there next year for our birthdays," Morgan said.

"It is a lovely place. Everything we saw was amazing. And the people were very hospitable. I told Ron, I want to go back again next year." Lydia showed them pictures from the trip on her phone.

"Yeah, we are definitely going there. Love the pictures," Hanna said.

"Other than a little traveling, we've been busy keeping the properties maintained and rented regularly. What's been going on with you young ladies?"

"Working mostly. I was promoted to Courtroom Presentation Specialist at my paralegal job at the law firm, so that takes up most of my time," Katrina said.

"I opened my interior design business, Designs by Hannah Allyn, last year, which has been prosperous."

"I'm still with the architectural firm. I also do some painting and drawing. I've had a dozen pieces of my artwork featured in various exhibitions in the past six months," Morgan said.

"Wow, it's great you all are excelling in your careers," Lydia said. "What do y'all do for fun? I remember when I was your age, we enjoyed doing all kinds of things, like going to night clubs, parties, amusement parks, and hanging out at the beach."

"We do some of those things. We meet up for dinner a couple of times per week. We also go to comedy clubs and concerts," Katrina said.

"Good, all work and no play isn't good for a fulfilled life," Lydia took a sip of wine. "Are you all in relationships?"

"Auntie, why would you ask that?" Katrina asked.

"Well, I talked to your momma last week and she said you broke up with your boyfriend last month."

"We did, and no I am not dating anyone right now." Katrina rolled her eyes and took a gulp of wine.

"A close friend of your uncle Ron has a nephew who started a new driving service here. He's in his early thirties and extremely handsome. I thought you all might need his services while you're here so you can enjoy the sights without having to drive up and down the peninsula." Lydia took another sip of wine.

"What a wonderful idea," Morgan said.

"Auntie, are you trying to play matchmaker? And did mom put you up to this?" Katrina frowned at Morgan.

"Why would you think that? He's single," Lydia smiled.

"I'm not interested in dating right now. If Hannah and Morgan want to have a driver while we're here that's fine," Katrina said.

"Great, here's his contact information. His name is Brandon Elliott." Lydia handed the business card to Katrina.

* * * *

You are appreciated.
Don't you know we love you sweet lady
Place no one above you sweet lady.

Brandon sang one of his favorite songs while driving around the OBX. *Buzz. Buzz.*

Brandon turned the music down and answered his phone. "Elliot Transportation. Brandon speaking. How may I help you?"

"Hi Brandon. I'm Katrina Collins. I'm in need of a driver for a few days while I'm in the OBX this week."

"Which days do you need services and how many people will be riding? Brandon pulled into a gas station to check his schedule.

"There will be three of us. Are you available tonight from six p.m. until about eleven and tomorrow at noon until midnight? We don't know our exact schedule for the rest of the week yet, but we'll need transportation most of those days also," Katrina said.

"Where are you staying and where are you going tonight?"

"We're in Kill Devil Hills. We want to go to JK's Restaurant and maybe to a nearby night club."

"Okay, it'll cost eighty dollars for tonight. All-day service from eight a.m. until midnight costs $400 per day. Half day service costs $200 per day. All scheduled services require half of the total at the time of booking," Brandon said.

"Okay, that seems reasonable."

"I'll text you the payment schedule with my website to book the services you want. You can pay the down payment. When I receive the payment, I will call you to confirm the times and days. Can I text the information to this number Ms. Collins?"

"Yes," Katrina said.

"Great, I just sent it."

"Got it. I will see you this evening at six," Katrina said.

"Thank you. Enjoy the rest of your afternoon," Brandon ended the call. *Man, if she's as sexy as she sounds, this will be a pleasant week.*

* * * *

"I booked the driver for tonight," Katrina smiled.

"What time will he be here?" Morgan asked.

Katrina was in deep thought and didn't answer right away. "Uh, six."

"Girl, what are you smiling about?" Hannah asked Katrina.

"Nothing."

"Nothing my behind. I've seen you smile like that before. Brandon must have impressed you on the phone," Hannah said.

"He had the smoothest, sexiest voice I've ever heard," Katrina blushed.

"Okay, Miss I'm not interested in dating right now," Morgan said mocking her.

"I didn't say I was interested in dating him. I said his voice is sexy and he was pleasant to talk to," Katrina giggled.

"Girl, whatever. We have plenty of time to get groceries before Brandon arrives. There's a grocery store a few blocks away." Morgan checked google maps on her phone.

They drove to the store not wanting to walk back carrying the groceries. They had gathered most of the items they wanted and were in the dairy section. Katrina was getting the milk, eggs, and cheese when she collided with a man causing her to drop a carton of eggs.

"I'm sorry sir," Katrina said stooping to pick up the eggs.

"It's my fault, I wasn't paying attention." The man turned to help her.

It can't be him. Katrina stopped picking up the eggs.

She stood up facing the handsome man with dark brown skin, brown eyes, and a strong jaw line standing in front of her. Flustered, she dropped the package of cheese.

"I'm so clumsy today," Katrina said.

"Let me get that for you." The man handed her the cheese, her fingers bushing against his.

Morgan and Hannah approached them with the shopping cart, avoiding the eggs splattered on the floor.

"Hey girl, what's going on?" Morgan asked.

"We bumped into each other, and I dropped the carton of eggs," Katrina said.

"It was my fault," the man said. His voice was deep and smooth.

"Katrina, didn't you book our driver for the week with Elliott Transportation?" Morgan asked, noticing the Elliott Transportation logo on his shirt.

"Katrina? Katrina Collins? I thought your voice was familiar. I'm Brandon Elliott, your driver."

"I thought so when I heard your unique voice," Katrina said.

"It's a pleasure meeting you, sorry it was over eggs and cheese. I will see you ladies in a few hours," Brandon smiled and walked away.

"Damn, he's fine!" Katrina said.

"Yes indeed." Hannah raised an eyebrow.

"Oh, my goodness, you sure didn't lie about his sexy voice." Morgan fanned her face with her hands.

"What are the odds of us running into each other like that," Katrina said.

* * * *

The friends put the groceries away then showered and dressed for dinner. They shared a bottle of wine while waiting for Brandon to arrive.

Clink. Clink.

"Here's to us meeting in yoga class fifteen years ago. The love and respect we have for each other is a bond which nothing can break. You are my sisters. I love you both. Happy birthday to us!" Katrina raised her glass to toast.

Morgan and Hannah joined the toast then they all hugged each other tightly.

"What did you think of Brandon?" Katrina asked.

"He seems nice, although we only met briefly," Hannah said.

"I agree, but it was weird meeting him like that," Katrina said sipping her wine.

"Lydia mentioned Brandon's uncle is a good friend of her husband. Ask your uncle Ron about him," Morgan said.

I'll talk to him tomorrow," Katrina said.

Buzz. Buzz.

"Our handsome driver has arrived," Katrina said after receiving a text on her phone.

* * * *

Brandon arrived at exactly six p.m. When the ladies approached his SUV, he greeting them and opened the doors. Morgan and Hannah climbed in the backseats, leaving Katrina to sit in the front seat.

"How long have you been in the transportation business?" Katrina asked.

"Eight years. I was a chauffeur for seven years in New York for rich and famous people. My mom became ill last year so I moved to Virginia to be close to my parents," Brandon said.

"My aunt said you recently started your transportation business here," Katrina said.

"That's correct. After my mom recovered, I decided to give it a try. Who's your aunt?"

"Lydia Walker, she's married to my uncle Ron Walker. Uncle Ron is close friends with your uncle.

"Yes, I have met them. They are good people," Brandon said. I'll have to thank her for referring you to my company."

"Do you live near the grocery store we were at earlier?" Hannah asked.

"Yep, I own a house around the corner from there." Brandon turned into the restaurant parking lot.

"Would you like to join us for dinner?" Morgan asked.

"No, I don't usually mix business with pleasure."

"Come on, our families know each other. And we would like to have you at our birthday dinner," Katrina said.

"Well, in that case I would love to join you ladies. Whose birthday are we celebrating?"

"All of ours. Our birthdays are in the same week, so every year we do something to celebrate together," Katrina said.

"That's cool." Brandon pulled into a parking space. When they entered the restaurant, the hostess seated them. The waiter took their orders and their food arrived thirty minutes later. During dinner, they got to know more about Brandon, talking and laughing until the restaurant closed. While driving back to the beach house, they listened to music. Traffic was heavy but moving at a steady pace. A pickup truck was in front of them.

"What do you like to do when you aren't driving?" Katrina asked.

"I enjoy going to concerts, comedy clubs, the beach, professional sporting events, and just relaxing at home," Brandon said.

"What the—"

Bam. Screech.

"Hold on everyone!" Brandon maneuvered his SUV dodging the tailgate flying in the air and repeatedly striking the road. As a body rolled from the bed of the truck Brandon slammed on the brakes, stopping the SUV seconds before the body hit the front end of the vehicle.

"Oh, my God!" Katrina screamed, holding on to the handrail.

"What the heck!" Morgan squeezed Hannah's arm.

Hannah stared at the windshield with tears streaming down her face. Brandon backed up and pulled to the side of the road.

"Call 9-1-1," Brandon said to Hannah and Morgan as he and Katrina got out to see if the person was dead.

"She's not breathing, but she has a faint pulse." Katrina started CPR on the victim.

Watching Katrina, Brandon's face starts to pale. Morgan and Hannah stand beside him. Police arrived and began securing the area. EMTs took over resuscitating the victim, but she passed away at the scene.

"Are you okay?" Katrina looked at Brandon.

"No, the woman was my customer. I dropped her off at a house on the beach about twenty minutes before I picked you up."

* * * *

Police took witness statements from everyone at the scene. Katrina, Hannah, and Morgan corroborated Brandon's account of events. They took him to the police station to obtain a statement about his interaction with the victim. Katrina called her aunt.

"He didn't harm that woman," Lydia said. "He is loving and caring from what I know about him."

"Auntie, have Uncle Ron call Brandon's uncle to let him know. Brandon needs an attorney. I told him not to talk to the police anymore without one present."

"Yes, I'll have Ron call right away."

"Thank you, we're on our way back to the house. I'll let you know if I hear anything else," Katrina said.

* * * *

The friends caught an Uber home from the scene. They sat in the living room discussing what happened.

"That was the most bizarre thing I've ever seen," Katrina said.

"Yes, I thought Hannah was going into shock, by the way she sat there staring straight ahead not saying a word, just crying." Morgan hugged Hannah.

"We need to help Brandon clear his name in this," Katrina looked at her friends.

"You think he's innocent?" Hannah asked.

"Yes, I know we just met him but after spending time with him at dinner, I don't see him doing this."

"I agree."

"What can we do?" Morgan asked.

"I don't know yet. We need to hear Brandon's side and even see if they are going to charge him with anything. Let's try to get some sleep for now."

The next morning, Lydia, Ron, and Brandon's uncle stopped by the beach house to give the friends an update. Lydia introduced everyone.

"Good morning, ladies. This is Brandon's uncle, Jason Elliott, and my husband Ron."

"Jason visited Brandon this morning at the jail. He wanted to update you and ask you all some questions," Ron said.

"When I spoke to Brandon and his attorney, the attorney said the woman was stabbed but the coroners must determine the cause of death. The police obtained a warrant to search his house and car last night. They didn't find anything that ties him to the murder, and he may be released today. Brandon said he talked to Katrina around noon, then he ran into you at the grocery store around one p.m.," Mr. Elliott said.

"Yes, everything is correct. He told me at the scene he had dropped the victim off at a house further down the beach twenty minutes before picking us up," Katrina said.

"That wouldn't have been enough time for him to stab someone, hide the body, clean up and pick us up on time." Hannah sipped her coffee.

"Exactly. His website scheduler would show a record of where he was supposed to be and the times he was supposed be there," Morgan said.

"It's circumstantial because it doesn't actually track his whereabouts," Katrina said pacing the room.

"Brandon also mentioned there was a man flying a drone near the house when he dropped the women off," Mr. Elliot said. "Maybe he picked something up on the drone camera but didn't realize a crime was being committed.

"It's a longshot but worth trying to find the owner of the drone," Katrina said. "We can take a walk down the beach to see if a man is out flying a drone."

"It was nice meeting you ladies. I wish it were under different circumstances. If you find anything, please let me know and go to the police with it." Mr. Elliot left, closing the door.

* * * *

"It's a beautiful day for a walk down the beach. Are y'all ready?" Katrina asked.

"Yep, let's go."

They walked two miles not seeing anyone flying a drone. The women sat down on a bench to rest and wait. After an hour, they began walking back towards the house.

"Do you hear that whirling noise?" Hannah asked.

"I just hear the waves crashing against the shoreline."

"There it is again," Hannah said, pointing towards the sky.

"Look." Morgan shouts seeing a drone flying in the distance. "The person operating it could be anywhere."

Katrina started jumping up and down waving her arms around.

"What are you doing?" Morgan asked.

"I'm trying to draw attention to the operator of the drone."

Morgan and Hannah began copying Katrina. After a few minutes, the drone descended close to them.

"We need your help!" Katrina yelled into the face of the drone.

A man carrying a controller walked towards them and landed the drone at their feet.

"How can I help you beautiful ladies?" The man asked.

"A friend needs your help. Were you flying your drone around here yesterday after five-thirty?" Katrina asked.

"I sure was. Why?"

"Were you recording all your flights?"

"Yes, I record all my flights from take off until landing. I usually review the recordings later to help me practice and correct errors in my precision."

"Have you looked at the recordings from yesterday?"

"Not yet, let's look now. What are we looking for?"

"We need to see if a woman was stabbed or possibly in danger," Katrina said.

The man played the recording. Nothing out of the ordinary happened.

"Thank you for your time. Sorry to have bothered you." Katrina turned to walk away.

"Hang on a second. I have something." The man showed the women a different recording.

"Bingo," Katrina said.

The man took the recording to the police station. The video showed the victim arguing with a man who looked nothing like Brandon. The man forced her into a truck like the one the victim's body rolled from. The video was recorded at seven p.m.

* * * *

After the police reviewed the video, they released Brandon.

Katrina called Lydia. "Brandon has been cleared and released. Can you bring Uncle Ron and Mr. Elliot to the beach house? We can tell you everything that happened."

When they arrived, Katrina told them what transpired at the beach.

"I'm thankful for all of you pulling together to support me and help me prove my innocence. I'm not sure how things would have turned out if the three of you wouldn't have gone down to the beach," Brandon said.

Later that evening, Katrina and Brandon had dinner at a local sports bar. A breaking news announcement came on the TV.

A man has been arrested and charged with second degree murder of a woman whose body rolled from the back of his pickup truck. An argument ensued after the woman refused to go back home with her estranged boyfriend. The man forced her into his truck. He later stabbed her to keep her from escaping. The man put the woman in the bed of his pickup truck planning to drive her back home when the tailgate fell off the truck and the victim's body rolled out of the truck bed. The woman died at the scene.

"I'm glad the police arrested him," Katrina said.

"Me too. I don't know how I'll ever repay you."

"I think free rides for the rest of the week should cover it," Katrina smiled winking at Brandon.

A DEAD BODY IN THE HALL

PENNY HUTSON

A WOMAN'S SCREAM pierced the air. Charlie smashed his shin into the wooden leg of a Chippendale settee as he hurried through the old-fashioned and overcrowded drawing room. "Damn it!" He winced but kept moving. Someone always got hurt at these parties. Several men barreled down the main hall from the back of the large colonial-style house as Charlie reached the front entrance.

The maid pressed against the front door and pointed at the floor. "He's dead! He's dead!"

A grey-haired man in an expensive dark suit lay face down on the red and gold oriental carpet. An upturned black bowler hat lay a few feet away. Charlie knelt by the man and turned him onto his back. "It's Martin Van Croft."

A woman in a bright red party dress and single red feather sticking out of her headband pushed past the men now crowded in the narrow hallway. "What's happened?"

Charlie glanced up at the woman. "We just found him lying on the floor."

The woman in red reached for her chest. "Is he dead?"

Charlie felt the man's pulse and put an ear to the man's lips. "I'm afraid so."

"Oh my God! What do we do now?" A strained expression crossed her face.

Charlie peered up at the woman. It was the nanny for Van Croft's children. *What was her name?* When everyone continued to stare at him, he sighed. "Someone call the police."

"Right." Swinging a red feather boa over her shoulder, she hustled out of the hall. Several other women from the party now trailed after her.

Standing up, Charlie waved the men closer. "Let's get him off the floor, gentlemen."

"Wait," said Louie Legstrum. "Should we move the body before the police arrive?" Charlie had watched Louie cozying up to Van Croft all night, begging for a spot in the jazz band at Van Croft's Cavalier Hotel down on the oceanfront. Probably hasn't had a gig in months.

The men gawked at Charlie, as if he's in charge.

Charlie motioned to Henry Kim who's holding an unlit cigarette. "You're Van Croft's friend. What do you think?"

Henry blinked a few times and shrugged. "I don't guess it'll make much difference. Technically, you've already moved him. Can't see the harm."

Charlie peered at Van Croft. "I just can't stand to see him sprawled out on the floor like this."

Strings of "yeah, yeah," and "sure, sure," reeled out of the men like fishing lines. Avoiding eye contact with each other, they lifted the body and carried it into the sitting room.

"Easy, gentlemen," Charlie said as they lowered Van Croft face-up onto the couch. Charlie grabbed a blanket heaped on the arm of a chair and covered the dead man's body and face. "Alright, everyone, let's continue in the living room. More space in there."

Charlie closed the French doors of the sitting room, after everyone shuffled through the dining room, past the table still cluttered with half-empty diner plates and champagne glasses, and into the larger living room with soft couches and chairs.

Henry Kim wandered to a side cabinet and opened its ornately carved doors. Glass bottles clinked as he searched the shelves inside. He returned clutching a clear glass decanter of amber colored liquid. "Thought we all could use something a little stronger than champagne." He managed a lopsided grin. The unlit cigarette now clenched between his teeth. "Considering the circumstances, I don't guess our host will mind." He poured himself two fingers worth and held the bottle up. "Anyone else?"

The men filled their glasses as the women filed silently into the room.

The nanny rushed in behind them. "The police are on their way." She plopped into an over-stuffed chair. "Now what?"

Charlie blew out a long breath. Why can't he remember her name? He was usually good at that.

"Well, someone do something." Mime Marlo, the only silent film star at the party, sashayed into the room and perched on the arm of a large leather chair near the other guests already seated. Some stood near the bay window that faced the beach now hidden by the blackness of the night.

Charlie admired Mime's walk. Shoulders and hips swaying. Was it all an act, or was she just naturally confident? Charlie couldn't decide but loved the way her gold-colored sequined dress clung to every curve.

"Has anyone tried to figure out what happened?" The film star glared at Charlie.

"You mean who killed him?" Charlie narrowed his eyes and suppressed a grin. Man, she was good-looking, even with the blonde wig, but not so smart.

"Maybe he just had a heart attack." Vera Low, the oldest woman in the group, adjusted her oversized hat which slid down her forehead.

Charlie cringed at her fake fur stole and accent. Where did she find that awful brown ballgown and cream-colored puffy hat—the 1800s? Maybe her grandmother's attic?

When no one answered her, Vera huffed. "Well, did anyone check?"

"What are we, doctors now?" Henry Kim held out his empty hand.

Charlie suppressed a groan. "I didn't see any wounds."

"Maybe he was strangled?" The film star held up a slender black cigarette holder. An unlit cigarette sticking out of its end.

"Wouldn't that leave a mark?" The nanny lifts a shoulder.

"Yeah, I suppose." The film star wrinkled her nose. "Dumb question, huh?"

"Better question. Where's the butler?" Henry Kim poured himself another drink.

Everyone glanced around.

"I saw him in the kitchen right before the scream." The nanny tossed her boa over the back of her chair. "This thing is so itchy."

"How long before?" Heny Kim asked.

"I don't know. Maybe five, ten minutes."

"Plenty of time to make it to the hall, strangle him, and high-tail it out of here."

Great. Another genius. Charlie sighed. Thinks he knows who did it without any evidence.

"Let's not make any accusations just yet," he said. "Why don't we all say how we know our host, Mr. Van Croft?" Charlie produced his well-rehearsed smile and looked at his watch. Where the hell were James and Arthur?

"Good idea." The nanny plucked off her high-heeled shoes. "These things are killing me."

No one spoke. Their gazes flicked around the room and at each other. Some fumbled in their handbags or pockets. A few pulled out their invitations to the event.

For crying out loud. Charlie exhaled loudly. Guess he'd have to start. "Well, I'm Mr. Van Croft's financial adviser." Several eyebrows lifted at this news. "We all know the butler and, of course, the maid." He gestured in her direction.

She nodded and curtsied several times, switching directions with each bow. A few of the men whistled.

"Alright," said Charlie. "Can we take this a little more seriously, gentlemen?" They'd probably had too much to drink. "As far as I can tell, we still have no idea who the murderer is." He looked directly at Henry Kim, who didn't appear to get Charlie's meaning.

"Then why don't you enlighten us?" Henry Kim cocked his head. "You were the first one here. Seems to me you had the most access."

Charlie didn't point out Van Croft was still alive when all the guests had arrived. "The maid is here much more than me."

"The butler's always here, too." The maid jammed her fists into her paunchy sides and scrunched up her face.

Charlie smiled. Good girl. Quick thinking.

The butler suddenly appeared in the doorway. "I go home every night at eight p.m. She's here all the time." He pointed a finger at the maid. "She lives on the third floor."

"That doesn't make me a murderer!" The maid stormed over to the butler and jabbed a finger into his chest. "You're the snooty one. Think you're better than us. And it's no secret you despise Van Croft after you found out he's only leaving you the silverware and tea service when he dies. Not a penny of his millions."

The butler's face contorted in anger. "Twenty-five years of loyal service." He straightened his spine, cupped his hands together and grimaced. "Yes, Mr. Van Croft. Right away, Mr. Van Croft." Then, his mouth twisted in disgust. "And how does he repay me? Ack!" He waved his hand as if swatting a fly. "You're the one who had an affair with him."

"Liar!" The maid grabbed the feather duster hanging from her belt and flung it, hitting the butler on the shoulder. The duster fell to the floor.

The butler kicked it aside and pursed his lips. "Don't try to deny it. I saw the way you looked at him, like a love-sick teenager! Then, you found out he wasn't leaving his wife. In fact, you were going to be fired right after tonight's party."

"Says who?" The maid leaned closer to the butler.

Charlie stepped between them, extending his hands like a referee. "Easy, now."

The two glared at each other a moment longer, then turned and retreated like boxers to the opposite corners of the room.

"Another round of drinks?" Henry Kim held up the decanter and grinned.

"Great idea. C'mon fellas. Let's get a refill." Charlie motioned the men over. He needed to give James a few minutes. "Good time to powder your noses, ladies. The bathroom is just down the hall."

"Alright, girls. Who's first?" Vera Low stood up, pulling her stole tighter.

"After you," said Mime.

"We're right behind you." The nanny pushed a flap of hair off her cheek.

The women's heeled shoes clicked on the wooden floor, as they sauntered through the dining room.

Charlie was the last to refill his glass, as the nanny waltzed into the living room. He glanced at his watch. "I think that's everyone." He then raised his voice. "Don't know what's taking the police so long." His eyes met the maid's. "So, let's keep going, shall we?" Charlie motioned to the nanny. "How do you know our host?"

"I'm the nanny for Martin's... I mean, Mr. Van Croft's children."

"How very interesting!" An unfamiliar voice boomed into the room.

Everyone turned. A policeman stood in the doorway, holding a Billy club. Charlie relaxed. About damn time.

Speaking in a perfect French accent, the policeman strode closer to the nanny. "Do you usually get invited to your employer's private parties, Madame? Maybe you know more about ziss murder than you're telling."

"I'm just as surprised as you."

"We shall see, mademoiselle." The policeman tilted his chin to one side. A gleam of excitement sparkled in his eyes. His shiny coal-black hair and mustache were combed and waxed to perfection. "Allow me to introduce myself. I am Inspector Morris of the Princess Anne County murder squad, and these are my sergeants Staff and Willard." Two men dressed exactly as the inspector entered the room, as if on cue.

Charlie crossed his arms and leaned against the wall. This guy was good.

"Let us not jump to conclusions just yet, eh?" With mustache twitching, the inspector slid the club into his belt. "First, if someone would be so kind as to direct me to the body."

Charlie pointed toward the dining room. "He's on the couch in the sitting room, just through the there."

The inspector crossed the dining room and entered the sitting room alone. He closed its French doors behind him. His officers positioned themselves on either side, as Charlie peered through the living room doorway. In a few minutes the inspector came out and whispered to the policemen. They saluted, then hauled the covered body out of the room and down the hall.

Entering the living room, the inspector faced the crowd. "I'm afraid I cannot determine zee exact cause of death at ziss moment. We will have to wait for za surgeon to examine za body. However, without any obvious wounds or bruising, I suspect poison of some kind." He motioned to the dining room. "Shall we?"

The women settled into stiff-backed dining room chairs scattered around the large table. The men remained standing. A few leaned against the wall or doorway.

The inspector took a deep breath. "First, I will need a list of everyone here, tonight."

"Miss Haskins can get you that." Charlie nodded at the maid.

"Yes, sir." She whirled and hurried out.

"Very good, Monsieur. Why don't you start by telling me what's happened here tonight?"

"Of course." Charlie recounted the events of the evening, repeating as many of the names and occupations he could remember. The maid returned with the list. "Thank you, Miss Haskins." Charlie handed the sheet of paper to the inspector.

The inspector examined the list. "Where is Madame Low?"

Vera raised her hand.

Charlie wiped his mouth with the back of his hand to hide a smile. From his position across the room, a fruit bowl in a painting on the wall directly behind Vera appeared to be sitting on top of the poor woman's outdated hat.

"Ah! And how do you know Monsieur Van Croft?"

"I've been commissioned to paint the family portrait."

"So, you're an artist?" The inspector stopped to stroke his chin. "And you're being paid by our illustrious host?"

"That's right."

"Perhaps…" He raised his finger. "You think not enough?"

"Not true!" Vera Low stood as if to give a vigorous defense but deflated like a punctured balloon. A nervous expression crossed her face, and she sat down. "Besides, how would killing him help me?"

Her accent was gone, or maybe it was a different one. Charlie couldn't tell.

The inspector smiled. "Maybe he knows some secret you wish to hide."

"Don't be ridiculous!" The artist scoffed.

"And you Monsieur?" The inspector turned on his heels to a man leaning against the wall's burgundy and gold striped wallpaper. "You are?"

"Leroy Jones. Van Croft's lawyer." He smiled smugly, as if that information alone absolved him of any suspicion.

"Maybe he's the one not getting paid enough." Vera frowned and pointed at the man.

"Sorry." The lawyer crossed his arms. "Attorney-client privilege." He smirked.

"Thank you, Monsieur Jones. Where is Monsieur Kim?"

"Over here." Henry raised his glass. "I was a personal friend of Mr. Van Croft."

"And what do you do for a living?"

"I'm a millionaire banker." He shrugged. "What can I say. I invested wisely over the years."

Leroy Jones, the lawyer, laughed. "If you're the killer, at least we can't say you did it for the money."

A few others joined in but stopped when the inspector frowned.

"What about you?" Charlie gestured to a morose fellow leaning against a pillar by the hall. Unlike the other dark suited men, he wore a baggy tan coat and pants. His hands sunk deep in the coat's large outer pockets. The brim of his tweed cap nearly covered his eyes, and a toothpick stuck out from the corner of his mouth.

"Eddie." The man's face was impassive.

"You got a last name?" the lawyer asked.

"They call me Lucky Eddie." He rolled the toothpick from one side of his mouth to the other, as if gauging whether to say more. "Let's just say I'm Mr. Van Croft's right-hand-man."

"Excellent!" The inspector raised his chin. "Then, I suppose you can tell us who would have wanted him dead."

"Nope." Eddie's face was unreadable, his body stock still. Did he know the answer or just not telling anyone? How infuriating.

"Okay," Charlie pressed his lips together. *They needed to hurry this up. They were behind schedule.* "Who's next?"

"I'm Louie. Uh, Louie Legstrum?" He said as if unsure of himself. "Jazz musician. I play sax at the, uh—" he glanced at a paper in his hand. "Cavalier. A hotel down at the oceanfront?"

"Classy place. You must be good." The nanny smiled flirtatiously.

Louie lifted his palms. "I suppose."

"And you must be Madame Marlo?" The inspector peered at the actress.

"That's right. How'd you know?"

"You are the only female left on the list who has not yet spoken."

"Well, aren't you the smart one?" Mime batted her long eyelashes.

The detective winked at her. "And how do you know our host, Mademoiselle?"

"Mr. Van Croft was a patron of the arts. He comes to the studio from time to time."

"I never heard of any movie studio around here." The young, sandy haired man with attractive sideburns and reddish goatee turned to Henry Kim. "Have you?"

"Can't say that I have." The cigarette in Henry's hand was still unlit.

The film star widened her eyes and shifted her body toward the young man. "And who might you be?"

"Bill Burston. Newspaper mogul. Nice to meet you."

"Mutual, I'm sure." She adjusted her necklace, clearly pleased with the man's response.

The others laughed at the newspaper man's puzzled expression. Mime seemed not to notice.

"Let's see if we can find some evidence?" Charlie made a circular motion with his hands. *Come on, we don't have all night.*

"Ah, but of course." The inspector sniffed. "Now that I have questioned everyone." He extracted a handkerchief and cleaned his spectacles.

"What kind of evidence?" Vera Low asked.

"Where's good ol' Sherlock when you need him?" Henry Kim laughed and sipped his cocktail.

"Just look around." Charlie swished his hand back and forth. *Did they think he was just going to hand everyone the evidence?* "You'll know it when you see it." He widened his eyes at the maid and Lucky Eddie. The maid scowled at Charlie. Eddie rolled his eyes.

Vera Low stood and clapped her hands. "Split up everyone."

"No, that's how the killer always gets his next victim." Mime Marlo frowned. "Stay in groups of two or three."

"Excellent idea, Madame." The inspector bowed slightly. "I'll stay in here with Monsieur Charlie and search the dining room."

"We'll take the kitchen." The nanny tugged on the film star's arm.

"We'll go upstairs." The maid strode out of the room with the butler close behind.

"I hope there's no basement," said the newspaper man.

"Not at the oceanfront," said Charlie. "You hit water about two feet down. Remember, we're at sea level."

"That makes sense. Let's take the garage." He tapped Henry Kim on the arm with the back of his hand.

"No need to mess around in there," said Charlie. *Did he remember to lock it?* "Why don't you two take the back porch and yard?"

They nodded and headed for the back of the house. Everyone else hurried out of the room, as if in search of some treasured prize.

Now alone with the inspector, Charlie strode across the room and peered out into the hallway, then whispered back at the inspector. "What the hell took you so long?"

"Have you tried putting this on?" The inspector adjusted the collar of his uniform.

"Poor thing." Charlie shook his head, then smiled. "Nice accent, though."

"You like it?"

"The guests are eating it up."

"Do I really sound French?"

"Who cares?" Charlie stepped closer to the man and lowered his voice. "Just stick to the plan from now on, and we all get out of here on time."

"Excuse me!"

Charlie and the inspector whirled around.

The nanny and the film star were standing in the hallway, looking apologetically at the two men.

"Ah, Mesdames!" The inspector straightened and extended his arms toward the women. His French accent back in full bloom. "Have you found some-zing?"

"I think so." The film star held up a large brown wallet. "We found it in the kitchen."

"So, you have located our first clue," said the inspector.

The women squealed in delight, as they pranced over to the inspector. He gestured for them to place the item on the table.

"Good job, ladies." Charlie inclined his head. "Have a seat while we wait for the others."

Vera Low burst into the room. "We found this!"

"It was in the hallway," said the musician right behind her.

She held out a broken, unlit cigarette.

"Please." The inspector pointed to the table. "If you'll place it here."

She gently placed the cigarette next to the wallet with an air of triumph, as if pleased with herself.

Henry Kim rushed in. "Inspector." He waved his hand wildly. "Come look at this."

Inspector Morris followed him out of the room, signaling for the others to remain where they are.

"Must have discovered something out back," said Charlie.

A moment later, Kim, the inspector, and the newspaper man returned. "Just as I suspected!" Morris shouted. "Footprints leading up to the back porch and dirt by the back door."

"How does that help?" The musician's brow furrowed in confusion.

"We shall get to that, Monsieur Legstrum." He glanced around the room. "Who is left?"

"Jones. Van Croft's lawyer." Charlies paused, then raised his voice. "And Lucky Eddie, the butler, and the maid."

"No need to yell." Lucky Eddie sauntered into the room, baggie trench coat hanging loosely open. And without a word, he held up a small black box.

"Rat poison," said the inspector dramatically.

Lucky Eddie placed it on the table with the other items. "Found it in the trash can in the kitchen."

"Very interesting, Monsieur. Very interesting, indeed."

"I wonder where the maid is?" Charlie pokes his head out of the room, as if looking for them. *Come on people, we don't have all night.*

Hurried footsteps clicked on the wooden stairs. "Sorry, sorry!" The maid rushed into the room with the butler close behind.

"Alright," said Charlie. "Did you find anything?"

"Of course we did." The maid tilted at the waist as if bowing and with a flourish handed the inspector a small gold item. "Found it in the master bedroom right below some painting of a man on a horse."

The room was silent as the inspector raised the item to within an inch of his face and rotated it slowly. His forehead wrinkled. Then, as if jolted by an electric shock, his eyebrows shot up and his eyes widened. Then, he lowered the item. One corner of his mouth lifted ever so slightly. "The last clue."

"How do you know that?" Henry Kim picked up the decanter he'd carried from the living room.

"As you shall see, Monsieur Kim, these items will be sufficient to direct us to our killer." The inspector placed the item in his breast pocket. "Let us begin with the rat poison."

"What about that gold piece? Looks expensive."

"All in good time, Madame Marlo." He picked up the box of rat poison from the table. "Has anyone seen a rodent anywhere in the house, tonight?" He glanced around the room.

"Maybe the stuff is working?"

"Perhaps, Monsieur Jones, but I suspect another reason. And when combined with all that we've collected here, you shall see zat they all lead to one irrefutable conclusion." He crossed the room and handed the box to Lucky Eddie. "Tell me, Monsieur, has the seal been broken?"

Eddie flipped open the top. "Yup."

"And do any of its contents appear to be missing?"

Eddie shook the box and peered inside. "About half empty, I'd say."

"Ah! So ziss confirms my first analysis that our dearly departed host was likely poisoned. And here we hold the very murder weapon in our hands. Would you agree Monsieur Kim?"

"Sounds reasonable," said Henry Kim

"And do you not find it odd that such an item was discovered in the trash can?"

"That'd be the first place I'd throw it, if I'd used it to kill someone." Kim laughed.

The inspector turned to Lucky Eddie. "And what made you decide to look through the kitchen garbage bin, Monsieur?"

"Like the man said. That's where I'd have put it. I mean, who'd think to look there?"

"Apparently you, Monsieur."

"Just what are you implying?" Appearing to lose his calm for the first time all evening, Lucky Eddie stepped away from the column.

"It is not I, but the evidence that implies."

"Pssh." Eddie waved his hand dismissively and leaned back against the post.

"Now that you mention it, kind of odd that he went directly to the kitchen and found that box of poison straight away," said Henry Kim.

"No proof that's even what killed Van Croft," said Eddie. "We haven't heard back from the doc yet, have we?"

"And what about you, Monsieur Burston?" the inspector swiveled toward the newspaper man. "You've said very little all evening. As an investigative reporter, I find this very odd."

"Wait a doggone minute now! You're the fancy-smancy detective."

"Inspector."

"Whatever. You're supposed to figure out the crime."

"We also have footprints in the dirt and on the kitchen floor. Would you say those prints came from a man's or a woman's shoe, Monsieur Burston?"

"Definitely a man's."

"And your reasoning?"

"All the ladies are wearing high heels. Those are wide flat prints with ridges, like the men's shoes."

"Excellent deduction, Monsieur." The inspector continued to pace. "Would all of the gentlemen here tonight be so kind as to lift your shoes?" The inspector paraded by each man as they lifted one foot and then the other. He stopped in front of Lucky Eddie, who didn't move.

"So, I went for walk after dinner. A free country, ain't it?" Eddie shifted in place but did not lift his shoes.

"It is indeed, Monsieur Eddie, but a man is dead, and we are all suspects."

"Innocent until proven guilty. Ain't that right, Mr. Jones?" Eddie directed his gaze at the lawyer.

"Well, yeah, sure but like the detective said."

"Inspector."

"Sorry. Like the inspector said, a man's dead. So, it's a different ball game now, buddy."

"Agreed. So, unless you are confessing to zee murder, Monsieur, I suggest you show us the bottoms of your shoes."

Eddie turned his head from side to side before pushing away from the column. Slowly, he lifted one shoe to reaveal wet sand caked to the sole.

"Look at that," said Vera Low. "And he had the poison, too. He's clearly the murderer."

"I got no reason to kill Van Croft."

"Monsieur Eddie is correct. No motive has been identified. Let us complete our examination of zee evidence before we decide, Madame." He picked up the broken cigarette. "Only two people have had unlit cigarettes with them tonight. Monsieur Kim and Madame Marlo, our beautiful actress."

Mime closed her eyes and bowed her head slightly.

"And we can all see that Monsieur Kim's cigarette is still in his hand, but Madame Marlo's is missing. Is it not?"

Mime lifted her black cigarette holder. "Sure is." Her voice rising unnaturally. "Must have fallen out. Easy to do, you know. And what does that prove anyway?"

"By itself? Nothing. But combined with our other clues, you shall see a different picture." The inspector started to pace again. "You and the nanny were the first to return. You, Madame Marlo discovered this wallet." He retrieved it from the table. "Correct?"

"Hey!" Lucky Eddie reached in his pockets. "That's my wallet!"

"Indeed, it is, Monsieur. Where exactly did you find this Madame Marlo?"

"In the kitchen."

"More specifically?"

"On the floor." Her voice quavered.

"Were you not with someone else when you discovered it?"

"Yes, but she was searching in the pantry with her back turned when I picked it up."

"How convenient, Madame."

"It's the truth!"

"Unfortunately, I believe it is not. We still have one more piece of evidence." He plucked the golden and jeweled item he had pocketed earlier. "This, Madame Marlo, I believe belongs to you."

The film star grasps the left side of her dress.

"It was on you when you arrived this evening. Was it not?" The inspector raised his eyebrows.

"How'd you know that?" Henry Kim asked. "You weren't here when we arrived."

"True, Monsieur, but if you examine the left side of Madame Marlo's evening dress, you shall see two small holes about the same distance apart as the width of this brooch." He held up the item.

The newspaper reporter marched over to the film star and examined her dress at close range. "I see it." He turned back to the inspector. "Let me have that pin." He took it, examined it, and held it up to the spot on the dress. "You're right. Look."

Several others stepped closer and murmured in agreement.

"So, I lost my pin. What of it?" Mime rolled her eyes.

"You did not just lose it, Madame. You lost it right below the hidden safe in Monsieur Van Croft's bedroom on the night he was murdered. And there are traces of what appear to be rat poison on it."

Several guests gasped.

"So far, Madame," the inspector continued. "Three pieces of evidence are connected to you."

"It's his wallet." She pointed to Lucky Eddie.

"Which you stole from his pocket earlier tonight in order to frame Monsieur Eddie."

"You can't prove that!" Mime Marlo said.

"Ah, but I can, Madame. Sergeant, would you be so kind as to hand me Madame's purse?"

The sergeant picked up the black and gold satin purse and gave it to Morris, who pulled out a thin black wallet. He passed it to the sergeant. "Please tell everyone to whom this wallet belongs."

The sergeant opened the wallet. "It's Mr. Van Croft's, sir."

"It is indeed, Sergeant."

"I forgot I had it. I swear!" said Mime. "I was going to put it back."

"So, you admit taking the wallet," said the lawyer. "Why?"

Mime Marlo's eyes darted back and forth. "I, uh, discovered Van Croft in the hall before anyone else. I shook him. Tried to wake him up. Turn him over. But he was too heavy." The film star swallowed and stood up. "I need a drink." She turned to Henry Kim who was standing near the bar. "Would you mind?"

Henry stared blankly for a few seconds. "Oh, yeah. Sure." He scooped up an empty glass from the counter.

"Make it a double, please." Mime smiled tightly at the group.

Kim poured the drink and shuttled it over to her.

"Go on," said the inspector.

The woman downed the entire drink, winced, and wiped the corners of her mouth. "When I realized he was dead, I pulled out his wallet." She paused, then spread her hands out. "He was faced down. I couldn't tell who it was. You guys all in black suits. Then I heard someone coming down the stairs." She scanned the room and put down the glass she was still holding. "I panicked. I ran. I was going to put it back, but they carried him into that room, and I never got another chance."

"Unlikely," said the inspector. "You took Monsieur Van Croft's wallet for the $500 it contained. Then you took Monsieur Eddie's wallet with the intention of producing it as evidence found near the poison in the kitchen trash bin to make it look like he was the murderer instead."

"Not true! I've no reason to kill Van Croft."

"Ah, but I am afraid you do, Madame."

Mime Marlo froze but said nothing.

"When Madame Haskins retrieved the guest list for me earlier tonight, your name was not on it. And no Mime Marlo works at the film studio here either. Isn't that right Sergeant?"

"Yes, Inspector." The policeman straightened instantly into attention and stepped forward. "I spoke to the stage company manager myself, sir."

The inspector nodded and the sergeant stepped back.

Mime tossed her head and attempted a smile. "It's a stage name. Only the director would know it."

"Forgive me, Madame, but I do not think so. You showed up at to-night's party uninvited and unknown by anyone except our dearly departed. You are, in fact, the sister of Mrs. Van Croft who knew about her husband's affair and his plans to divorce her. You and your sister had a great deal to lose if that happened. I suspect your sister promised to share the millions she would inherit in exchange for poisoning him tonight."

"So, that story 'bout his wife being out of town pro'bly not true." Henry Kim's words slurred slightly as he reached for a half empty bottle of champagne on the table. "Wouldn't you agree, Inspector?"

"We will know soon enough. Police have already been dispatched to the Van Croft summer home near Little Island Park and her parents' house in Smithfield."

"Waste of time. She's on her way to some Caribbean Island by now." Leroy Jones waved a hand dismissively and pointed to the film star. "Leaving you holding the bag."

"Not to worry, Monsieur. We will find her sister. And she will be prosecuted to the fullest extent of the law."

Mime Marlo searched helplessly around the room. Then, her face registered anger. "That lying, cheating, philanderer deserved to die. Why should my sister and family suffer for his adulterous life? My sister's a good woman and a good wife."

"So, Mesdames and Messieurs, here we have our murderer." The inspector held out a hand in Mime's direction.

Loud applause burst out in the room.

"I knew it was you!" Vera Low snapped her fingers.

"I thought it was Lucky Eddie over there," said the nanny.

"I knew it had to be either you or the maid." Bill Burston stood up and clapped the inspector on his back. "Nicely done."

"I coulda sworn it was old Charlie. Seemed to know too much if you get my meaning." Henry Kim shook Charlie's and then the inspector's hand.

"I was beginning to wonder if anyone of y'all were gonna get it." Charlie shook his head.

"Well, I'm glad I came. Even though I didn't guess right." The musician scratched his head. "Such a beautiful house on the beach, too."

"Thanks so much, everyone." Vera Low hugged the maid and the butler. "You guys were the best actors."

"Most definitely." Mime Marlo blew them kisses.

"I agree." The nanny looked around. "Now, where are my shoes?"

"Loved the 1920s theme! Perfect for a murder mystery dinner theater." Henry Kim downed the last of his drink.

Then, the inspector, Charlie, Lucky Eddie, the butler, the maid, and the sergeant joined hands and bowed together. Everyone clapped again.

"We're glad you chose to be with us while on your vacation in Virginia Beach. Another round of applause for our actors tonight." Charlie motioned to the other players.

"Wait a minute," said Louie, the musician. "Weren't there two sergeants?"

"Indeed, there were, Monsieur. Very observant. Did no one notice that when the sergeants left with the body, only one policeman came back?"

Everyone shook their heads.

"Apparently," said Charlie. "No one noticed that Lucky Eddie had not been here during dinner, either. Arriving mysteriously only after our sergeants left."

"So, one of them changed into Lucky Eddie!" Vera Low slapped her thigh.

"Correct, Mademoiselle."

"What happened to Van Croft, then?" Henry Kim asked.

The inspector lifted his hat with one hand and yanked off his wig with the other. Then, dropping the wig to the floor, he ripped off his fake mustache and glasses to reveal that he was indeed Van Croft now in a police uniform. No one had recognized him, either.

THE HALLOWEEN HIT

KIMBERLY R. THORN

IT IS a cool and breezy Halloween night on the Chesapeake Bay. A few hours ago, all was quiet at the old Oceanview Carnival. All that could be heard was the constant swish and foaming of the water as it washes up on shore and then retreats back into itself. That was until…

Sharmi grasps the blood-stained baby blanket in her gloved hands. As her hands shake, she lifts it up to her nose. The unmistakable mercury scent of dried blood confirms her worse nightmare.

Detective C. Hunt interrupts her thoughts. "What is it?"

As she snaps to, she shows him the soiled baby blanket. "The bastard hurt the baby."

"But where is the baby? We've looked everywhere. There are no other bloodstains except where the victim went down. If there was—"

Sharmi is suddenly blinded by a white light and Hunt's words are omitted by a deafening scream. She braces herself for what comes next as her vision quickly turns into vivid imagery of the park. Except, Hunt isn't there this time. All she sees is the source of the screams. A small woman runs past her while holding a baby and cries for help. Right as she passes Sharmi, a soiled baby blanket falls out of her arms to Sharmi's feet. Staring at the fallen blanket, Sharmi snaps back to reality and the bloody blanket she has in her hands.

"Sharmi, are you okay?" Hunt's words startle her. "Was it a vision?"

"Yes, it was, I'm okay," she responds with a shaky breath and then a sigh of relief, "I think the baby is fine. Apparently, his mother was also here when it happened and took him to safety. The blood here is of the victim, not the baby."

Hunt opens the evidence bag, and replies, "Well, that's some good news to this whole fiasco. Go ahead and put the blanket in this and I'll get it checked out to be on the safe side."

As she puts the blanket in the bag, she laughs at Hunt and says, "You don't believe me again, huh?"

"No, you know I believe in your power, er, sorry, I mean abilities, but my captain doesn't. He wants the cold hard facts. I just thought it would save us both a lot of trouble to go ahead and get forensics to test it."

"Point taken. I guess you wouldn't have called me here if you didn't believe me. Can you take me to the victim?"

"Come with me, he's this way right in front of the Ferris wheel." Hunt points in the direction the woman was running from in the vision.

While they make their way over to the Ferris wheel and then through the yellow police tape, Hunt updates her.

"Looks professional. One shot to the middle of his forehead. Pretty messy. But who can shoot like that besides a professional? I mean, really, one shot? And what the hell was he doing here? The carnival was closed for Halloween, thank goodness kids were out trick or treating or no telling how many deaths we would have."

"True. But if it's a professional hit, it would seem to me that he would have been the only intended victim. You didn't find any other shots? No bullets struck anywhere else?"

"No, nothing. It *has* to be a professional." He looks down at the body and sighs. "Poor bastard didn't have a chance. It just pisses me off. And to find out he has a kid, makes it even worse."

Sharmi bends down to look at the wound. Hunt is correct, one shot to the center of his forehead and blood everywhere. "Must have died instantly. Anything on him? And do we know who he is?" she asks as she looks again at him and around him.

Hunt takes out his small, spiral notebook from his top jacket pocket and reads, "Steven Marshall of Lowry Lane in Peyton Gardens just down the road. That's all we know so far based on his driver's license. Still trying to locate his car."

A man on the opposite side of the body looks up from where he was squatting to examine it. "Detective Hunt, I'm pretty sure the cause of death is just as it seems. Fatal shot to the head, one to be exact. I say he died instantly as you correctly assessed." He nods to Sharmi. "It looks as if the bullet went through his brain. I'll of course perform an autopsy, but I think what I'll find will not be any surprise. It looks as if, based on what I can see, that it was a high-powered rifle."

"Sharmi, this is Dr. M. C. Denton, he's the medical examiner for this case." Hunt gestures towards the man still squatting down.

"Nice to meet—" Sharmi starts.

"Wait a minute." He quickly cuts her off as he fixates on something in the distance. He stands up and turns around to face directly opposite where the body still lays. He holds out his left arm with his index finger pointed out and thumb pointed upward, his right eye shuts, and he adjusts himself until he stops pointing at the top of the Haunted House. "That's about 500 yards away, so I'd say that is where your murderer was when he took the shot."

Sharmi and Hunt look in the same direction with their mouths sightly open in disbelief and then look at each other, in surprise.

Hunt immediately moves over to the nearest uniformed officer and orders him along with a few others to follow him to the Haunted House roof. Sharmi is close behind him.

Denton yells, "Can I take the body with me? Are you done with it, Detective?"

"Yes. Dr. Denton, it's all yours, I'll of course look forward to your autopsy results in a few hours," he yells back.

Denton grinds his teeth. "You know that is unrealistic. An autopsy takes time to be sure it is done right. You cannot rush it. But I can say that I'll put a rush on it and get started as soon as I get the body back to the morgue." As he's walking away with this bag, he mumbles to himself, "It's okay if I work all night, I mean I don't have anything better to do with my life."

Once they all are on top of the Haunted House, everyone starts going into four different directions. It is a huge roof, so Hunt is glad he had three others to help him search. He has no idea how big it could be as he didn't remember it being such a long ride. Each of them looks around their prospective areas scanning for anything out of the ordinary and find nothing. Hunt turns around just as Sharmi is blinded by the bright light again.

She sees the back of a short, stocky masculine figure dressed in all black. Laying on his belly exactly where she is currently standing on the roof of the haunted house with a huge high-powered rifle on a short stand. She then is looking through the sight directly at the victim as he smiles at someone straight ahead of him on ground level. Sharmi jumps as she hears the shot then the bone shattering through the victim's skull making him fall backwards instantly. As the vision finishes, she turns around to see Hunt and the two uniformed officers staring at her.

"What," Sharmi asks in confusion.

Hunt answers, "I'm asking if you are alright?"

"Yeah," Sharmi answers haphazardly as she is still processing her vision. She keeps looking forward toward where she saw the victim take the hit. Still trying to get her thoughts together after the shock of what she has just seen.

Detective Hunt's cell phone chimes. "Hunt, what have you got Alveraz? Oh really? We'll be down there in a minute. No, we found nothing on the roof. But go ahead and send forensics up here. See if they can find some fingerprints. Then have forensics meet me there. Hopefully I'll be done by then."

As Hunt disconnects his call, he looks at Sharmi again and asks, "What did you see?"

Sharmi shrugs. "Not much, but the killer was laying right about where I am standing. I can't see a face, only the back of him and I'd describe him as stocky and short is all I've got."

"Ok," Hunt says to Sharmi as he turns to two uniformed officers. "You two stay here and seal it off."

"Sir, yes sir," they both respond as they start to rope off the area with yellow police crime scene tap.

Hunt continues, "You heard what Sharmi said, so have forensics dust for prints over where she is standing. And when they are done here, send them to me at the spider ride. It looks like forensics will be working overtime tonight. There is much need for them at the amusement park, it seems."

Both uniformed officers stop just long enough to nod their confirmation and then continue to tape off the area.

"Sharmi, come with me, please."

As Hunt leads her from the roof of the Haunted House, he explains, "Alveraz called to say that the owner of the carnival is here and while she was checking everything, the owner noticed a bullet lodged in a wooden sign telling patrons how tall they have to be to ride the spider ride."

"Lovely," is Sharmi's only reply as she picks up her pace to keep up with Hunt.

Once they reach the spider ride, Alveraz already has the area taped. Hunt nods to Alveraz as he walks up to the sign and sure enough there is a bullet lodged into it. Hunt inspects it as close as he can, "damn, looks like a .308 Winchester. But we didn't see the shell up on the roof." He furrows his eyebrows in thought and scratches his head before pulling out his phone to call Dr. Denton.

"Hey Doc, the bullet has since turned up. But I just can't understand it. If the killer was five hundred yards away and the bullet was found about another hundred yards away but towards the left of the body. I just don't understand it. Something isn't adding up."

"What caliber bullet was it?"

".308 Win."

"Ahhh, that explains it then. That caliber would mean the murder weapon would be probably a Remington 700, bolt action, would be my guess. They can hit a target up to 1000 yards. That would explain the size of the bullet hole, and the damage to the victim's brain. It could also explain the trajectory of the bullet after it hit the victim too. But again, I can't confirm it until I complete the autopsy, remember? I'm getting ready for it now."

"So the bullet would have changed direction slightly after it went clear through the victim taking it off of its otherwise straight course."

"Yes, you've got it. But that gun isn't something that most people use, Hunt."

"Damn it, that's what's been bugging me all along, we're looking for a—"

"Professional," both Hunt and Dr. Denton, said at the exact same time.

Sharmi's head pops up to look at Hunt while he is still on the phone with Dr. Denton.

"We're sending the bullet to you, please hurry with the results and let me know if you find anything."

Hunt turns to Sharmi. "While we wait, let's look around to see if we can find anything else."

* * * *

Several hours later, as they start to finish their investigation of the carnival, Hunts phone rings.

"Yeah, Dr. Denton, what have you got for me?"

"Just as I suspected, one fatal shot to the center of the skull. Hit the brain to kill him instantly. Didn't find anything else abnormal. Healthy young male. He had a bit to drink but nothing remarkable. He was certainly not drunk at all. That I can safely say."

"Thanks, doctor for the quick autopsy. Any word on the baby blanket?"

"Yes, it is the victim's blood."

"Ok that's good to hear, at least the baby is not hurt. No prints were found on the roof of the Haunted House and no prints were found on the bullet."

"You are correct that it is a .780 Win and it is the bullet that killed the victim. It is a perfect match to the wound to the victim's head."

"Great, that means it is definitely someone who knows what they are doing so everything is wiped clean."

"I would say that that looks to be correct."

Hunt and Denton are still talking when Alveraz walks over to Sharmi.

"Sharmi,' he starts talking as he turns and points towards a tall, lanky, blonde with her long hair in a French braid down her back, 'that beautiful young lady behind the police tape wants to speak to you. She says she knows you and needs to urgently speak with you.'"

As Sharmi looks at her, the young lady waves back, Sharmi winces like she has a sudden pain.

"Yes, I know her, she's my nosy neighbor's daughter. They always think that they know something that can be of use to me in the investigations that I help you all with."

"Oh, well do you want me to get rid of her?"

"No, it's probably best if I speak with her or she'll be here waiting for me. They are impossibly stubborn when they think or want to be of help but don't really KNOW anything."

"I completely understand. My aunt was the same way. Thought she always knew something useful to help our cases. Never anything but pure gossip," he laughs as he remembers it, 'of course, may she rest in peace. I miss that ole bird, truth be told," he continues to smile as he walks away.

Sharmi walks over to the woman with disgust on her face as she gets closer to her. She grits her teeth and sneers as she says, "why are you here? What do you want?"

The young lady smiles as she responds, "My money, Sharmi."

"Keep your voice down, you idiot."

"I want my money," she whispers. "Now."

"How can I give you the rest of your money now when I'm still working," she continues quickly before the other woman has a chance to respond. "Don't you think it would be a little suspicious for me to be seen handing over an envelope to you here, where a murder just occurred. Of which, someone that was supposed to do it, didn't actually do it," she spat at the woman with all of the hate she could muster, without drawing attention to herself.

"I have no idea what you are talking about."

"You know damn well what I'm talking about, I saw a short, stocky man pull the trigger, you bitch. It wasn't even you. You didn't do what you were paid—I mean supposed to do."

The blonde looks at Sharmi with disbelief in her whole face, not just her eyes, "Wait, hold on a minute, how do you know it wasn't me? That would mean that you are a real—"

"Yes, I am a real psychic," Sharmi cuts in and grins, "I saw your friend in a vision and knew that it wasn't you. Not the same build at all, and masculine. Anyway, the rest of your money is in my apartment. I left the key under the flowerpot in front of my door. Go get your money from my nightstand, and then leave town. I don't want to see you again."

"You have to admit,' she laughs, "it was a great plan."

"But why didn't you do it yourself?"

"I couldn't trust that you wouldn't turn me in, this way the job still gets done, I get paid and split a little with my partner, and you can't pin it on me to help your career."

"Why would I? Never mind, it doesn't matter now, as you say the job is done. That bastard Steven thought he could beat on a woman and get away with it, didn't he? And don't worry about Deborah and the baby. I'll take care of them."

"Wait, don't tell me you're gonna… I don't, well you know, kill kids," as she turns around to see who is nearby.

"No, don't be silly, they are just as much his victims as I was once, I'll look out for them. As a matter of fact, they are safe now. They are far away from here getting the help they need at a shelter, and he can't hurt them anymore. Long ago, I told him the last time he hit me that if he EVER hit a woman again, that I'd personally make him regret it. He just laughed in my face."

ACKNOWLEDGEMENTS

The authors would like to thank Teresa Inge and Yvonne Saxon for their time and talent in editing the book. Their attention to detail in proofreading and editing each manuscript contributed to a well-crafted collection. A special thank you to Kimberly R. Thorn for gathering the stories and to Allie Marie and Michael Rigg for reviewing final edits. Additional acknowledgement goes to the Mystery by the Sea chapter and Sisters in Crime for their support, and Wildside Press for publishing the book.

ABOUT THE AUTHORS

DAWN BROTHERTON retired as a colonel after 28 years in the Air Force. Now she spends her time writing, crafting, coaching, and teaching. Her wide range of interests has expanded into her storytelling with books for all ages. Her 19th book will be released in March 2024. She teaches for Osher at the College of William and Mary, presents webinars for Military Writers Society of America and Sisters in Crime, and volunteers as a reviewer for York County's Reflection contest for literature. When she isn't using her words, Dawn is in her craft room, quilting and painting or taking online classes.

JUDITH FOWER is a retired jail discharge planner who once sang opera. Her stories in *Coastal Crimes, Mystery by the Sea, Virginia Is for Mysteries*, Volume III, and *Rock, Roll and Ruin* are available on Amazon. Her first novel-length mystery is *Lie About Yourself.* Blog posts can be enjoyed at sandinourshorts.blogspot.com.

The Retirement Gift, published under pen name J. Johonnot, takes a light look at the many disruptions the retirement transition brings. An upcoming story collection of "senior noir" imagines what her retired neighbors are hiding. You can message her @JudithJohonnotFowler.

MARIA HUDGINS is the author of the Dotsy Lamb Travel Mysteries, the Lacy Glass Archaeology Mysteries, two Mutt Mystery novellas, and several short stories. A former high school science teacher, she loves to travel and has visited all the countries that serve as locales for her stories. She has worked on an archaeology dig in the Isle of Man and a dinosaur dig in Montana. Maria lives in Hampton, Virginia and vacations every summer on the Outer Banks of North Carolina.

PENNY HUTSON began her writing career as a newspaper reporter at the ripe old age of seventeen. After studying under award-winning author Tony Ardizonne in the creative writing program at Old Dominion University, she became an English teacher and later school librarian for middle and high school students in the Virginia Beach City Public School system. Now retired, she spends her days creating spunky characters and twisted plots for her historical fiction and mysteries. She is a member of the national Sisters in Crime organization and its local chapter Mystery by the Sea. Although she lives in Virginia Beach with her husband, she loves to travel around the world and spend time with her grandson in southern California.

TERESA INGE grew up reading Nancy Drew mysteries. She is a member of Sisters in Crime, Short Mystery Fiction Society, Virginia Writer's Club, and Hampton Roads Writers. Teresa is an author in over a dozen anthologies including V*irginia is for Mysteries, Mutt Mysteries, Coastal Crimes, and Promophobia, an Agatha award-winning collection.* When not writing, Teresa can be found showing her 1955 Thunderbird at car shows. She resides in Southeastern Virgina and can be reached on social media and her website, teresainge.com

SHERYL JORDAN is a writer of fictional mystery. She has a bachelor's degree in criminal justice. Sheryl is a Burnsville High School Hall of Fame 2023 Inductee. She is a member of the Sisters in Crime National Chapter and the SinC Mysteries by the Sea Chapter Secretary. Her works include her novel *"Manipulation, Money, and Murder."* She has contributed to several anthologies and is working on a female trucker novel series. When Sheryl isn't writing she enjoys reading, spending time with her husband, family, and friends. She also enjoys traveling and watching football and basketball.

ALLIE MARIE is an award-winning author who grew up in Virginia, where her favorite childhood pastime was reading Nancy Drew and Trixie Belden mysteries and led to a career in law enforcement in the US as well as overseas.

After retirement, Allie embarked on a quest to fulfill a long-time dream—to write mysteries and crime thrillers. Ancestry research, however, inspired *The True Colors Series*, a paranormal mystery series with modern local settings and colonial history that has garnered multiple awards, followed by a spinoff collection, *The True Spirits Trilogy*. Her standalone historical mystery, *Return to Afton Square*, bridges the two series. She has contributed short stories in various genres to several anthologies.

Those other planned mystery stories? They still patiently wait for their turn. Besides family, her passions are traveling anywhere, any time, and camping with her husband Jack.

MAX JASON PETERSON (they/Mx., maxjasonpeterson.wordpress.com) is a professional member of Sisters in Crime, SFWA, and HWA. With mysteries in *Mystery Magazine* (including one that earned the cover illustration), *Seascape: The Best New England Crime Stories 2019*, and *A Study*

in Lavender: Queering Sherlock Holmes, Max has over 500 stories, poems, art, and articles published under bylines that include Adele Gardner (gardnercastle.com), with a book, *Halloween Hearts*, released by Jackanapes Press, https://www.jackanapespress.com/product/halloween-hearts. Known as Max to friends and family, this genderfluid, bi night owl can be found reading comics with cats or shooting b&w film in the noir nightscape.

MICHAEL RIGG is a retired Navy Judge Advocate who recently retired from a long career as a civil servant. He writes stories set in two disparate locations: Virginia and New Orleans. Mike is a member of Hampton Roads Writers, as well as the Sisters-in-Crime national organization and its Southeastern Virginia Chapter—Mystery by the Sea. Mike is the author of a novelette, *Ghosts of the French Market*, and has short stories in several anthologies. Visit him on Facebook at: facebook.com/michael.rigg.author or on his website: michaelrigg.com.

KIMBERLY R. THORN serves as the vice president of Hampton Roads Writers and treasurer of Sisters in Crime, Mystery by the Sea chapter. She writes articles for community newspapers and contributes to several blogs. She has a poem that is painted on the Elizabeth River Trail in Norfolk, Virginia, and a poem in the poetry anthology "Things I Know Now." You can reach her on social media at thepennedscribe.

www.ingramcontent.com/pod-product-compliance
Lightning Source LLC
Chambersburg PA
CBHW012151260626
47155CB00020B/3569